Urban Tango

A Novel by Regina Neequaye

Copyright © 2015
Regina Neequaye
All Rights Reserved.

LIBRARY OF CONGRESS CATALOGING-IN-PUBLICATION
DATA HAS BEEN APPLIED FOR

ISBN 978-0971886001
LCCN 2015907358

Printed in the United States of America

Cover art: SelfPubBookCovers.com/Island

ACKNOWLEDGMENTS

I would like to give thanks to my creator. To my husband, Lamar Crowell, you are the best. I would like to thank my mother, Marjorie Renee Monnigan Reynolds, who gave me the gift of compassion. To my children, Reynolds, Jordan, and Monnighan, you guys have been my inspiration. To my sisters, Denise, Shela, and Vonetta your support and love is abounding

CHAPTER 1

I stand in front of the bathroom mirror in awe of Stacy's reflection. She lies on her stomach in the middle of my bed. Her full breasts are almost flat to the mattress. Her thick, black hair is haphazardly spread across the fluffy, down pillow. The covers have slid down exposing half of her rotund, firm chocolate bottom. I flush the used condom down the toilet and wash my hands. I am en route to her, holding my hard-on in my hand, ready for round two when her phone rings. She quickly leaves the bed and retrieves the phone from her purse. The curve of her hips, her toned, slightly bowed legs, and her firm, round breast turn me on. I stand close behind her and attempt to get her in the mood again. She moves my hand from between her legs and quickly grabs her robe.

"Shush," she places her index finger in front of pouty, succulent lips and whispers, "it's Ming Lee." I quickly move to the side fully out of view of the phone's camera. She accepts the request for a video connection and places the phone on the desk. The thin face Chinese woman with a British accent appears on the tiny display. She and Stacy trade a few niceties before quickly getting to business.

Mr. Ye is requesting an impromptu date with his personal companion. He has developed a strong affinity for his special young friend. He normally visits once per month; however, this will be the second for the month. I have never met Mr. Ye. I have never spoken to him. All communication is through Ming Lee and Stacy. Stacy informs me of the time and date of his arrivals, and I coordinate the transportation with one of my drivers.

Mr. Ye is my favorite client. He receives special services. He transfers twenty-five thousand dollars to my offshore account in the Caymans every month to keep his companion personal. He is a top shelf client who pays for top shelf service. I immediately call Courtney. The phone rings three times and goes directly to her voicemail. I hang up and dial her cell. Again, the call goes straight to voicemail.

"Fucking bitch!"

"What's wrong?" Stacy ends her call with Ming Lee, quickly scrolls through her text messages, and places her phone back in her purse.

"We are going to have to do something about Courtney!"

"Besides you and me, who do you know is awake at 5:00 o'clock on a Saturday morning? She is probably asleep. Mr. Ye's plane does not land until 8:00. He is not expecting Ashleigh until 9:00. That is five hours from now. We have a lot of time. Calm down." She walks to the bathroom and stops in the middle of the threshold. "Do you want to join me?"

"You know I do not do romantic and mushy." She laughs; she and I both know I am not joking. I have made it perfectly clear on more than one occasion this is a business with benefits arrangement. We both agree this works for us since we are together so much. Due to our line of business, we cannot afford serious outside relationships with people who will need accounts of our time. She sometimes forgets, but I have no problem reminding her and keeping her on track.

I lean back deep into the pillow. I am restless. My mind is occupied with Courtney. I replay Courtney's behavior for the last month or so in my mind. My anger bounces between Courtney's fuck ups and Stacy for not keeping her cousin in check.

The sound of the shower annoys me. She has the acupressure massage at full blast. The bathroom door is closed, but I can still hear the sound of the water hitting hard against the stone walls in the shower. I can only imagine what it is doing to her flesh. I dial Courtney's number again. She does not answer. I throw the phone hard against the mattress and leave the bed.

"What are you doing?" I open the bathroom door and find Stacy squatting in front of the vanity.

"I am looking for shampoo. I need to wash my hair."

"I don't have any!" I push her away, close the vanity door, and turn the shower off. "Don't go through my things!" I step over her wet body and walk to the toilet and relieve myself.

"I am not going through your things. I need to wash my hair." She pulls strands of her hair from the shower cap and brings them to her nose. "My hair smells like your sweat." She laughs. "I have a few days before my next salon visit."

"Don't go through my shit!"

"You are uptight. You should calm down. Call another driver."

"They are all tied up." Her nonchalance fuels my agitation. I flush the toilet and wash my hands. She follows me to the bedroom. She removes the shower cap from her head; a mass of thick, jet black hair falls out of the cap and down her back. She bends forward and gathers her hair to the top of her head and wraps a rubber band around it. The long, bouncy ponytail makes her look like a teenager. She loosens the towel; it falls to the floor. I expect to see bruising and discoloration from the massage jets, but her chocolate skin is flawless. The sight of perfect, firm melons on her chest makes my nature rise. I am too focused on Mr. Ye, his companion, and Courtney to do anything about it.

"I am going to leave now. I have errands to run. I will catch you around noon at the Chicken Shack. You do not have to pick me up. I will drive myself." She squeezes her perfect body into tight jeans, pulls her T-shirt over her head, and throws her bra and panties in her purse. I grab my robe and walk downstairs with her. She hugs me; I am uncomfortable but reluctantly return the embrace. She gathers her shoes and leaves.

I call Courtney again as I crack two eggs and drop them in the hot skillet. The call goes to voicemail. She has no more times to fuck up. I get rid of trouble before trouble starts. According to the rumor mill, she is using street pharmaceuticals again. I started to take care of her when the rumors first surfaced, but Stacy pleaded her case and convinced me the rumors come from people who do not want to let go of the past. I agreed with Stacy for a while, but I could no longer ignore the rumors when she almost fucked up a thirty thousand dollar deal a couple of months ago. She was a no-show for a very wealthy new client who paid fifty percent down for a companion for a five-day Mediterranean cruise. Lucky for Courtney, Stacy found a replacement. The replacement was not an exact match. The skin color was a half-shade darker than Courtney's. Her no-show cut into our profit, as I gave the customer a twenty percent discount for his inconvenience. This business thrives on repeat customers, and customer service is my number one priority.

My goal is to give our customers exactly what they want. I hired one of the best programmers in the world to build and maintain an encrypted website so secure, the government's best programmers cannot hack into it. With the exception of Mr. Ye, my first and favorite international client, our clients log in, enter the desired dates to meet with their companions. The client has the option of choosing from a variety of characteristics, including eye color, hair color, hair texture, and skin pigmentation. Profiles of available companions and their sexual specialties populate. The client chooses his companion and wires the money to my off-shore account in the Caymans.

I guarantee my services. I would have made Courtney disappear for fucking up, but she is Stacy's cousin. I gave her a second chance. I limit her job to transportation, and she is fucking that up. I run a tight ship. My staff knows I don't play. In this business, everyone has to be on their game one hundred percent. Drug addicts and alcoholics lack discipline and have no place in this business.

I check my text messages as I walk up the stairs. Lailah, my children's mother, thanks me for the extra five grand I deposited in her account yesterday. She texts a picture of Kaycee, our eight-year-old daughter, and Jonathan our four-year-old son. I stare at my children's pictures and sometimes allow myself to dream, for a moment, that one day I will share a home with Lailah and my children with the white picket fence, the two car garage, and a dog named Fido. In reality, I know I am not equipped to be a husband or father. I see them when time permits. Besides, Lailah is too special to be affiliated with this game. I don't want her or the kids exposed to this life.

I straighten the covers, sit on the bed, and catch the last of the morning news. I am restless and cannot sit still. I pick up Stacy's wet towel from the floor and make a mental note to remind her to pick up after herself. I stare at the phone and contemplate dialing Courtney's number again. She has my mind fucked up. She is a distraction. If she is using, she risks bringing unwanted attention to our organization. Something has to be done before she fucks it up for everyone. We have a multimillion dollar business. If the business continues to grow, I project in a year or so we will have a billion dollars in sales. Several national and international players depend on our business to stay discreet. A drug addict is unpredictable and has no place in this type of business. I take a quick shower and slide into an old pair of jeans. I open the vanity, slide the fake backing to the side, open the safe, and remove a few bills from a stack of cash hidden under a small manila envelope.

I have been out of the street game for years, but I never gave up my pass. I drive to Buckhead and stop at an old acquaintance's house to make a quick purchase, then drive to the train station. I park my car at the Lindbergh station and ride one stop to the Buckhead Station. I exit the train with my sun visor pulled close to my head. My sunglasses cover my eyes. I stop at the neighborhood store and pick up bread, milk, eggs and enough canned goods to fill two grocery bags, and walk three blocks to her sky rise apartment. I walk towards the side of the building, careful to keep my face away from the cameras. I inconspicuously wait with the two bags filled with groceries in both of my arms for a resident to enter or exit the building. I have digital access, but I don't want this visit recorded. I walk the ten flights of stairs to her apartment with my head turned away from the security cameras. I knock on the wooden door, but she does not answer. I pull my sleeve over my finger and press the numbers on the keypad to unlock the door.

The smell of rotten food hits me like a ton of bricks as I enter the foyer. I am filled with anger when I notice a sink filled with dishes and a sea of empty takeout containers on the counter. I kick a plastic garbage bag half-filled with trash to the side as I make my way to the living room. I walk to the front of the leather sofa and find Courtney sprawled out in her bra and panties. Her hair is wet and slick to her head. Mascara is smudged around her puffy eyes. I look at my watch; it is 8:00. She should be dressed and ready for the day. I stand in front of her. She does not notice my presence until I raise her arm. Tiny black holes the size of a pin head mark the inside of her arm and the back of her hand.

"Jefferson" It takes several minutes for her to focus. She attempts to stand; she grabs the side of her head, then slowly sits down. "What's up baby?"

"You tell me; I had a job for you. I have been calling you all fucking morning!"

"What time is it?" She uses her fingers to remove thick, crusty sleep from her puffy eyes. She struggles to focus on the crystal clock on the side of the table. "Damn, baby I am sorry. It won't take me long to get ready." She slowly stands and pulls her arms high over her head exposing unshaven armpits. I step back and away from her as the putrid smell of musk from her underarms mixed with the stench of unwashed ass assaults my nostrils. "You have a job for me?"

"Don't worry about it baby. The client has been taken care of."

"I am sorry, Jefferson. I had a late night. I hung out with some friends from Vegas I have not seen in a while." Her apology is sincere, but much too late. "I will be on it next time." She stands, stretches, and walks to the bathroom. She appears to not notice she is half-dressed; her only clothing is her bra and panties. I follow close behind. She opens the medicine cabinet, removes a white pill from a folded napkin, and pops it in her mouth. She grabs an open bottle of water from the shelf over the commode. "It's a muscle relaxer."

"You need something stronger? I got what you need right here." I reach in my pocket and remove a baggie of uncut heroin and dangle it in front of her.

"Jefferson, you got me wrong." Beads of perspiration congregate on her forehead. She scratches the inside of her arm incessantly. Thick saliva forms in the corners of her mouth. "You know I know better. I don't do that shit anymore." She is so focused on the baggie in my hand, it is as if she is talking to the baggie instead of me.

"That's not what I heard. My Buckhead connection says you are a regular for heroin and ecstasy." She turns away. Her nervous tics confirm she is a heavy user. "I hear you got fired from the nonprofit for not calling and not coming in for an entire week. Everyone has to keep a job to look on the up and up!" I look around at the upscale downtown condominium she rents on paper from my offshore corporation. "How will you explain your ability to pay this high ass rent if you are ever questioned?"

"You're right, Jefferson, but it wasn't my fault. Those people…" She cannot complete a thought or finish a sentence. "I don't know what you heard, but I am not using." I step closer to her. The stench of metabolized heroin seeps through her pores. She steps back and away from me. She loses her balance and falls in the bath tub, landing with both feet in the air. I grab her feet and spread her toes. Black marks surrounded by puss-filled blisters sit in the cracks between her toes. "Courtney, you know better!" I throw her foot to the side. We are both startled by the loud echo as her feet hit the shower.

"I am so sorry, Jefferson." She puts her hands together as if she is praying. "Shit got so hard. You know my mother will not allow me to visit my kids and…"

"It is okay; don't worry about it. Has anyone been here?" I look around for evidence of lowlife drug dealers and desperate drug addicts. I open the bathroom closet and find size 12 men's Timberland boots. I look under the cabinet and find two different bottles of male cologne. An oversized men's Obey sweat shirt and a dingy pair of hi-end designer jeans lay unfolded on top of the hamper.

"I swear on everything, I am sorry, Jefferson!" Her lips quiver as she speaks. Her carotid artery beats so hard, it looks as if there is a jumping bean in her neck. "I will pull it together; ain't nobody been here but my brother. I never cop here." I feel like smacking her across the face for insulting my intelligence. Her only brother is locked up, doing a ten-year bid for stupid shit.

She grabs the handle on the side of the bathtub and attempts to pull herself out. I stand and watch her struggle. After several unsuccessful attempts, she lets go of the handle and falls back in the tub. I offer my hand; she takes it. I pull her out. She stands close in front of me. "I am really sorry." She flirtatiously bats her eyes. "Let me make it up to you." She smiles, showing yellow, decaying teeth as she rubs her thin body against me. She takes my hand and leads me to the bedroom. I grab the open bottle of water and willingly follow. She grabs what looks like a month of dirty clothes from the bed and throws them on the floor. The drugs have made her lose her mind. She knows, and everyone who works for me knows, with the exception of Stacy, I don't get down with employees.

"Don't worry about it, Courtney; everything is cool." Dark circles surround her eyes. Stress lines cover a prematurely aging face that was flawless two months ago. "I am going to make you feel good; take your mind off of everything." She lies on the bed and leans back on two oversized pillows. I sit next to her and open the small baggie filled with uncut heroin. She quickly opens the night stand and pulls out her gear. She is so anxious she doesn't notice the thick black leather gloves that cover my hands. Her hand trembles as if she has a neurological disorder. She struggles to get the rubber band around her arm.

"Let me help you, baby." I take the rubber band and tie it as tight as I can. I remove the syringe and metal spoon from my pocket. I place the heroin on a spoon, mix in a couple of drops of water, melt it with a lighter, and fill the syringe with as much of the warm, bubbly liquid it can hold. I rub my thumbs over her desecrated veins, find a good injection spot, and insert the needle.

"Slow, baby, you got to do it slow." I ignore her and quickly push all of the poison in her arm. She leans back against the upholstered leather headboard. Her eyelids flutter and slowly close. A euphoric smile stretches across her face. After several minutes, she slowly opens her eyes and stares at the wall. I almost pity her. She was never smart, but she had a perfect body and a beautiful face. Small craters now cover her honey brown cheeks. She lost a lot of weight much too quickly, causing the elasticity in her skin to diminish. Courtney very much needed her good looks to make up for her lack of intelligence and common sense. She has no self-confidence and is a magnet to losers.

Her head falls to the side. She struggles to hold meaningful conversation. The heroin that flows through her veins is pure and uncut. Her eyes slowly roll back in her head. Her gaze is peaceful. She mumbles, but her words are inaudible. I sit in the chair next to her bed and watch the clock.

"This is some good shit! You got a little more?" The high is wearing off. Her speech is still slurred and labored; it is as if the space in her mouth is too small to accommodate her tongue.

"Sure, baby, anything for you." I sit on the side of the bed, tighten the rubber band around her limp arm, empty last of the poison from the baggie onto the spoon, and melt it. I siphon the liquid in the syringe and stick the needle in her arm. Her mouth curves into a slight smile. Her head slowly falls back against the headboard. Her breathing is soft and slow, almost like a sleeping baby. I look at my watch. Five minutes have passed. Her body jolts forward and begins to shake uncontrollably. She is stiff as a board. Spittle, thick like milk, flows from her mouth. Her head falls forward; her chin sits awkwardly on her chest. Her eyes are wide open; I take my glove covered hand and close her eyes. I leave the needle stuck in her arms and turn off the lights. I grab the empty baggie and cigarette lighter and place them in a pocket of the jeans that lay on the hamper. I wipe down everything my hands touched and leave with plenty of time to transport the companion to my favorite client.

Chapter 2

It is 4:30. I have completed five of the ten tasks on my "Things To Do" list. Osei hates when I bring work home, but I have to do what I have to do. He used to be my biggest supporter and number one fan. He has changed and become resentful of the time and energy I spend advancing my career. I reluctantly shut down my computer and shove files in my briefcase. My cell rings. I ignore it and organize my desk for next week. It has been ringing off and on for the last hour. The constant ringing is annoying. I grab the phone, change the setting to vibrate, and drop it in my pocket, but the caller is persistent. The vibration from the phone drives me crazy. I reach into my pocket, feel for the decline button, and forward the call to voicemail. It is killing me not to answer. It's Friday; I meet Osei and the kids for dinner every Friday after work. I should have left thirty minutes ago to avoid rush hour traffic. I lock my file cabinet, grab my things, and walk to the elevator. I reach the parking deck, and the phone begins to vibrate again. I remove it from my pocket and look at the display. It is Detective Davis. I throw my things in the backseat of my car, sit in the driver's seat, and reluctantly return the call.

"Detective Davis," he answers after the first ring.

"Why are you blowing up my phone? It's Friday, and it is almost five o'clock." I glance at my watch. I should not have returned the call. Time is quickly passing, and there is a pit bull waiting for me with my children at Benihana's.

"Ayanna," he chuckles. "You are just as married to that chair in the District Attorney's office as I am to mine at Precinct East." Unfortunately, my husband will probably agree with him, but the truth is that chair in the District Attorney's office will lead to greater opportunities.

"Quiet as it's kept, Detective Davis, I have a life, and it is waiting for me at Benihana's."

"I know; but give me a few minutes. I have a surprise for you. I will be at the detention center in two minutes. Meet me in front of the Intake Desk at the female entrance. You will not believe who is sitting handcuffed in the back of my car."

"Who is it?" I turn my wrist inward and glance at my watch again. Time is quickly passing.

"It is a surprise, a big one; I will see you in two minutes." If I am late for dinner, there will be hell to pay, but business is business. I leave my car in the garage, grab my purse and clipboard, and jaywalk across the street to the detention center. Davis is at the Intake Desk when I arrive. A handcuffed female dressed in high end fashion stumbles in front of him. She looks out of place amongst the other female detainees waiting in line to be processed into the jail. "This is one of my presents to you." A female detention officer escorts Davis' prisoner through the X-ray check point. Detective Davis instructs the detention officer to pat her down and take her to an interrogation room on the female side of the jail.

"Who is she?" I don't know where he is going with this and wonder why he believes his detainee is a present to me. "Where did you find her?" The handcuffed female with blue eye shadow and two shades too light pink lipstick smudged on her lips looks more like a child than a woman. Her body looks out of place in the high end Gucci Stilettos and the body fitting black dress. I can't think of the designer, but I have seen this dress in one of the high-end fashion magazines I subscribe to.

"We detained her during a prostitution sting at one of the five star hotels in midtown; an undercover officer saw her leave the hotel with a suspicious, middle-aged Asian male before getting into a white Range Rover."

"She does not look like a typical streetwalker." I inconspicuously glance at her shoes and examine the intricate stitching and the logo; they are authentic. Her high end, sexy and classy attire is not usually worn by common prostitutes. "I hope you arrested the men as well."

"We arrested the man in the white Range Rover."

"Only one of them?"

"We tried to detain and arrest both men." I look over my glasses. Davis looks over his. "The Asian gentleman is a foreign diplomat. He refused to answer questions. Within minutes of detaining him, a representative from the Chinese embassy was on the scene. After he flashed his credentials and requested diplomatic immunity, we had to release him to his embassy. We believe the white Range Rover belongs to her pimp."

"Oh." I try not to be rude, but I hope like hell he has not interrupted my evening to inform me of a pimp and his hooker's arrest. The pit bull and my kids are waiting for me. I am in no mood for confrontation. Last Friday, Osei blew a fuse because I was 15 minutes late.

"And guess who the pimp is?" I balance my weight on one leg, fold my arms across my chest, and wait for disclosure. "Jefferson Thomas." My thoughts travel from zero to a hundred in minus two seconds. I quickly glance at my watch. Osei and the kids are expecting me in less than ten minutes, but this is the best news I have had all day. Jefferson Thomas, as he is now known, is one of the cockiest, ruthless criminals that have crossed my path. He seduced many of the occupants in City Hall with campaign funds and monetary bribes. He is Ivy League educated with a thuggish modus operandi.

He, along with his suit wearing crew of thugs, turned Mason Hills, Dixie Falls, and half of the Fourth Ward into a zombie land of oxycodone, crack, and meth addicts. He and his cohorts single handedly destroyed what was once a strong and affluent, upper middle class, African American community. Most of the businesses in the communities were owned by black people who actually resided in the community. The community was home to the largest concentration of educated blacks in the nation; however, education and affluence could not compete with residents who became the dope fiends that lived in the community or the fiends that came into the community from the suburbs to purchase illegal drugs. The dope fiends ran customers of once thriving businesses away. Jefferson and his cohorts used politicians he bribed with campaign contributions and City Hall staff on his payroll to change zoning codes. Locally owned boutiques, bookstores, and flower shops were replaced with pawn shops, liquor stores, and other cash-based businesses that were fronts to funnel proceeds from illegal activities. Between the constant thievery and the turf shootouts, many family-owned businesses that were part of the community landscape for decades were forced to board up and close shop. The demographics of the community quickly changed. Residents who could afford to leave left in droves. Many high-priced homes were boarded up and abandoned. Those that remained lived in self-made prisons. Security firms made a fortune. Windows covered with burglar bars and steel doors became the norm. Because of his connections, Jefferson got away with his illegal enterprises for many years.

He travels in the right circles amongst politicians, bankers, and big money investors. He inconspicuously slithered his way onto many civic boards and charitable organizations. He is able to disguise his nefarious ways by sponsoring events for underprivileged youth and the elderly in the community. His enterprise would have continued to thrive until the neighborhood was zoned a weed and seed community. An influx of mostly white, upper middle class to wealthy homeowners desiring quick and easy access to downtown purchased properties and became active in the community and eventually voted the old guards out of political office. The politicians that remained realigned themselves with the new guard and were forced to act as he expanded his enterprise and drug addicts started showing up in classrooms in some of the most prestigious, private schools in town.

The District Attorney's office worked with the police department and spent hundreds of thousands of dollars trying to build a case against him. When we finally had enough evidence to get an indictment, the witnesses began dropping like flies. Those he did not manage to kill or have killed were so afraid that even under the threat of racketeering charges and possible federal indictments, they refused to testify. Without crucial testimonies, there was no choice but to withdraw the indictment.

I was crushed. Jefferson Thomas was my first unsuccessful prosecution. He became an instant celebrity. He slandered the District Attorney's office and the police department in the many media interviews after the dismissal. His lawyer filed over two hundred ethics complaints against me and the District Attorney's office. Answering each complaint was extremely time consuming and stressful. The grueling hours of interrogation from the ethics boards were so overwhelming that I was prescribed three different medications to deal with the stress.

"So we get another shot?" I glance at my watch as I walk down the hall to the interrogation room. At this point, I am ten minutes late to dinner. Ten minutes or an hour will not make a difference. Osei has very little tolerance for tardiness. I am going to get the cold shoulder regardless; it might as well be worth it.

"Hey, Ms. Sexy Prosecutor you're still looking good girl. It has been a long time since we last tangoed." He licks his lips and scans my body from head to toe as I enter the bright interrogation room. His cold, dark eyes make me uncomfortable. "I thought that African would have you on lockdown, barefoot and pregnant again. I haven't seen you in years. How is the family?" His slick smile makes me want to throw up. "How is that pretty little girl? If my calculations are correct, she should be about eight. Am I right?" He attempts to stand; the officer shoves him back in his seat. "Watch yourself, man!" Jefferson is sitting, yet his head and the standing detention officer's head are almost level.

"Don't get up again!" The officer is unthreatened and unmoved by Jefferson's tall and muscular physique, as he knows cadres of his fellow detention officers are on guard outside with batons and Tasers, ready to invade the tiny interrogation room at a moment's notice.

"Motherfucker!" He brushes his shoulders and stares intensely at the detention officer. "This cost more than your monthly salary."

"Donate it to charity; you won't need that suit where you are going." The detention officer continues to stand at attention and is completely unmoved by Jefferson's antics and attempt to intimidate.

"Where are we going, Ayanna?" He ignores the detention officer.

"Mr. Thomas, please address me as Ms. Williams. We are not personal acquaintances."

"Oh, it's like that?" His eyes are lifeless, cold, and void of all emotion; his fake smile disappears. "You cost me a fortune in legal fees. You have made several attempts to ruin my good name. The way I see it, we are connected like family. Fuck the formalities!" His mouth widens into a smile, but his eyes are blank and remain dark and deadly. He looks at the clock on the wall, then at the Rolex on his toned, muscular arms. "You should check that clock; it is off a few seconds. Why am I here? Where is that young lady I picked up? Is she okay?" A disingenuous expression of concern designed to mock is plastered on his dark, chiseled face. "I don't remember exactly what she said, but she said something about someone harassing her and needing a ride. Did she get to her

14

destination?"

"You are funny." I wrap my arms around my clipboard and hold it tight against my chest. "I believe she will testify you are her pimp. Mr. Thomas, this is low even for you. She is 14, maybe 15? You may be looking at other charges as well. We don't play the pimp game in this city! We're especially tough on lowlife thugs who pimp children."

"Ayanna, oh, I forgot. Excuse me. Ms. Williams, you are funny. Pimp? Please don't insult me. Do I look like a pimp?" He laughs as he extends his arm outward revealing a diamond ring so big, it had to be custom made. "I am a self-made businessman. You tried to destroy me, yet I am still successful. Pimp? Ask her she will tell you; she said something about someone harassing her or something. Hell, I really can't remember. I was simply doing my civic duty assisting a young lady in distress. I am just a concerned citizen trying to help a fellow citizen in need."

"Mr. Thomas, that's your story; stick to it. I hope that works out for you, but I have every intention of ripping that story to shreds, just as I plan to rip you to shreds."

"Still a tiger, I see." He roars like a vicious feline and puckers his lips. "I look forward to it, Ayanna. I look forward to this second dance." His cold, dark eyes are piercing. They emanate an evil so powerful, I cannot maintain contact. "Just make sure you follow the rules this time. We don't want another scandal in the District Attorney's office. I am sure you do not need another ethics investigation." The smirk on his face is nauseating. "I was speaking with one of the city council members the other day. I hear, in spite of the number of cases you have lost lately, City Hall still has big plans for you. You don't want to ruin that." I glance at my watch to avoid eye contact. I hold my clipboard close with one hand and open the door with the other. I take a quick look at my nemesis and exit the interrogation room.

Osei is going to be pissed. I should call and explain my tardiness, but at this point, it is useless. I walk down the musty hall to the female interrogation room on the other side of the building. The child dressed like a celebrity at a red carpet premiere looks out of place sitting in a brown, lopsided, wooden, hard back chair. Her expensive stilettos lie recklessly on the stained concrete floor. Her skinny legs dangle under the grey, metal, graffiti covered table.

"Hello, I am Mrs. Williams. I work for the District Attorney's office. If you don't mind, I need to ask you a few questions." I place my clipboard on the table and slowly move the wooden chair next to her away from the table. I discretely take in her facial features as I sit in the chair. Up close, she looks about twelve, and no older than thirteen. She still has those last stubborn remnants of baby fat in her cheeks.

"Look bitch, I ain't got shit to say!" She crosses her legs and leans back in the chair. "Take my ass to juvenile hall!" Her voice has the pitch of a child much younger than the seventeen she is claiming to be.

"Well, it's not that simple. Since you say you are seventeen, we will have to put you in the adult population."

"Bitch, please!" She stands, pops her neck back and forth while making various designs in the air with her finger. "I know my fucking rights. Get your ass to a fucking phone, call juvi, and tell them to pick my ass up!" She pops her neck and waves her index finger back and forth with each syllable. "I am a damned minor! Y'all mother fuckers need to stop fucking asking me so many damn questions! I need to see my damn lawyer!"

"What is your lawyer's name? I will call him for you." I remove my phone from my pocket. My eyes are glued to my clipboard as I wait for her to provide the phone number. Her antics are so hilarious, it is hard for me to contain my laughter.

"Fuck, I don't know, that's why I got a damn lawyer!"

"I don't understand why you guys have this baby behind the glass! You should have the pimp and the John behind this damn glass!" Miss Thing and I both jump in our seats as Mary, the bohemian county social worker, abruptly enters the interrogating room in her signature flowing dashiki. She has worked for the county much too long and really needs to consider retirement. A new crop of juveniles have entered the system, yet she behaves as if we are living in the time when kids came in the system for stealing from the grocery store, truancy, or running away from home. This new crop are gun toting, dope dealing, and angry as hell. "This city is a hub for human trafficking. We should be looking her up in the system, trying to figure out where she belongs." She folds her arms across her chest. "Mrs. Williams, you are out of order! You are aware it is against regulations to question a minor without a representative from child services present."

"The minor states she is 17."

"Well, it is obvious she is not."

"About time someone with some fucking sense!" Little Ms. Thing sits down, pops her neck one last time, folds her little arms across her not so developed chest, and rolls her eyes so far back in her head, her eyeballs almost disappear.

"We arrested Jefferson, your pimp." I ignore Mary's diatribe and continue the interview.

"Pimp?" She slowly slides to the back of her chair; her demeanor changes. She appears genuinely confused. "Who is Jefferson?"

"I am not someone for you to play with! You and your pimp were arrested together! You are well acquainted with Jefferson Thompson!" I move closer; our faces almost touch. "I am going to have him released, and he is going to be angry. I am going to make him think you talked."

"Do you, bitch, I don't know anyone named Jefferson Thompson." She tries hard to maintain the strong, hard persona, but I sense fear seeping through her cracking armor.

"What will Jefferson do when he thinks you talked?" Her acting skills are superb. Her denial of Jefferson is almost believable. I stand and leave her sitting to mull over Jefferson's anger and the consequences of thinking she talked.

"Don't worry, honey; we are going to get you home." Mary behaves as if I am invisible. She sits in the chair on the other side of Little Miss Thing and gently wraps one arm around her shoulder. Her motherly affection to this wayward child annoys me. I am surprised Davis called child services so soon. If he wanted to give me an opportunity to have a productive interview with the child, he should have waited at least two hours before calling child services.

I leave and allow Mary her motherly moment. I rush out of the building and sprint across the street to my car, praying they are still at the restaurant. I am always late. I hate it, but I have to do what I have to do. My next career move is District Attorney, a move that will take me to the State, then Federal bench. Although I have lost my last three cases, the county and state brass continues to vet me for District Attorney upon D.A. Leslie's retirement. They still have faith in my ability to lead the District Attorney's office. I will not get there doing mediocre work. The last three not guilty verdicts surprised me. I can usually get the defendants to take a plea deal. The meanest thug will cry, beg, and plead for mercy when faced with a fifty-year sentence and will jump over backwards for a ten-year deal instead. Somehow, these last three defendants were able to retain lawyers. They were basic street thugs nickeling and diming marijuana and oxycodone pills. Two lived at home with their mothers, and one lived with his girlfriend.

They had 'hood money; but in real world economics, they were poor. Where they got the money for legal representation is a mystery; as long as the lawyers get paid, they could care less where the money comes from. I work hard to present good cases on behalf of the citizens of the county. If it takes working twenty-hour days, I will work twenty-one. My career path takes a lot of time away from the kids which is why I was surprised when Osei, who grew up with many nannies and housekeepers, refused my request for a nanny to help with the children. I understand his desire to be a hands-on parent, but when you can afford help, why not use it?

I glance at my watch. A burning sensation travels from my stomach to my throat. I reach in my purse for an antacid pill. My underarms are drenched with perspiration. The thought of dealing with Osei's attitude makes me anxious. I drive so fast that I hit the curve turning into the restaurant's parking lot. I quickly shift the transmission to park. I do not wait for the valet to come to the car. I jump out of the car, give the keys to the valet, and walk briskly inside. They are finishing dessert when I arrive.

"I am sorry. I got stuck at the office." He does not acknowledge me; I bend forward to kiss Osei on the lips. He turns away; my lips brush against his clean shaven cheek instead.

"Hey Mommy" OJ, as usual, is warm and happy to see me.

"Hi, Mom," Che' takes a queue from Osei and painstakingly greets me. Her greeting is dry and sounds as if it has taken every molecule in her body to get it out. Unfortunately, her demeanor is usual as well.

"You could have called." He makes no eye contact as he reads messages on his phone.

"I know; I lost track of time. I had to sit in on a very important interrogation and..."

"Are you going to order?" His tone is firm. He interrupts me as if I am one of his subordinates. I am not surprised; I expected his rudeness. Lately, I am surprised when he is cordial.

"I will have my meal to go." I scan the dinner menu for a

seafood entre. I feel guilty for missing dinner, but in this case it was worth it. Osei will have to understand that my career is flourishing and requires a lot of time away, but I will try to do better at managing my time. "How was work today?" I quickly change the subject in a futile attempt to change his ill mood.

"I thought we agreed to stop talking about work when we are spending family time with the kids." He finally makes eye contact, but instead of love in his eyes, I see contempt.

"Apologies." I take a sip of the warm wine in front of me. "Che', how was school?"

"Good" she answers never taking her eyes away from the smart phone Osei purchased for her against my wishes. Her directness is disrespectful. Osei usually corrects her, but he behaves as if he does not hear her. This child is only eight-years-old. I thought the "I hate my mom" thing starts at puberty. "I already told Daddy about school, but as usual, you were not around." Her wit and sarcasm is that of an adult. Osei can take full credit for the way Che' behaves, as she is often present when he puts me down. His insults are subtle, but Che' is smart and has picked up on the cracks in our once united front.

"I'll tell you about my day Mommy."

"Okay, baby, tell Mommy about your day." If it were not for OJ, I would not feel part of this family.

"It's time to go" Osei rudely interrupts OJ as he glances at his watch. He calls the waitress for the check. "You have a soccer game tomorrow. You need to get a good night sleep so you can kick a few goalies."

"OJ, you can ride with Mommy and tell me about it in the car on the way home."

Osei pays the check, takes both of the children's hands and leaves the table. "Daddy, I want to ride with Mommy." OJ attempts to pull away from his father; Osei tightens his grip. He exits the restaurant and walks towards the valet, dragging a resistant OJ behind him.

"Not tonight, your seat is in my car."

"Mommy has a seat in her car." Osei holds tight to OJ's hand, and ignores his protest as they stands in front of the restaurant and wait for the valet to bring his car.

"It's okay, OJ; tell me about your day on the way to soccer tomorrow."

"Hopefully, she can make it on time." Osei takes the keys from the valet. He secures the children in his car and leaves me standing alone at the entrance as I wait for mine.

Chapter 3

I am alone in the dark, waiting for the valet to bring my car when I feel my phone vibrate. I glance at it; I have a message from Trevor Bordeaux. I quickly delete the message and turn off my phone. Trevor is becoming careless. He knows I do not answer his calls after 5:00. He is becoming too needy. He is forgetting the business aspect of our relationship. I remain focused. However, Osei makes it very easy to stray. He is fast becoming the husband from hell. I would have thought Osei would have waited until I am secure in my car before leaving me standing alone under a pitch black sky. He should have waited; instead, he immediately drives off with the children. His behavior has been strange for the last couple of months. He is short-tempered, and he never passes up on an opportunity to disagree and debate some of the most mundane issues. I am not one to walk on eggshells, but lately I find myself tiptoeing around him. I am not apprehensive when it comes to discussing significant issues, but I simply don't have time for dumb shit.

We are an intelligent, focused, regimented, and disciplined family. Osei is out of character. Lately, the kids come home with ice cream and other sweets. We agreed, before the children were born, they would not have refined sugar, pork, red meat, or dairy products. Yesterday, I walked into the kitchen and found Che' and OJ indulging in an ice cream sundae. I did not question Osei. I wanted to, but I was not in the mood for debate and unnecessary confrontation. I am still recovering from our confrontation two weeks ago when he allowed Che' to watch an extra hour of television on a school night on what is supposed to be a children's channel.

"Osei! Do you see what she is watching?" I was in the kitchen and happened to hear a prepubescent male voice discussing making out with a girl.

"What are you talking about? This is a kids' channel!"

"Che', turn it off!" She did not move and continued to watch television. "Now!" My elevated voice stirred no reaction from her; instead, she looked to Osei for subliminal clues to navigate her next move. I walked in the den, grab the remote, and pressed the off button.

"Mom!" she yelled so loud, if I believed in corporal punishment, I would have smacked her.

"Che', go to your room and get a book!" He left the computer where he was playing games with OJ, snatched the remote from my hand with such force, one of my freshly acrylic nails broke. He pressed the on button, then threw the remote so hard, it bounced off the sofa and onto the ottoman. "Osei! Have you lost your mind?" I was shocked and felt threatened by his display of aggression. I had never witnessed that side of him before. This is not how we operate. We agreed to always be a united front and never disagree in the presence of the children.

"It's not a big deal! It's a kids' show! Stop being uptight!" His pitch is loud. His posture is stiff; anger emanated from the face that was once the home to the most inviting and radiant smile. I stepped away from him. The room is silent. OJ's eyes were wide and glued to mine. Che' is unmoved. She leaned back in the chair, crossed her legs, and continued watching the inappropriate television show. Osei returned to the computer with OJ. I walked my shocked and defeated ass back to the kitchen and finished dinner. I let it go and attributed his attitude to the hard time he is having at the firm.

Some executives, both black and white, do not know how to relate to an unwavering black man. Osei is an uncompromising professional. He is all business. His designs are seamless. He is the best engineer in the firm. No one can complain about the quality of his work, but he refuses to play the game. Yes, what you know is important for success, but if you want to play with the big boys, who you know is equally important. Working hard is definitely part of the game, but the big players know a lot of deals are made outside of the office. His three-generation, rich colleagues constantly invite us to mini-vacations on their yachts in the Caribbean and all expenses paid vacations in the Hamptons. Osei is unimpressed. He always declines and uses the kids as an excuse not to attend events outside of work. My parents would be more than happy to watch Che' and OJ. Unlike Osei I play the game inside and outside of the office. I often attend events alone, as Osei has no interest in parties or gatherings. My name is on the VIP list of every political event in the county. I am on a first name basis with every politician in City Hall. My connections in City Hall have allowed me into elite circles with many local and national officials. I have an agenda that goes far beyond the District Attorney's office. I am in it to win it. I have no choice but to win; there is never a warm reception for losers.

He resents me. I feel it. I don't know the origin of this resentment, but I feel it. He takes advantage of every opportunity to put me down. He belittles my law degree and my profession. I often think of leaving the marriage, but the single parent demographic will be a career killer for me. Besides, I would rather be a widow than a single parent. I have changed from the woman he met in college. I am more driven, more goal-oriented and moving up rapidly in the District Attorney's office. I spent a lot of time studying key players in the political game. I know the game and play it well. I attend the black tie affairs, political fundraisers, and the occasional weekend getaway. I make it my business to know the names and faces of the key players in the city, county, state and federal government. Whatever it takes to be number one, I am on it.

He often accuses me of changing for the worse and insinuates I am out of balance. His accusations have no merit. He was attracted to my drive when we first met, but of late he has become threatened by it. I will not allow him to stop me. Networking with the top brass, a weekend getaway, or spending happy hour with co-workers is part of the game. It's all about making good connections. I don't accept every invitation but feel no guilt leaving the children to attend social events. Children should not prohibit parents from having a social life. "Me time" is important as well. I will admit that I enjoy and engage in "me time" much more often than Osei, but this is how he obviously wants it.

Lately, when I return from my excursions, I am greeted with a funky attitude and subtle accusations of infidelity. It is never blatant. Osei is too smart for that. He has become passive aggressive. He denies it, but I know a passive aggressive personality when I see one. When he is angry, he ignores me. I can be deeply engaged in a conversation with him, and in the middle of our conversation, he may walk away and leave me talking to myself. Or if I ask a question or make a comment, he sometimes pretends he does not hear me. I have barred him from my office because he is rude to my staff. Our relationship is in a spiral decline. He has accused me of having an affair with the District Attorney as well as other colleagues in my office. I find the accusations hilarious and borderline insulting. My eyes are set on prizes bigger than the county District Attorney office. He could learn from my playbook.

"Osei," I would sometimes suggest, "there is nothing wrong with meeting the guys on the golf course."

"I guess not, if you like golf. I don't like golf. That is the most boring sport in the world." I have unsuccessfully tried to convince him he would move up faster with his firm if he reached out and engaged more with top management.

"Babe, it is a way for other executives to bond with you."

"They do not share my bed or my home. We don't need to bond. I am doing my job. I am doing a good job. I generated over eight million in business last year alone. Fuck them!" He refuses to see his unwillingness to compromise shorts him some of the perks less productive engineers enjoy.

I am thankful for him in spite of the way things are going in our marriage. He is everything any woman would want in a man. Osei was not my first choice, but at the time, he was my best choice. Unlike the black American men I dated in the past, Osei did not downplay my dreams. He dreamed with me. In his world, glass ceilings or pre-set limitations do not exist. When we first met, he was everything I thought I wanted spiritually, intellectually, and physically. He caught my attention the first time I laid eyes on him. I was having lunch with Fatima, an upper classman in the law program. She briefly introduced us. He is not as tall as I generally like men. I would not have known he was from the continent until he opened his mouth and greeted Fatima. It turns out they are both from Kumasi, Ghana. He did not fit my idea of an African. I admit; I had my stereotypes. I am an intelligent woman, but I was influenced by television images of starving African children with extended bellies and women with elongated breast and protruding nipples walking with baskets balanced on their heads. I was not expecting him to live in a hut, but I did not expect his background to be as privileged and cultured as it is.

I became attracted to his unique style. He wears clothes by

designers unheard of in America. Yet he is not flashy. His father is an architect and owns a construction firm. He makes a fortune with government contracts throughout Africa, the Middle East, and Europe. He is a descendant of hard work and sound business dealings. Osei is very exposed and exudes a confidence I had never seen. He attended boarding school in London and has vacationed all over the world. He is the epitome of a global citizen. He introduced me to fine wines, exotic foods, and to an Africa I never knew existed. He is rich, educated, and successful. I deserve him and all of the perks that come with him.

When we first met, I was involved with a popular fraternity brother. He had a promising future in the corporate world. He came from a sound family, but his pedigree was minuscule in comparison to Osei. My ex-suitor was heartbroken, but I play life to win. Osei was a smarter choice.

I am not the exotic arm candy many high players use to accessorize, but what I lack in exotics, I make up with my brain. Everything is cognitive for me. I have watched women use their hearts to make lifelong decisions. I have seen my sister, Dee, ruin her life by loving men with her heart and not her brain. That is not who I am. Love, for me, is a cognitive decision. I decided I would be rich as a young child and knew my brain would get me there.

I learned the difference between thinking people and compassionate people in my early years. Thinking people seem to have money and are able to enjoy the good life. My parents are not rich. My father works as an insurance adjuster at a Fortune 500 insurance firm. When we would attend the annual Christmas parties at the CEO's house, my heart was always filled with envy. As a young child, I wanted and felt that I deserved the best of everything. Allie, the CEO's daughter, was always kind to me. She would invite me to her suite in their mansion. I pretended to like her. She may have made a good friend but I was so envious of her life that I could not stand being around her and begrudged having to attend the annual company events at her home.

Resentment against my parents would build up inside of me every time I was forced to endure Allie's company. I wondered what my parents lacked that I could not live in the mansion with a suite of my own. I figured it out by the time I graduated high school. My parents were feelers; the thinking gene totally eluded them. I was determined to be different. I surrounded myself with the smart kids in school. I did what the smart kids did. I put myself in situations where I knew I would be amongst the winners. Osei is the jackpot for now.

Osei does not have to flash. Class is natural to him. His presence is powerful. All eyes are on Osei when he walks into a room. He was a very unique experience for me. He showed me a deeper meaning of relationships that had nothing to do with physical attributes, or emotion. Osei was my first win, but not my last.

I work hard to prove I am worthy. Osei would be okay if I stayed home and raised our children, but I want him to always know I am a good decision, and until lately I have been successful. He complains that I spend too much time away from home and my priority should be my family as opposed to my career. However, I am a stickler to my goals. I worked hard to make the grades to get accepted in Ivy League to position myself for the good life. Osei is my first experience with a man with money, but not my last.

Though we are at odds and come from totally different backgrounds, Osei and I are alike in many ways. We both have a desire to leave the shadows of our families. I worked very hard to move beyond basic middle class status. Osei worked hard to move beyond familial cultural expectations. My determined spirit hooked up with the rebel in him, and we became inseparable and in sync in many ways.

I am not and most likely will never be a perfect fit with his family. I met his wealthy and well-connected family for the first time after graduating from law school. Osei surprised me with a three-week vacation at the family vacation home in London. I can't say it was a positive experience. Disapproval lurked in his mother's wide set eyes the first time she laid eyes on me. She was not unkind. She served great food and ensured my living quarters were clean and tidy, but she did little to conceal her disdain. Her eyes were uninviting and held a keen look of suspicion.

"*Sika digger*," were the first words that came from her full, dark lips. It took several years for me to learn she was referring to me as a gold digger. Although she speaks fluent English, when she spoke to Osei in my presence, she spoke in Twi, their native language. Osei would respectfully respond to her in English; Mrs. Badu-Bonsu would continue her conversation in Twi as if I were invisible. His sisters, an almost exact replica of their mother, were standoffish and very formal. However, Mr. Badu-Bonsu, his father, was very attentive. He was very engaging with very intelligent conversation.

Mr. Badu-Bonsu is flamboyant. Expensive gold accents big, dark, well-manicured hands. He is Ivy League educated in the states, but unlike many of his fellow countrymen who would have given their right arm to stay in America, he returned to Ghana and built a small empire. He has vacation homes in the south of France and Morocco as well as a palatial home in his native Kumasi and a compound in Accra. Osei's mother was promised to his father when she was seven-years-old. He returned from America and married her.

Mrs. Badu-Bonsu's demeanor was strange. She did not speak to me in the presence of her husband. Actually, she did not speak with her husband in my presence either. I have never observed the formality I observed with the Badu-Bonsus. From my black American perspective, their family is a web of strange relationships. Osei has several siblings. His mother is the mother of four of Mr. Badu-Bonsu children. Mr. Badu-Bonsu has seven other children with three different mothers. Astonishingly, two of the children from different mothers are the same age. Mr. Badu-Bonsu is well into his sixties, yet his youngest child is five years old. All of Mr. Badu Bonsu's children are welcomed in the home. Although some of the siblings have different mothers, I could detect no rivalry.

Local and foreign dignitaries, politicians and business men and women were in and out of the home for various meetings or as dinner guests. Dinner at the Badu-Bonsus was an extravagant event. Mrs. Badu Bonsu's children and their families were always at dinner. The children from other mothers came sporadically. The maid served our meals; however, Mrs. Badu-Bonsu served her husband. The food was a smorgasbord of local fresh fruit and exotic entrées. There was a lot of boisterous laughter and conversation between the men. The women were demure and talked quietly amongst themselves. I had no interest in their petty conversations. Engaging with the men in the family was a better fit to my personality.

I took special notice when Nana, accompanied by her mother and father, entered the sitting room. The Gucci bag that hung from her healthy, toned arms was gorgeous. Her freshly braided hair was pulled away from her chiseled face in a tight chignon. Her makeup was flawless. The designer jewelry perfectly accented her honey brown skin. Korkor, his sister, introduced her as a cousin, but I could tell from the vibe, she was not a blood cousin. Her affect was flat with Osei. She greeted the family with a warm embrace and a kiss on each cheek, but she simply tilted her head in Osei's direction. I also noticed Osei greeted her differently than he greeted other visitors. He was lively and vibrant with visiting old friends; but with Nana, he was reserved.

Mrs. Badu-Bonsu's eyes lit up when Nana entered the room. She affectionately shouted, "*Babea*!" I found it strange that she referred to her as daughter when she was introduced as cousin. She continued to speak to Nana in her native language until Mr. Badu-Bonsu clapped his hands, spoke in a harsh and scolding tone in Twi, and then continued his conversation with me in English.

I learned a lot about Osei from observing his easy interaction with his multi-ethnic, wealthy friends and his close relationship with his complicated family. I immediately knew becoming a member of this family would provide status and open many doors. However, Mrs. Badu-Bonsu had other plans. She prepared a daily itinerary for me to keep me away from the home. It was evident when special guests were present, she was not comfortable with the black American guest. I brought it to Osei's attention, and he assured me that was not the case. However, I found it strange she always sent me away alone with the driver. She never accompanied me, but she ensured I visited every known site in London. Finally, after spending almost the entire vacation away from me, Osei and I took a sightseeing trip together. Mrs. Badu-Bonsu did everything she could to stop it. She pretended Atta, the driver, was unavailable and requested Osei, without me of course, drive her to brunch. Osei was adamant that we would spend time together and arranged for Kwaku to escort her instead. She was so angry she canceled the brunch date.

Our trip to the London Eye sealed our relationship. The London Eye is located on the River Themes. It resembles a Ferris wheel, but instead of open bucket seats, there is a capsule that can hold up to twenty people. Unlike a Ferris wheel, you stand and walk around inside the capsule. The London Eye is so tall, it allows for a bird's eye view of tourist sites such as Buckingham Palace and the London Bridge.

"Osei, this is beautiful! I have never seen anything like this!"

"Yes, it is fascinating. You can see over twenty miles of the city from the capsule. I believe it took about seven years to build it." He kisses my forehead. "Marry me, and I will show you many magnificent and fascinating things." He removed a flawless, five carat, princess cut diamond from a box and placed it on my finger. I always knew I would marry well and would accept no less than two carats, but this was beyond anything I imagined.

"Osei, I don't know what to say." I use the back of my hand to wipe the tears away.

"Say yes" His smile is confident, yet nervous.

"Yes!" I yelled so loud, I startled the other passengers in the adjacent capsules.

He announced our engagement to his family over dinner. His father and brothers were happy and excited. Mrs. Badu-Bonsu immediately left the table. She screamed "*Sikka Digger Tuutuuni!*" Her daughters left the table and ran after her, leaving me alone with the men. Mr. Badu-Bonsu politely smiled, excused himself from the table, and followed his wife and daughters. There was loud conversation between Mr. and Mrs. Badu-Bonsu in their native language. Loud echoes from the door opening and slamming shut permeated the house. Five minutes later, Mr. Badu-Bonsu returned to the table with the Mrs. and their daughters following close behind. He stood at the head of the table and proposed a toast in honor of our engagement "We welcome you into our family." His smile was wide and genuine. Mrs. Badu-Bonsu kept her face covered as much as she could to hide the river of tears that flowed from her eyes.

Mrs. Badu-Bonsu kept her distance from me after our engagement announcement. I was happy for the downtime, as the many outings she arranged began to feel like work. I enjoyed meeting many of Osei's childhood friends. I enjoyed the shopping spree sponsored by Mr. Badu-Bonsu, but I was happy when the trip ended.

After returning from London, Osei and I found perfect jobs in our respective fields. Osei landed a six-figure position in a global engineering firm. I landed a close to six-figure position in the District Attorney's office. A year after graduation, we were married. His father insisted we get married in Ghana, but I wanted my family and friends to attend. Unlike his family and friends, mine could not afford to travel to Ghana for a wedding. Mr. Badu-

Bonsu and all of his children attended, but Mrs. Badu-Bonsu became afflicted with a mysterious illness at the last minute that prevented her from traveling the nineteen-hour, first class flight to Atlanta.

Our lives were well planned and executed. Two years after the wedding, I became pregnant with Che'. I agreed to another baby two years later to get it over with. I honestly never wanted children. I'm not vain, but I like my body. I work out five days per week, and to be honest, I don't like being pregnant. When I am pregnant, it feels as if my body has been invaded by an extraterrestrial. Pregnancy, for me, is not the pleasurable experience many women describe. Osei wanted four kids. I negotiated two.

Until now, we have never had problems communicating. We are both very driven and feed off each other's energy. This dissension began around the time he did not receive a well-deserved promotion to partner at the firm, and I was promoted to Senior Assistant District Attorney. Osei has engineering designs better than most engineers. He works harder than anyone in the firm. When a younger, less experienced, less educated fraternity brother of the vice president's wife's Junior League member's son made partner over him, he was beyond insulted. Osei is not a docile man. He was unhappy about the decision, and everyone in the firm knew it.

"Next year!" he yelled so loud, I had to move the phone away from my ear for fear of bursting my eardrum.

"Osei, calm down; you are at work!"

"I don't give a shit! Fuck that racist son of a bitch!" The racist son of a bitch is Rahm, his immediate manager. Osei and Rahm have never gotten along. I am sure if Rahm could fire Osei, he would. Osei is a major asset; he has global connections that generate millions annually for the firm. Firing Osei would be career suicide for Rahm. I have always liked Rahm. I think he is smart and has a good sense of humor. Osei thinks his career rides on White Boy Fraternity connections and believes Rahm to be highly overrated at the firm. I don't agree with Osei. I think Rahm knows his stuff, and what he does not know, he is smart enough to hire someone like Osei who does.

"Osei, this is not the way to behave on your job. You must maintain your reputation. Take the rest of the day off and meet me at home. We can gather the children later."

Chapter 4

The pungent aroma of cannabis hits me hard in the face as I enter the garage. I exit the car and leave the garage door open to help get rid of the odor. I have begged him not to smoke in the house, but he has convinced himself it is harmless. I explain it may be harmless, but my career dictates I am not to be around or associated with any illegal activities.

I have explained to him a million times that his ganja source will eventually get caught. He dismisses my concerns as paranoia. He believes he is safe from law enforcement because he rarely smokes and his supplier is Ghanaian. He does not understand loyalty; it means nothing when one is faced with a lengthy prison sentence. Some defendants will turn in their own mothers out of fear of doing time. I walk into the den and place my briefcase and purse on the brown leather ottoman. The smell hangs in the air and permeates the entire downstairs. He sits at the end of the sofa with his feet propped on the leather ottoman.

"I am not going back!" He brings the glass with a shot of brown liquor to his nose, swirls the liquor around in the glass and swallows it in one quick gulp. His eyes are red. "Fuck them!" His speech is slurred.

"You are not a quitter. You have to go back." I walk behind the sofa and rub his shoulders. I softly kiss the back of his neck, slip my hand under his shirt, and rub my fingers over his nipples. "We have a mortgage, private school fees, two notes on luxury vehicles, and credit card bills to pay."

"Yeah, this is not my country." His smug, arrogant tone makes me uncomfortable. I have never seen this side of him. "I can work for my father. I don't have to put up with this racist, good old boy shit! Car notes? Mortgages? What the fuck is that? My father will wipe out all of our debt tomorrow if I ask."

"I thought you wanted to make your own money. Be your own man." I nibble on his ear and slowly push his shoulders down until his back is firmly pressed against the sofa. "You are always downing your brother, Kwaku, for not making it for himself." I slowly walk around to the front of the sofa. I remove the hair pins from my hair. The French roll at the back of my head unravels and my hair falls onto my shoulders. I purposely prop my weight on one leg so my toned and shapely thigh on the other is exposed through the slit in my skirt. I seductively pose in front of him and slowly open my blouse one snap at a time.

"Me and Kwaku are different." He is calm and very attentive to my subtle strip tease. "Kwaku never left. In retrospect, there was no need to leave. We had everything we needed and wanted in Ghana and Europe." He grabs his crotch, squeezes his thighs together, and leans deep into the sofa. He lights his spiff again and deeply inhales then slowly exhales clouds of smoke that hover in the air.

"Put that away! I can't be near that!"

"You have to stop being so square! You don't work for the fucking CIA! It is just a civil fucking service job, for God's sake!" He ignores me, places the spliff between his lips and inhales again before he reluctantly puts it out. His insults are becoming more frequent and blatant each day. I want to change my mind and go back to work, but I dig down deep and find sympathy to give him relief from the bulge in his pants. I bend forward, loosen the button, and unzip his pants. He lifts his hips so I can slide them down. He rubs my face as I slide to my knees. I take in as much of him as my mouth will hold. With each up and down stroke, his shaft hardens until it is rock solid. I stand, step out of my tights, pull up my skirt, and straddle him. He steadies his hard-on in his hand as I slowly slide onto it. I move my hips slow, then faster to keep up with his rapid, deep thrusts. My arms are tightly wrapped around his thick neck. I inconspicuously glance at my watch. Five minutes have passed. I am honestly not in the mood; this is for Osei. Making love is the last thing on my mind. I would rather work developing strategy to put Mr. Thomas behind bars for life.

I glance at my watch. We are at the six-minute mark; I tense my body as if I am having the orgasm of all orgasms. Soft moans escape my mouth. I beg him to thrust harder. I pant and feign physical exhaustion, hoping he will quickly climax. My head falls on his shoulders as if it weighs a ton. Osei is still erect. I make a mental note of the tasks I plan to complete tomorrow then make a grocery list in my head. It usually takes three to four minutes for Osei to climax after I orgasm when he is tense, but we are now past the ten-minute mark. He grabs my hips and holds me in place while he pushes up and deep inside of me. Finally, his entire body shudders then stiffens. I feel a river of warm liquid flow inside of me. I intentionally wait a couple of minutes before moving. I attempt to get up. His grip around my waist is tight.

"I want to hold you." He holds me tighter while planting soft kisses on my neck. "You should stop faking it."

"I was not faking."

"I can tell when you are faking." He is lying because if he could tell, his self-esteem would be damaged. I fake it seventy-five percent of the time. He would never want to make love to me if he knew how often I fake it. I continue to plan my strategy. I try to wiggle out of his arms, but they are wrapped tight around my waist.

"I want to feel you in my arms."

"I will be back. I need to wash this stuff off me." He releases his grip. I use my tights to wash away the sticky stuff that flows down my leg as I walk to the bathroom. He follows and joins me in the shower.

"I am going home." He barely twists the nob for the water to flow. The water is almost too hot, but this is how he likes it, so I tolerate it. He turns around, and I lather his back.

"What?" The silence is so thick, you can cut it with a knife. I rinse the suds away from his deep chocolate skin and turn around so he can lather my back. Surely he knows this is something we should talk about before a decision is made.

"I need to go home. We haven't been home with the kids in a while. It will be nice to go home for a while. They need to see their family again."

"Can't your family come here? I don't know if I can go. I just made Senior Deputyt District Attorney. My hard work is paying off. I am next in line for District Attorney, and I have a really big case to prosecute."

"What?" There is a strange accusatory tone in his voice. "When?" His stare is hard and intense; it feels as if he is scolding me with his eyes.

"I just found out today." I am lying. It is strange; I feel guilty.

I have no idea where these feelings of guilt originate. Osei has always been in my corner. We bathe in each other's success. "I was going to tell you." He turns the water off and steps out of the shower. I turn the water back on and rinse the lather off. I cannot read the expression on his face. I do not know the emotion tied to his expression. It is one I have not seen before. "I will take time off and go with you." I turn the water off and step out of the shower. I don't know the source of the insecurity I feel, but I did not want the children to travel to Ghana without me. I should welcome the opportunity to be alone to work on my case. My last three cases received not guilty verdicts. Colleagues whispering about my skills at the water cooler are beginning to affect my self-esteem. It is important that I win this case against Jefferson Thomas.

"Thanks, Ayanna, I really need that. I really need you right now. Besides, we need a vacation. Pop has hi-speed Internet in his home office. He has videoconferencing; you can do your precious little job while you are there." His negative, combative attitude quickly returns. He continues to dry his body, then throws the towel on the floor next to the pile of clothes he removed earlier. He knows this is not acceptable. I am not the maid, and the one we have is not due for another two days.

"I am going to get the kids." I wait for him to pick up his mess. Instead, he puts on a pair of jeans and a T-shirt, grabs his keys, and leaves. I look at the mess. My first instinct is to leave it. I hate clutter and cannot function in disorder. Leaving his stuff on the floor will only torture me, so I gather the pile and take it to the laundry room.

The house is quiet. I want to simply sit and enjoy the serenity, but the children will be hungry and expect dinner when they walk in the door. I totally resent this cooking thing. We need a full-time maid and nanny, but he is against people coming into our home around the children. It took an act of Congress for him to agree to a maid coming two days per week. I skip down the spiral stairs to the kitchen. Osei does the majority of the cooking, but the two days per week I am scheduled to cook are simply too much. I hate this part of family life. Cooking and house cleaning is not something I enjoy, especially when we make enough money to pay someone to do it for us. I open the freezer and notice an unopened package of ice cream bars hidden behind the vegetables. I throw the ice cream in the trashcan, grab chicken breast and mixed veggies, and make stir fry.

I am startled when my phone beeps. It is a message from Trevor. I do not respond. It is almost 6:00, and he knows I am with my family. I erase the message and make a mental note to remind him not to send messages after 5:00. I am in the kitchen finishing dinner when I hear the garage door open. OJ runs directly into my waiting arms. Che' immediately goes to the kitchen, opens the freezer door and slams it shut. She stomps to her room and slams her bedroom door. I hate to admit it, but I am joyous from her disappointment. Osei walks past me; he mumbles something inaudible that sounds like a hello before he runs up the stairs. I don't bother to ask him to repeat it. I just want the day to be over and pray he will soon return to himself.

OJ sits at the bar stool while I cut fresh fruit for dessert. He is talking so much that initially I do not notice the television is on in the den. I enter the den and find Che' sitting in the leather chaise diva style with the remote comfortably in her hand, flipping the channels.

"Have you lost your mind? Television is not allowed until after dinner and homework! You know this!"

"Daddy said I could." She turns away from me and continues watching the television. I grab the remote and turn off the television.

"Wash up for dinner! After homework, you will get your hour of television!" I thought I would have to drag her out of the seat because it takes her ten seconds too long to move. Lucky for her, she uncrosses her legs, stands, and stomps to the bathroom

Osei enters the kitchen as I finish setting the table. He is silent and unengaging. Che' appears angry at the world. The only chatter comes from OJ. I don't know how long it takes to get over the disappointment of not getting a promotion, but I hope Osei gets over it soon. His sulking is driving me crazy.

After dinner, I clean the kitchen and go straight to bed. He usually comes upstairs with me after the children go to bed, but he remains downstairs in the den watching television.

"Mommy" I wake up to find OJ prying my eyelids open with his fingers. "Wake up." I look at the clock; it is six o'clock. Osei's side of the bed has not been touched.

"What's wrong, baby?"

"I peed in my pants." He looks down at the wet spot on his

pajamas.

"It is okay. Go to the bathroom, and I will be there in a second."

He stands in the tub, as I run the water. He is talking a mile a minute as I bathe him. I respond but really have no idea what he is talking about. It is early, and I am perplexed that my husband did not come to bed last night. I finish with OJ then take a shower. I put on my clothes and go downstairs, where I find Osei fully dressed in the kitchen, making breakfast for the children. I greet him, but he ignores me. I kiss the children, grab my keys, open the garage and leave.

Not making partner was the last straw for him. He deserves to make partner, but he feels entitled. I try to explain to him that many people, particularly black people in this country, do not get what they deserve. We make the best of things. Besides, we cannot complain; we are firmly upper middle class and enjoy more perks than the average family of any ethnicity.

Chapter 5

"Ms. Williams" I am in the middle of an important meeting when Kate knocks on the conference room door. She stands in the threshold. I excuse myself from the meeting.

"Yes, Kate." My foul attitude is purposely transparent.

"Ma'am, it's your husband; he says it is important." Her voice quivers; her hand trembles as she passes the cordless phone to me. I close the door to the conference room, step into the hall, and take the call.

"Yes Osei, is there a problem?" I am annoyed. I try to set a good example for my subordinates. When it is time to meet, it is time to meet. With the exception of a life and death emergency, interruptions are not allowed.

"I need you to meet me at the post office in the Federal Building. They will not allow me to get the replacement passports without you."

"What passports?"

"Passports for Che' and OJ. They need passports to travel out of the country. Remember we lost their passports last year?"

"Osei, you have got to be kidding me! I am at work in a very important meeting! I can't leave now! What is the urgency?"

"When can you meet me?" He ignores my protest.

"I am at work! This can wait until I get home!" I hang up the phone, not too hard to attract the attention of my colleagues, but hard enough for Osei to know I am miffed.

"Kate, don't interrupt my meeting again! If anyone calls," I stress *"anyone"* and furrow my brows to convey my sincerity, "please send them to my voicemail. As always, I will return all calls when I am finished with my meeting."

"Yes, ma'am."

I put on my poker face and return to the meeting. I fight to stay focused as my team provides updates on their cases. Osei's behavior is distracting. My team depends on my expertise and look to me for leadership in prosecuting difficult cases. Luckily, when I received this promotion, I implemented a policy of recording status meetings. I do not understand the urgency of this trip. After the meeting, I listen to five messages from Osei before I return his calls.

"What is the rush?"

"There is a lot to do before we leave, Yanna!" I had hoped he was not serious about this trip and prayed the idea of the trip was his need to blow off steam. I planned on organizing a mini-vacation for us to allow him to take his mind off work and regroup before he came up with this brilliant idea of leaving the country.

"Can't you talk to me when I get home? I was in a very important meeting, and I can't talk now because I have another meeting in five minutes. This is the big one for me!"

"Your job and career goals supersede everything, including me and the kids!" The pitch in his voice is high and deep. "We are mere backdrops on your stage, and I am sick and tired of it! If you want this marriage, things will have to change!" He has never given me the impression our marriage is on shaky ground.

"That is not fair, Osei! I have always supported your career! Why can't you support mine? Where does this hostility come from?" If it were not for his breathing, I would swear he hung up the phone. "I will see you when I get home."

I rush out of the office to the conference room for a scheduled meeting with D.A. Leslie. This is our third attempt at meeting. Each time, we have had to postpone the meeting due to a previous appointment that slipped his mind or an unexpected meeting he needed to attend. I stop outside of his office, adjust my clothing, and tuck loose strands of hair back into my French roll. I knock on the door to announce my presence before entering.

"Come in" He appears thinner than usual. Initially, there is no eye contact and his vibe is unwelcoming. His temperament is normally jovial. He usually stands and greets his staff when we enter his office. His appearance is normally impeccable, but he looks like he rolled out of bed and came straight to the office. Course, grey stubble sticks out of his pores like porcupine needles. He looks as if he has not shaven in days. His tie is normally straight and perfect. It is loose with noticeable coffee stains. The top button of his shirt is unfastened, and a dark stains line the inside of his collar. His rugged, unkempt appearance makes me uncomfortable.

"Good evening, sir." If he returned my greeting, I did not hear it. I pass the manila folder with the case report to D.A. Leslie. It feels as if my arm hang in midair for hours before he takes the file from my hand. He leaves his desk and finally takes a seat at the conference table. I follow him. I turn on the projector, place my memory stick in the computer and join him at the long, mahogany wood conference table. I start the PowerPoint presentation with Jefferson's current mugshot. I flip through fifty slides that highlight the evidence. "I admit, right now, it is mostly circumstantial and relies on the testimony of a twelve- or thirteen-year-old child. With the proper resources, I can build a solid case against him."

"Not enough." He flips through Jefferson's file, barely looking at the pages before he closes it.

"Are you serious?" I am cautious to keep emotion out of my voice.

"You don't have enough evidence. Everything you have is circumstantial." He taps his pen on the table then leans back in his over-sized high-back leather chair. "An unnamed Asian male seen with a skinny black girl that lies about her age or a skinny black girl that lies about her age getting into a car with a black male does not constitute a crime."

"Sir, I believe it does constitute a crime if the black male is involved in the Asian male sexually exploiting the skinny half-dressed black girl that lies about her age." The DA finds no humor in my sarcasm. "According to Detective Davis, the Asian male invoked diplomatic immunity, so the detective could not interrogate him and had no choice but to release him to his embassy. He is using his contacts at the FBI to identify the gentleman and his purpose in the states." He reaches for his smart phone and begins scrolling through messages. I feel small and inadequate but continue with the presentation. "Mary Beckham, the county social worker, is working with Ashleigh. We believe her testimony will…"

"The testimony of a runaway hooker?" He folds his hands behind his head and leans back into his chair. "Did the girl identify Mr. Thomas as her pimp?"

"No, she did not." I tuck a runaway strand of hair behind my ear. "As you know, pimps are cunning. She claims she does not know him, but we are working with her to win her trust and…"

"You want to hold him in spite of the fact the runaway hooker denies knowing him or the Asian male?" His constant interruption annoys me, and his apprehension in moving on this case surprises me. D.A. Leslie has supported all of my cases in the past. Until these last three verdicts, I had a one hundred percent conviction rate; a rate higher than any Assistant District Attorney in the county's history. The last three defendants did not accept a plea and opted for a court trial. The cases should have been a slam dunk, but the defendants were able to secure legal counsel.

"With all due respect, the runaway hooker is a twelve, maybe thirteen-year-old child. I believe this is going to pan out to something big. As you know sir, Jefferson Thomas does everything big. We owe it to the citizens of this great state to put him where he belongs. He is a co-conspirator in cheating the citizens of the county by purchasing the allegiance of many of our local and state politicians." I take a deep breath. "We cannot let him get away this time."

"True, he does everything big, but I just don't see the evidence. For now, you have to let him go."

"Let him go? Sir, you cannot be serious!" I stand, straighten my jacket, and walk to the water cooler to gather my composure. "Sir, this is the same Ivy League graduate responsible for a lot of crack babies in this city. Many who are now adults and wreak hell, havoc and mayhem on our city. We know he was responsible for reintroducing heroin in the third and fourth wards. He was king to all of the meth and crack addicts in zones five, seven and eight, and now he has changed his career to peddling little girls, and we just let him go?" I pause and take a deep breath. "Sir, he hides behind his friendships at City Hall and the capital. It is almost election time. The citizens of this county will be most grateful to their District Attorney for getting this pervert off the street." I sit down in the chair directly across from him. "The news media will be all over this. We had an abundance of evidence the last time we prosecuted him. Everyone was shocked when charges were dropped." I inhale, count to ten, and place the pesky runaway strand behind my ear again. "This is not like the last time. We actually have someone in our possession who can testify. Someone we can protect. Sir, this is more than a pimp and prostitute case. I will deliver. If you give me the resources, I will deliver." His delayed response makes me uneasy.

"I spoke with the mayor. He says you have already started to discuss the case with him." It feels like he is scolding me.

"I was not discussing the case." This feels like an interrogation as opposed to a status meeting. "Detective Davis and I were at Stoney's with Trevor Bordeaux, the State Attorney, when the major stopped at our table, and I simply mentioned that we may get another shot at Jefferson Thomas. As you will recall, sir, he attempted to make a mockery out of this office."

"Mr. Thomas has a lot of friends in the political arena. I would like for you to keep protocol and respect for the chain of command!"

"Of course, I fully understand."

"The budget is tight; I will do what I can to find the resources when you have something more. Right now, there is no funding for a case based on circumstantial evidence. We don't need the embarrassment that happened the last time we tried to prosecute Mr. Thomas; for now, he walks." He turns and stares me in the eye. "We cannot allow taxpayer money to be used to settle personal vendettas."

"Sir, I can assure you this is not personal." He stands at the opposite end of the table.

"I am going to go off the record. Mr. Thomas knows a lot of people in big places. There are people in those big places who believe you will make a great D.A. when my tenure is over. Don't fuck that up over some personal shit. I will do what I can to provide the resources when you produce something other than circumstantial evidence and conjecture."

"Thank you, sir. I will work with Detective Davis to get the evidence, build a case, and present it to you at a later date." I check my watch. It is 5:30. I grab my briefcase and laptop. It is my turn to get the children, and once again I am late. I hang my D.A. badge on the rear view mirror and speed down Interstate 20 to Grace Academy. I know I am past late. With the exception of two school buses and a black Mercedes, the parking lot is empty.

"Hello, Gail" She does not return the greeting. She raises her eyes over her glasses and tilts her head to the side. "I am here for Che' and OJ."

"Your husband picked them up hours ago." I hate this

woman. For some reason, Osei thinks the world of her, but I think her attitude stinks.

"Are you serious? He must have forgotten it is my turn." She sarcastically glances at the clock on the wall, as if I do not know it is thirty minutes after pick up. I leave the building as fast as I walk in.

"I am at the kids' school." I quickly call Osei as I walk to the car. I hear OJ and Che's voices in the background. "But you have them. You could have called and let me know you were getting them."

"Oh damn, it is your turn. I am sorry. Come home; I have a surprise for you."

"Surprise? What kind of surprise? You know I don't like surprises."

"Just come home." He ends the call before I can protest. I don't like surprises, but I am happy my husband is acting normal for a change. If he was still in his funk, I would probably check into a hotel to clear my thoughts. I have too much on my mind to deal with Osei's antics. I am obsessed with prosecuting this case. Surprisingly, D.A. Leslie is not behind me. He and I know I can build a strong case and get a conviction with adequate resources. It will be a challenge; Jefferson is embedded in the political circles. He won the last bout. I had no idea the extremes he would go to for survival. Although the ethic allegations were unfounded against me, it took a lot of time for the parties in my network to believe in me again. When your name is plastered all over the local news and reporters camp out in front of your subdivision to report on a political scandal, politicians treat you as if you have the plague.

I arrive home; the pleasant aroma of fresh ginger and fresh fish greets me as I open the door and enter the kitchen. Che' and OJ sit across from each other at the dinner table. Osei meets me with a glass Kistler Vineyard Pinot Noir. He places a soft kiss on my lips and takes my bags.

"Sit down; dinner is ready." I am speechless; we have been at odds for a while; I am apprehensive of getting too comfortable with his kindness.

"What's the occasion?" I sip from my glass as he brings the plates to the table for me and the kids.

"No occasion, a man knows when he is not treating his woman right. I've been an ass."

"You have been difficult lately." I smile, but I am in total agreement; he has been an ass.

"I've been going through some stuff lately. I have taken it out on you, and I apologize."

I blow a kiss in his direction. He blows one back. This is the family I can tolerate. The children take turns sharing the events of their day. Between filling their mouths with food, OJ and Che' debate which witch is more powerful in a children's story I never heard of. There is no tension between Osei and me.

"Truce?" We toast and sip our wine. He leans forward and places a soft kiss on my lips. "Che', OJ, go upstairs and get ready for bed." OJ wraps his little arms tight around my neck before going upstairs. Che' leaves the table and goes directly upstairs. If it were me telling her to prepare for bed, I would receive unwanted lip service; I would have to threaten her with consequences. I am not necessarily surprised, because my relationship with my mother was also strained; until my late teens, the sun set and rose on my father. I stand and reach for my plate. "No, let it be. I will clean the kitchen. Go, have your shower. I will be up when I am done."

"Osei, I love you." I almost mean it when the words leave my lips.

"I love you, too."

"I mean I really love you." I step in front of him, wrap my arms tightly around his waist and press my head firmly into his sculptured chest. His hands are full with dishes, but he returns my affection with a peck on my lips.

"Ditto, now go and have that shower; I will be up in a few."

I rummage through the drawers in search of a sexy teddy and matching undies. I cannot find anything suitable. Besides, I can tell from Osei's mood I will not need them. I shower and rub lotion all over my body. I am anxious and want to make love to my husband. It is not often that I actually want to. I have not seen Trevor in weeks, so I am in the mood. My body and mind are relaxed and waiting to receive my husband. I lay naked on my side of the bed as I hear him run up the stairs. He loosens the string in his pajama bottoms and allows them to fall to the floor as he locks our bedroom door. He removes his T-shirt in one swift move. He lies on his side, facing the night stand as he sets his alarm clock. I slide closer and rub my hand across his back down to his backside. His hard, muscular body turns me on. I desperately want to make love to my husband; the anticipation is killing me. I will leave the job at the office tonight and focus on my husband. There will be no faking this time. No mentally planning my work calendar or strategizing my next move. My thoughts are only of Osei.

His gentle touch against my skin makes me quiver. Images of my life when things were less complicated flash through my mind. I slide my hand across his chest. I stroke the ripples on top of his stomach, move further down, and rub my hand against his flaccid manhood. He rolls onto his back. I lower my mouth to his chest; his nipples immediately respond to the friction of my tongue. I roll over onto my back. He rolls over and gently lowers his body on top of mine. His rhythm is perfect. Our bodies are perfectly aligned; his hard-on strokes my G-spot perfectly. We are so in sync that we reach our destination simultaneously. This is the way I used to like to make love to my husband, simple and sweet. We lay still, holding tight to one another for what seemed like hours before letting go. I am too exhausted to wash the sticky stuff off. I use the top sheet to clean myself and make a mental note to change the sheets first thing in the morning.

"I have the children's passports." His breathing is still labored.

"How did you get them so fast?" I use the sheet to wipe the perspiration from his face.

"I paid an extra hundred bucks." He pulls the cover over my shoulder. "I want to leave in three weeks."

"Osei!" I quickly sit up. "That's not enough time. I have an important case I am working on!"

"The kids will be on summer break. This is a good time to go. The kids are out of school, everything does not have to revolve around your career. I have not purchased the tickets. I will purchase them tomorrow. If you can't join us now, then come later." A sharp pain travels from the bottom of my stomach to my chest. I roll away from him, open the night stand drawer and reach for the bottle of antacid tablets.

"You should stop taking those pills and go to the doctor, but you probably cannot make time for that either." I ignore his sarcasm. I am anxious at the thought of him and children leaving the country without me. I do not know the origin of this anxiety. I totally trust Osei with the children. He is more hands on than me, but I am not comfortable with Osei taking the children out of the country without me.

"Order my ticket. I will leave with you and the kids."

I slide close to him and roll into his arms. His body feels good next to mine. His alarm goes off. He presses the snooze button twice.

"Let's relax. We never lie in our bed and enjoy each other anymore." He pulls the bedcovers over my shoulder.

"I would love to, but work is calling me." I have other cases to prosecute, but this one will restore my reputation. I remove the covers and go to the bathroom. "Do you want to join me?" I stand in the threshold of the bathroom door.

"No, go ahead. I don't want to hold you up!" I ignore his saltiness. I close the bathroom door and enjoy the ten minutes of alone time. I leave the shower and dial Davis as I open the dresser and search for undergarments. "Can't you do that when you get to work?" Davis answers the phone. I quickly tell him I will call him back. I continue to ignore his saltiness. I gave him one hundred percent of me last night. He should be grateful. I get dressed, comb my hair and go downstairs to the kitchen and find the kids sitting at the table.

"Daddy will be down in a minute." I grab my bag, kiss the kids and leave. I dial Davis again to share the bad news as I back out of the garage.

"You got to be kidding me! We have the girl!"

"I know. He is questioning her integrity and believes no jury will believe her."

"Who is he to make that call? He has not talked to the girl. How can he ascertain her credibility without speaking with her?"

"He thinks it is personal for me. He is convinced my motivation is revenge. My last three cases ended in not guilty verdicts; he thinks I have something to prove."

"This is fucking personal to me. I will make a few calls. There are some folks in high places that owe me favors. Give me a couple of hours. He will miraculously have an unpaid speeding ticket in another county. We can hold him for a few days no matter what the D.A. says. I will see if I can get his paperwork misplaced."

"I have a special friend I have an appointment with that I believe can pull some strings as well. I will call you in a couple of hours." I end the call with Davis. I dial Osei and spend ten minutes trading niceties to ensure he is in his office. I stroll through my contacts and dial Trevor Bordeaux.

"Hello." His morning voice is sexy. "Are you on your way?"

"I am turning into the garage. Let me in." I have known Trevor Bordeaux since law school. He was the keynote speaker at Fatima's commencement. Her graduation class was small; the setting was intimate I made it my business to cross Trevor's path every chance I could get away from Osei. He is tall. His wavy, close shaven hair gives him a distinguished look. He is from old Negro money, passed down from white ancestry. He is a generational member of the Boule and has strong connections to the wealthy political class. He is a hit with the ladies. Trevor denies being a ladies' man. He is married but has been linked to several females in high places. His skin was soft and golden brown. Trevor Bordeaux is a hands on Attorney General and very personable; everyone at the graduation vied for his personal attention. I inconspicuously watched him the entire evening, trying to manipulate an opportunity to initiate a conversation with him.

"Osei," I kissed him on the lips "I am going to refresh our drinks." Trevor was finally alone at the bar. "Hello, Mr. Attorney General." I extend my hand. "I thoroughly enjoyed your speech."

"Oh" He turned around, stood up, and extended his hand. I was taken aback by the intensity of his light brown eyes. "Are you a member of this graduating class?"

"No!" I release his hand. He continues to hold tight to mine. "I will be graduating next year."

"And your concentration?" His smile is wide. His lips are slightly darkened. A faint odor of nicotine escapes his mouth.

"Criminal Law, I want to put the bad guys away."

"Let me get out of your way." He sits back down. "I am a bad guy." We both laugh. I inconspicuously look around to ensure Osei is preoccupied.

"Honey, are you ready?" A thin, light complexioned woman who could almost pass for Caucasian comes from out of nowhere and wraps her arms around him. She marks her territory with a kiss on his lips.

"This is my wife." I extend my hand. She reluctantly takes it.

"And your name again?" He leans forward.

"Ayanna Williams."

"This is Ayanna Williams." His eyes were flirtatious; he behaved as if his wife were not present. Mission accomplished. I have his attention. "Ayanna will graduate next year." His wife was unimpressed.

"It is nice to meet you, Anna."

"Ayanna" I correct her. "My name is Ayanna."

"Forgive me." She placed her left hand over her heart to ensure I see the rock the size of Gibraltar on her hand.

He kissed her on the forehead, but his eyes were on me. He motions for his security team. A tall, bald white male walks to the bar and stands next to Trevor. "Honey, let me say goodnight to everyone, and I will meet you at the car. Geoffrey, please escort Mrs. Bordeaux to the car."

"Don't be too long." She waves and puckers her lips.

"Of course not, dear, I will be with you in a minute." He removes his business card and places it in my hand. "Call me if you need advice in navigating your career. I mentor several law school graduates. I would love to be your mentor."

Trevor and I have had our special friendship for years. He gives good counsel and is always available to assist in providing strategic advice on my cases. I enter the security gate and drive in circles until I am at the 4th level of the garage. I love Trevor's man cave. I wanted to live in the heart of Buckhead, but Osei would not agree. He wanted the subdivision in the suburbs, as he was hell bent on creating the idyllic American family portrayed on television. I park in the visitor parking spot next to the elevator. He greets me at the door in his robe with a soft peck on the lips. The bulge underneath his robe pokes my stomach. He pushes his tongue so far down my throat, I almost choke.

"I miss you."

"I miss you, too Trevor, but this is a business meeting." I could not get in bed with him when I just made love to my husband a few hours ago. "I need help."

"Me, too." He points to the bulge protruding from his robe.

"Hey," I laugh, "this is business."

"Business? Was that what you were doing with the Secretary of Commerce at Stoney's yesterday? Taking care of business…" He laughs to disguise the seriousness in voice. I do not respond. He pulls me close, plants soft kisses on my neck and massages my breast. I step away from him.

"This is business."

"Can't blame me for trying." I sit on the sofa next to him. His eyes are glued to mine.

"Do you remember Jefferson Thomas?"

"Not directly; jog my memory."

"The loser responsible for the ethics charges against me and the District Attorney's office."

"The Ivy League graduate turned street thug?"

"That would be him. I have another shot at redeeming my name. He was arrested last week, but District Attorney Leslie will not grant permission to prosecute.

"Oh" He smiles.

"I need this opportunity."

"What is in it for me?"

"I am going out of the country for three weeks, when I come back, we can go away for the weekend." I grab my bag.

"Can I just taste it?" I feel guilty. I hate for him to beg, but there are rules to our situation.

"Trust, you do not want to do that." I kiss him.

"Your husband has been messing with my stuff." He laughs to lighten the mood but he is seriously getting too attached. He walks me to the door and stands in the threshold until the elevator door opens. I check my watch I am twenty minutes late for work. I rush to my car and speed out of the parking deck. I weave in and out of traffic en route to the office.

D.A. Leslie's parking space is empty. He is normally the first person in the office. I go through the motions of working on a few cases, but my mind is not in it. I want to give my undivided attention to Jefferson Thomas. He and his sycophants act as if they own the city. He looks legit, but he is not. I see straight through him.

I am sitting at my desk flipping through files when D.A. Leslie barges in my office and slams the door. His face is so contorted that he looks like a caricature. Wrinkles that would normally go unnoticed are visible and well-defined. I stand, not knowing whether to flee or fight.

"Mrs. Williams, I should fire you for insubordination!" His breathing is rapid and intense.

"D.A. Leslie, I do not understand." His disposition is almost violent.

"You had someone contact the Attorney General regarding Mr. Thomas! You have done enough to embarrass this office! Don't you think?"

"D.A. Leslie, sir, I honestly do not understand. I would never break the chain of command." I pray he cannot detect the elation in my voice.

"Why would the Attorney General insist on you prosecuting a case based on circumstantial evidence?"

"I don't know. Honestly, I had nothing to do with it. I have no idea how this happened." He slams my office door as he exits. A few seconds later, I hear his office door close so hard, it causes a vibration in my office. I am sure everyone is gathering at the water cooler to gossip about the possible reasons for the commotion. I do not leave my desk. Instead, I turn on my computer and type emails to staff members I have chosen to work with me on this case. Nothing but the best will do. Jefferson is good at manipulation. He is wealthy and will have the funds to fight a vigorous defense.

I am caught between a rock and a hard place. I wanted to stay in the states and work on this case with Davis, but in a few days we will be on a flight to Ghana. I brainstorm a formidable prosecution in my head as I make appointments to get the required vaccines for the trip to Ghana. I leave the office after lunch and spend the last half of the workday shopping with Osei, purchasing items from a list his mother emailed him.

I am resentful for having to take time off for this trip. The State v. Jefferson Thomas deserves my undivided attention. Osei's inability to accept not getting a promotion is a distraction that is causing stress in my life. He and the children are happy and excited as they load our luggage in the shuttle. I am silent and withdrawn the entire trip to the airport. I sleep the entire flight.

When we finally arrive in Ghana, the children are so tired, it takes two days for them to recover. Mrs. Badu-Bonsu immediately takes over the care of the children while Osei enjoys the vacation and I work on my case.

Mrs. Badu-Bonsu is still very distant and guarded with me, but the love she has for Che' and Osei Jr. is apparent. She is very open and inviting with the children, especially with OJ. She can't keep her hands off him. Osei never gave me the impression that he is from one of those backwards families that treasure boys over girls, but it is obvious she has a stronger affinity for OJ. She is not unkind to Che'; in fact, she is very loving. It is obvious there is a difference, but she is very protective of both children. She does not allow the maids to come near the children. Initially, I thought this was the lovingness from a grandmother. But there is something about her attention to the children that makes me uncomfortable.

Titi, Mr. Badu-Bonsu's personal assistant, escorts me to Mr. Badu-Bonsu's amazing home office. He has upgraded his office since my last visit. His flat screen computer monitor is the largest I have ever seen. His new 50" Video Conference Monitor is less than one-eighth of an inch thick. Osei explains he gets all of the electronics from China years before they are sold to the public. The backdrop behind his desk is a hand carved wooden mural. I have never seen a piece of art so massive and detailed. His Internet is faster than my service in the states. Osei is right. He has everything I need to conduct business.

"Mommy" Che' and OJ sit across from one another at a small table in the sitting room, stuffing their mouths with spoons filled with homemade mango sorbet. OJ is playful and inviting, as usual. Che' has that "*Gotcha*" look. The children are not allowed to take food out of the kitchen at home. I want to instruct them to go to the kitchen, but this is not my house. Mrs. Badu-Bonsu is still very formal with me, and I do not want to overstep my fragile boundaries by imposing my household rules in her home.

"Are you enjoying your grandmother?" They nod their heads affirming the love Mrs. Badu-Bonsu has for her only grandchildren. Though Osei's family is distant with me, they are very loving and catering to the children. I expected Mrs. Badu-Bonsu to have the grandmotherly love for the children; however, the affection the sisters display is overwhelming. I am becoming uncomfortable with the attention the sisters give the children. Every time I carve out a moment to spend with the children, Mrs. Badu-Bonsu or one of the sisters calls for them. I should be grateful because this case needs my undivided attention. It is not often a prosecutor gets a second shot at bringing a ruthless, politically connected criminal like Jefferson to justice.

I am working, but Osei is having a ball. I have not seen him this relaxed in a long time. Childhood friends who have heard through the grapevine that he is visiting stop by daily. I, on the other hand, spend my days reading Jefferson's criminal history from the last case in hopes of finding something I missed and searching online public records to find anything that leads to his financial holdings. My evenings are spent teleconferencing with my prosecution team. D.A. Leslie is right; the evidence is not enough to hold him without a bond, nor is it enough to get an arrest warrant or an indictment. We need the girl's testimony to build an airtight case. Jefferson will do everything to cover his tracks. He knows I know how he operates. He knows I will not stop. He tried not to show it, but he is worried. This is bigger than a pimping case. He does not operate on that level. He does not play low money games.

Jefferson is flash and bling. He mixes and mingles with the political class, but he is a tortured soul with no substance and a shattered moral compass. Where you see Jefferson, big money is following close behind. He likes big money, and the sex trade is a billion dollar business. Atlanta, Georgia is the sexual trafficking capital of the world; these escapades often involve young children. The perpetrators are brazen; they advertise sexual services right under our nose. The buyers and sellers have their own underground language. A simple ad in the paper for a tune up in their world has nothing to do with an automobile. His operation is complex. My team has perused many local magazines and thousands of Internet sites but cannot find one source to connect Jefferson to any of the sleazy known escort type sites. As I suspected, there is nothing typical about his operation.

"Are you going to work the entire visit?" He stands in the threshold of the sliding glass door. The breeze from Lake Bosomtue feels good; it blows the sheer linen pants close to his skin, revealing the outline of his well-toned thighs. I quickly click the exit button, and Jefferson's face disappears.

"Of course not, but I have to prepare for this case. I have to make a conference call in five minutes." The alarm from the door, that has been held open too long, beeps. He moves away from the sensor. The automatic sliding door opens a few inches, then closes. I dial into the conferencing system and wait for the participants.

"Hello." Mary is the first participant to dial in.

"Hello, Mary, how is Little Ms. Thing?"

"Ashleigh is not cooperating. She will not disclose the names of her parents. She is adamant about it. I am guessing there must have been some form of abuse in her home."

"Still in juvi?"

"Yes, but we are going to transfer her to a group home as soon as there is an opening."

"How is Ghana?" Linda, an Assistant D.A., wanted to travel with me, but I knew better than to ask. Osei does not have a friendly disposition and does not take well to strangers.

"It is lovely, but honestly I have not had time to enjoy it. Have you requested the warrants to search Mr. Thomas' financial records? I want to know where he lives. What kind of property he owns? Bank accounts? Stocks? Bonds? We need an all-inclusive warrant to search his house. Make sure the search warrant covers his computer hard drive and phone records. He will hire the best attorneys, so everything has to be in order."

"Yanna!" The electric sliding door opens again. "We will have lunch outside!" His tone is authoritative as if he is a drill sergeant shouting commands. I ignore him and continue with the call. He continues to stand in front of the sensor. The door remains open. The loud laughter and conversation is distracting, but I do my best to ignore it.

"Mary," I turn my attention from Osei and back to the conference call. "We need to work on getting Ashleigh to testify. I will talk to the D.A. about getting funds for private therapy. We need to put a team together so we can locate her parents.

"She will not budge on disclosing the names of her parents or where she is from. Honestly, we are not sure her name is Ashleigh." I attribute Mary's slurred speech to a bad connection. It is 8:00 in the morning stateside, much too early to drink. "There is no need to schedule a counseling session. We have one on staff she is scheduled to see next week."

"Ms. Williams, can we go through the Missing Children Database? I think that will be the only way. Her fingerprints came back clean. She has no juvenile record."

"Linda" I feel as if I have a bull's eye in the back of my head. Although I am doing everything in my power to ignore Osei, he is intentionally distracting me. "That could take forever." There are over two hundred thousand missing black people in this country. Many people are unaware because missing black people rarely get media attention.

"Why not use our interns to go through the database?"

"Good idea. Set up space in the empty office next to my office. Have a technician from computer support install as many computers as possible, and put them to work. Okay, ladies, we will talk in a couple of days." I thank the participants for their time and log off.

"What?" He is taking his passive aggressiveness to another level.

"What? My friends who I have not seen in years bring their families to visit, and you barely take time to acknowledge them! Can you behave like a wife for a few weeks?"

"You know I am working!"

"You did not have to come! If your little job meant that much to you, you should have stayed home! You had the option of coming later!"

"My kids were not traveling out of the country without me!"

"Really?" A surreptitious smirk beams across his face. "It is not like you spend time with them anyway. Everything in your fucking life revolves around that simple fucking public servant job!"

"Are you serious?" I walk from behind the desk and stand in front of him. "Just because your career is not moving in the direction you would like, don't you dare take your frustration out on me! Unfortunately, I don't have a rich daddy I can run home to just because shit does not go my way!"

"Is that what you think?" He steps so close to me. I can feel the heat from his breath on my face as he talks. The veins in his temple protrude. His chest unnaturally extends outward as he takes deep, angry breaths. There is an aggression in his voice I have never heard before. "Woman, if you only knew."

"If I only knew, what are you talking about?" Contention and condemnation fill his eyes.

"Quiet! Lower your voices! You will upset the children!" Mrs. Badu-Bonsu enters the office, directing her chastising, suspicious look towards me.

"Clean up! Lunch will be served in thirty minutes." His tone is harsh and very aggressive. I do not respond. Instead, I leave the main house, go to our quarters, and take a quick shower. I sit and meditate for several minutes to gather my thoughts before joining the family for lunch.

Lunch is the usual overabundance of food. The Badu-Bonsus could probably wipe out hunger on the entire continent with the food they throw away. I sit amongst the women as they engage in small talk. It is out of my nature to compare jewelry and clothes with other women. I find their conversations boring and of little substance. I couldn't care less about blue diamonds or pink diamonds or which European country has the best boarding schools or who received special invites to the presidential palace. I am in my own world sitting amongst the chattering women when I overhear Osei and his father making plans to travel to the family compound in Accra.

"We are leaving?" I panic. "How long will we be gone? I have another conference call to make before I can put things away."

"Don't worry." Mr. Badu-Bonsu shares his classic, radiant smile. "I have better, more modern accommodations in Accra." He softly taps my hand. Somehow, I am always sitting next to Mr. Badu-Bonsu. I am grateful because, as always, he is the only person in the Badu-Bonsu family who is warm and shows genuine kindness. Mrs. Badu-Bonsu and her daughters are distant and behave as if I have the plague.

Chapter 6

I am anxious. She is making major moves right out of the gate. I should have been released on my own recognizance the same day I was arrested. She has no evidence that I have committed a crime. She is a lone renegade. Her boss is too smart to fuck with me on this level. I should have not been housed in a cell block with inmates already found guilty of heinous crimes, waiting in jail for transport to maximum security prisons. She is the puppeteer manipulating the strings. I could have pulled my own strings, but I was denied my right to one phone call. For some unknown reason, none of the phones worked on the cell block. She or someone she knows produced a fake warrant for a fake unpaid ticket from a southern county I have never visited. I was stopped for a seatbelt violation three weeks ago. I was ticketed and released; there were no outstanding warrants for me.

I am happy and relieved, yet angry when the detention officer shouts, "Jefferson Thomas! Roll up!" I am released after it is miraculously discovered the unpaid tickets were not mine. Somehow, two numbers on the ticket were mistakenly inverted. The mistake was conveniently discovered one day before my civil rights would have been deemed violated. Ayanna does not know how to lose. She has not learned. One would think almost losing her career would have taught her a lesson.

I am anxious and ready to go home. My skin itches. I am funky as hell. Showering was not part of my routine. I sneaked quick showers when the other inmates were asleep, which was rare. Between the street lawyers offering advice on criminal cases and the gut-wrenching screams from scared, weak young men getting initiated to the frequent violation they will face in prison, the noise was incessant and there were very few moments of quiet and stillness. Most of the time, I was funky. I would rather be funky than stand naked next to another man. The suit they threw at me is not the same one I wore when I was arrested. The suit does not belong to me. This cheap replacement is two sizes too small. I cannot zip the pants, nor button the shirt. My arms will only slide half of the way in the jacket sleeves. Ayanna is sending a message; I have received it.

"What took you so long?" I have been sitting on the steps outside in the hot sun for over thirty minutes. The heat and the funk from this suit have me in a fucked up mood. A myriad of foul names to shout at Stacy dance in my head. When she greets me with a wide, contagious smile, my lips cannot form ugly words to say to her. How can I? She simply followed the instructions I laid out years ago. If either of us ever gets arrested, we will stay in jail until after the first court hearing, to appear as if we are hard up for cash. I stay off the financial grid as much as possible and do nothing to get on Uncle Sam's radar. On the books, I am a small, sometimes struggling business owner, and a model citizen. I donate to local and state political campaigns. I provide food from my restaurant to the homeless. I created a non-profit that raises money to award two four-year scholarships per year to disenfranchised students in economically deprived zone four. I try to keep a mean disposition when I enter the truck, but I can't. Her smile is contagious.

"Stop being evil, and don't curse me! Remember, we are trying to be better people." She is beautiful, and though I hate to admit it, I am happy to see her. "You know I am having a hard time. I really needed you to hold my hand when I was making burial arrangements for Courtney. She was my favorite cousin." Tears form in her eyes. "I can't believe she got back on that shit. She was doing so well. Thank God they made an arrest. They were able to get a fingerprint off some of the items found in her apartment. The fingerprints matched some low life drug dealer the police have been trying to arrest for a while. My aunt says the thug has already accepted a plea." She stares straight ahead with both hands holding tight to the steering wheel. "I can't believe she overdosed." Her flawless chocolate skin is inviting. I am almost tempted to kiss her.

"I can't believe that shit either. I don't understand why you did not know she was using again. You spent enough time with her to know the color of her shit!"

"She never did anything around me. She knew I would have never gone for it. I would have had her back in rehab if I had known."

"Junkies are like that. They are very cunning." I rub my hand up and down her leg and squeeze her thigh. "We will send money every month to her mother for her kids." I know my generosity to Courtney's kids will make Stacy feel better.

"Jefferson, you would really do that?" She begins to cry. "I really appreciate that. Courtney may have had her problems, but she was my cousin and best friend. We grew up together."

"Hey," I change the subject. I am not into emotions. Courtney was a threat to our enterprise and had to be taken care of. "You still did not tell me what took you so long. I don't look good in orange; I can't believe my ass got caught up in this shit. I was too careless."

"You told me not to come until after the first hearing."

"Yeah, that was three weeks ago."

"I didn't think you wanted me to come right after court. I bet you held it down, baby." She leans over the console and puckers her lips. My eyes say, "Bitch are you crazy!" She knows lip locking is not our thing. She rolls her eyes and slides back in her seat. "Jefferson, do you ever think of making our relationship official? I mean, I don't want to do this forever." I stare straight ahead. "Can't you see us getting our money right, getting totally legit, and having a couple of kids?"

"Any word on our product?" I ignore her; I want no part of her fantasy. Stacy is fully aware of our rules of engagement. Besides, we are in a dilemma. It is time to be serious. We cannot allow Ashleigh or whatever her name is to talk to the police. I know the girl is scared shitless. Stacy subtly threatens every companion. She strongly emphasizes if they get caught, it is because they have done something wrong. We are an exclusive upscale operation. We don't advertise. We are a word of mouth enterprise. We deal with clients who have just as much or more to lose. My employees are treated very well. They are provided the best accommodation, best clothing, vacations and sick time off. As long as business is taken care of, they are free to come and go as they please. Our high-end clients pay astronomical fees for our services. There is no room in this business for fuck ups. I have a lot invested. I do not employ people to dish out the punishment to a fuck up. On those rare occasions when someone fucks up, I inflict my own form of punishment. When that happens, it is over. There are no second chances in this business. Stacy is the face of the business. As a rule, the companions never see me. If they see my face, there is trouble, and my face is the last face they see before the lights are permanently turned off. Courtney was the exception; she was like family. The girl is also an exception; she is worth a lot of money.

"No, they still have her. Don't worry, she knows better than to talk."

"Yeah, according to the D.A., she is a twelve or thirteen. She is not sixteen!"

"And?"

"And that can be some real motherfucking time. I am not going to the pen. I can't do hard time. We will not do business with your North Carolina connection again."

"He seemed all business. I thought he was cool. Me and his sister kicked it hard before she left Las Vegas and moved to North Carolina. He was scary as hell, but he seemed to be about business."

"How in the hell did he not know her age? I told you, no girls under sixteen. If some shit goes down, sixteen in most states is the age of consent."

"There was a lot of pressure to find the right companion for Mr. Ye. No matter how young we tried to make the girls appear in our portfolio, he was not satisfied. The deal was too sweet to let go." She squeezes my hand. "Don't worry about it. The D.A. and the cops are bluffing. How the hell do they know how old she is? Trust me; she ain't saying shit. Besides, I am sending a couple of girls on the inside to remind her to keep her mouth shut. She is in juvi. They'll be transferring her to a group home soon. I will find out which one in a couple of days from my connection. We will bring her back. Don't worry; I got this." She unzips my pants and begins to massages my piece. "Stop thinking. I don't want you to think about anything but me."

"Don't worry? I am not worried. You had best be worried. I will check you if this shit turns bad. We run a high end operation and cannot afford these types of slips."

"I know, but the China man has specific needs. All of the companions in our portfolio were too old or too fat. You said my life depended on not losing this client. You put a lot of pressure on me."

"And I meant that shit, too." She is massaging the right spot. I close my eyes, get comfortable in my seat, and enjoy the manual stimulation. "Make sure you keep your eyes on the road."

Stacy is not my woman; she is my chick. I don't trust her as far as I can throw her. I don't trust women, period. The closest I have come to allowing a woman in my heart is Lailah. I would have kicked Lailah to the curb had I not found she was pregnant with my child. I am not gay. I don't get down with men. But a woman ain't nothing but a bitch, and I don't trust them, plain and simple. Give them an inch, they will take ten thousand. These whining bitches nag about men being dogs, but they will sell their asses to the highest bidder and not bat an eye.

"J, where is your mind?" I try to focus on releasing, but my mind is racing one hundred miles per hour.

"Just keep doing what you're doing." I place my hand on top of hers and guide it to the right spot. "I can't wait to get you between the sheets"

"Are we going home, or do we need to go to the chicken shack first?

"Girl, I am going to…home?" I have told her on more than one occasion my house is not her home. Yes, she sleeps at my home. She has a key and security access, but this is not her house. She has her own crib.

"Well, to your house…"

"You are getting too comfortable, and that can be dangerous!" Stacy is the only woman who knows where I live. My kids' mother does not know my residential address. Stacy has a few pieces in my closet, but my house isn't her fucking home. "Don't get too comfortable with me." She has fucked up my groove. I push her hand away and adjust my shit in my boxers.

"You know what I mean. Why are you uptight all of the time? I know it's not my home."

"I am not uptight. I just want to make sure we stay on the same page." She pulls the Range Rover to the gate. She places her index finger in the reader. A thin red line scans the tip of her finger. The metal gate slowly opens into another world. I play a harsh game, but the proceeds from that hell provide a five bedroom six bath mini-mansion on Heavens Row. I look around at the ten palatial homes that make up the subdivision and wonder what the rest of the owners do to live this good. I don't know their sources of income; I bet they are not punching a fucking clock.

The sweet scent of myrrh greets me as I remove my shoes at the door and step on imported mahogany wood floors in the foyer. I scan through a pile of mail stacked on the accent table next to the staircase. I am proud of my home. I am proud of my accomplishments. The odds were definitely stacked against me, but I beat hell out of those odds. I take two steps at a time to my bedroom, with Stacy one step behind me. I peel my clothes off, jump in the shower and wash the jailhouse filth off my skin while Stacy is on the phone handling business. She is a professional. She convinced me to stop the low level escort type service and take the business global. The low level escort business comes with too many risks. Advertising on the Internet and ads in local newspapers attract basic money. Our operation is upscale. We don't deal with household names. Rappers, actors, or athletes do not have the money to acquire our services. Our clients own the people who own the household names.

I walk out of the bathroom and drop the towel in the hamper as I pass the closet. I notice her clothes have taken up almost half of one side of the closet. I make a mental note to remind her to remove some of her things and take them home.

She is lying across the bed with her robe slightly open. I crawl in bed next to her. Her body is firm, yet soft in the right places. I skip the foreplay and get down to business. I was on lockdown for twenty-one days, but Stacy gives it to me like I have been away for three years. She moves her ass in slow, perfect circles where I can feel every inch of her tight walls, then bounces up and down, thrusting hard just the way I like it. It takes everything I have not to explode. I am ruthless, but a gentleman. I let her get hers first. She straddles me, holding on so tight to my chest that her nails dig deep in my skin. Deep grunts escape from her mouth. Her body shakes so hard, it feels as if she is having convulsions. She slows her rhythm to catch her breath, then grabs my chest and continues to work until I am ready to release. My climax is hard and strong. My hard on dissipates, but she continues to move to make sure I release every drop. The sensation is so intense that I push her off me and onto the empty side of the bed. We lay still, both so exhausted all we can do is stare at the ceiling.

"We can't lay here too long. We are behind schedule. The Mexicans and Russians have recruited some in demand chicks." I want to fuck again, but Stacy, as usual, is back to making my money. "Gorbachev will meet us with their portfolios tonight."

"Mexicans come a dime a dozen. The border brothers and sisters do not believe in birth control."

"I didn't say the chicks were Mexicans. I don't know where they recruit them, but they have some good looking potential companions in their portfolios. I am talking those exotic looking chicks with piercing green eyes and olive skin that may not speak good English but are hungry for the dollar. You know, the kind the celebrities use as arm candy."

"Where did you say you met Gorbachev again?" She has been talking about Gorbachev for the past five months. According to Stacy, this Gorbachev is what she calls a globalist. His allegiance is not to a country, but to international money. He is known worldwide amongst the billionaires who own the underground economy.

"I met him when I worked in Vegas." She turns away from me. She does not like to talk about her life in Vegas, so I drop it. I leave the bed and hit the shower. When I come out, she has two suits lying across my bed. "Take your pick."

"The khaki colored one is cool." I grab it and take it off the bed; she takes it from my hand.

"I like the black one better." She removes the handmade silk paisley tie from the rack and passes it to me. "You look sexy as hell in black." She stands on her toes and places a soft kiss on my cheek. "I will be ready in 15 minutes." I have to admit, it feels good having her in my corner, and it ain't so bad waking up next to her, but she is not my kind of woman.

In another life and in another time, things could have been different. I would have been with Lailah or a woman like Lailah. Lailah is pure and wholesome. I imagine if I had a normal mother, she would want me to have a woman like Lailah, but my mother has never been normal. Mary Francis Thomas' mental illness changed the trajectory of my life and led me to a woman like Stacy. She comes out of the dressing room with a black dress that fits so tight, it makes her ass look like two perfect round melons extending from her back. I get a hard on looking at her, but there is business to attend to. I'll take care of this brick in my boxers later.

She stands in front of the full-length mirror and scans her body up and down, three hundred and sixty degrees from head to toe, to ensure everything is perfect. Stacy looks like a million dollars. She was Earl's woman. Earl was one of my top salesmen. He was popped with five kilos of cocaine in his possession. Lucky for him he never made bond, because I would have put a bullet in his head for keeping the product at his residence. I was about to join her old man. It kills me how these supposedly hard negroes will sing like a canary at the thought of doing a little time. After Earl's incarceration and my indictment, Stacy and I were both down on our luck. My street connections would not fuck with me after seeing my face flash on the nightly evening news. My political connections distanced themselves from me as if I had the plague. Even the politicians whose political campaigns I financed treated me like a pariah. After the charges were dropped, everyone assumed I snitched. I am many things, but I am not a snitch. I handled my business in a way that gave them no other choice but to drop the charges. Ayanna underestimated me and the length I would go for self-preservation. My only regret is I did not finish what I started. I should have taken Ayanna's ass out as well. Matter of fact, she should have been the first person on my list. I came for her, but God was with her.

She is cunning. She betrayed me. I introduced Ayanna to many of the movers and shakers in the political scene. We saw each other several years ago for the first time in a long time at the mayor's first inauguration ball. She and her husband were dressed to the nines and looked like the couple of the year. He sports a tailored suit, and she's rocking a form fitting high–end designer gown. Her hair was perfect. Her body was perfect, thin but shapely. Every strand of her hair was in place. The African was laid back; she dragged him around like a trophy. I found him rather snooty and stingy with his conversation. She was all over the place introducing herself as the new Deputy D.A. I was conversing with Grant, a highly paid and sought after political campaign manager, about starting a football tournament with the youth in the juvenile detention centers. She passed us on her way to the bar when we immediately recognized one another from college.

"Hello, you look familiar. Do I know you?" Her smile was bright. The pricey veneers on her teeth were so perfect, they almost looked real.

"Yes, I am Jefferson Thomas." I extend my hand. She reluctantly extends her hand. Her handshake was firm.

"Jefferson Thomas?"

"Yes, Jefferson Thomas." She knew me as Tyree Thomas at Ivy League. I legally changed my name to one more distinguished. Doors open for Jefferson that would have never opened for Tyree. I continued the conversation, as there was no need to explain my name change to her.

"Have you met Grant?" She tightens her eyes, as if she is having a hard time focusing. I continue the introduction.

"Actually, I have not." She extended her hand to Grant. She behaved as if she was running for political office. She was all smiles and flirty with Grant and behaved as if her husband was not two feet away when she found out he is the most sought after campaign manager in the country. She conversed with Grant in a way she did not with me. It was as if she had a hidden agenda or a clandestine plot against me from the onset.

Ayanna believes she and I are different. We are not. We are both opportunists. Everyone in our circle knows she has brains. She is smart, but her brain is not the reason she advanced in her career quickly. I introduced her to many of the heavy hitters in her network. We play with the same politicians to get what we want. I am invited to every political event held in the county. She was moving up and quickly becoming one of the elites in the county. She began attending many of the events I attend. Initially her husband joined her, but she slowly started attending events alone. She began to make cracks at my business and questioning my net worth. She joined alliances with some of my rivals and used information from some of my loose lip friends to pique interest in my business dealings.

She used a random misdemeanor arrest from a street hustler I do not know and have never seen in my life to create a trail to Earl and connected Earl to me. I should have taken her ass out when I had the chance. She violated a myriad of ethics regulations in her quest to destroy me. She withheld pivotal evidence. She tampered with witnesses. Her network is tight and supported her attack. No matter how hard my lawyers worked, and no matter how many motions they submitted to throw out the indictment, the judge always ruled in her favor. I was losing and had to take matters in my own hands.

The heavyset and most likely underpaid female security guard at the entrance to her subdivision is a joke. The black handcrafted iron gate that surrounds her subdivision is a sign of status and security, but it was not secure enough to keep me out. I followed her undetected for months. I tailgated behind her neighbor and entered the gated community. I was scoping out the neighborhood when I saw the African standing at the mailbox in front of their house. I noted the address. I left and went online and found a map to her house. I located an entry point through the woods where I could enter the subdivision undetected. I returned a week later. I parked my car at the Chamblee train station and walked three miles through thick woods that surround her subdivision. I sat in the woods for hours behind her house waiting. Her home is beautiful. The yard is immaculate. She scores a one hundred for creating the façade of the picture perfect family.

The African came outside and lit the grill. It is hard to believe she is part of this Norman Rockwell canvas. I often think to myself. "When does she have time to play wife and mother?" She attends every political event in the county. I started to take the African out just for principle, but that would have taken away the opportunity to get the bitch I came for. She tried to destroy an enterprise that took years to build. There were businesses that built their businesses off my businesses. She is responsible for many mothers now standing in the welfare line and many children growing up without their fathers. I came to make her uppity ass pay.

After several minutes, she walked onto the deck with a bowl in her hand. She opened the bowl and placed the contents on the grill. Her head was dead center in the cross hairs of my scope. My hand was firmly on the trigger when her round belly distracted me. Her pregnancy surprised me. I had to move my eyes away from the scope and look again. She covers it well. No one in our circle knew she was with child. I alternate aiming the muzzle at the African's seed in her stomach and her head. I was indecisive on who to hit first. It did not really matter. I place my chin against the barrel and my eye on the scope as I twist the silencer. Her head was in the middle of the cross hairs again. Just as my finger touched the trigger, a little round, brown skinned body ran from behind her. Ayanna sat at the table, grabbed a bottle of bubbles, and began to blow. The chubby little girl ran after the bubbles. I put the gun down and pulled out my binoculars to get a closer look. The child had her mother's eyes. Her angular nose did not belong to her mother or the uppity African she married. She appeared to be about two years old, the same age as my daughter. Her complexion was the same as Ayanna's. The child had a wide smile with deep dimples. I sat and watched the child and her evil mother for several minutes. I hate the bitch, but no child should have to ever witness and live forever with the image implanted in their brain of their mother with a bullet lodged in her forehead.

A strange feeling came across me as the little girl appeared to lock eyes with mine. I did not understand my reaction; I was not cursed with the weakness of having a conscience. I have no problem inflicting pain. As a child, when I became angry, the neighborhood's dogs would disappear. At one point, there were no live four-legged pets within a one-mile radius of my house. My heart beat hard against my chest. My mind raced back to August 2007, when Lailah gave birth to my first kid. My head fell hard against the tree. I sat for twenty minutes to catch my breath. I untwisted the silencer, placed the Glock and the scope back in the case. I walked through the woods behind the house. I scaled the fence of her subdivision and walked to the train station, filled with internal anger for not finishing the job.

"Where is your mind Jefferson? Your mind keeps wandering off." She pauses. "Did anybody mess with you in there?"

"Are you crazy? I am over six-feet tall, and all man. A ninja would have to climb on a ladder to get my ass."

"Are you sure? You know you can tell me. I will not judge you." I pinch her ass. I am uneasy that I allowed Stacy to get this close. We have formed a good team, and we do well together. When we got together, her man and her only source of income was locked down. I wasn't behind bars, but I was not free. She had to do what she had to do. I had to do what I had to do, so we joined forces. It was a reluctant move. Initially, I thought she was a snitch. She did not have the same connections as I do. Everyone, including me, could not figure out why she did not go down with Earl. She was in the house when the weight was found. Earl took ownership of all of the drugs, and somehow she came out unscathed. At any rate, she and I were flat on our asses.

"Money is getting low. The cupboards are getting bare."

"I can sell the rest of my high end handbags at an upscale

consignment shop. I can sell more of my jewelry."

"That ain't going to get it. It costs a grip to stay in this loft. I spent a lot of my money on high end lawyers and a fortune on recalibrating the thinking of the State's witnesses."

"Maybe we can move to something cheaper?"

"Baby" I am insulted. "I don't do cheap. How about you put this on, we will hit Tits N Tats, and get some real money."

"I think you have the wrong girl! I was Earl's woman!" She picks up the crotchless and assless cat suit, holds it in the air, and turns up her nose. "You do remember the man doing time for you that kept you paid!" She grabs her purse and walks towards the door. I feel her arm pop when I snatch her around. I use the collar of her shirt as a cushion to make sure there are no scars or bruising on her neck. I place my hands around her neck. Not too tight, just tight enough to restrict the oxygen flow. Her eyes begin to bulge. Thin, curvy red lines slowly form in the whites of her eyes. I release her just before she passes out. She breathes in deep and chokes as she quickly inhales.

"I hate to have to do that to you; next time you talk to big Earl, thank him for putting us in this position." She snatches away from me. I grab her again. She loses her balance and falls to the floor. "I am going to need you to put that pretty chocolate ass in this cat suit. They are waiting for us at Tits N Tats."

She slowly pulls herself off the floor, grabs the suit, and runs to the bathroom. She comes out of the bathroom with tears flowing down her cheeks. I have never given a damn about fucking tears, especially when money is at stake. The cat suit was made for her firm and curvaceous body. She is sexy as hell. My shit is hard as a boulder. I wanted to bend her over the sofa and hit it before we left, but money was waiting.

Tits N Tats is an exclusive club. Members are so-called ballers with familiar household names. Membership is ten thousand a year for vendors, and ten thousand for customers. Exclusivity is expensive. This was the best ten-thousand-dollar investment I have ever made. I made my money back in three nights. It did not hurt that Stacy is smart. She recruited three girls for our business venture the first week and bought her way off the stage and back into my bed.

"Damn, baby, you look good." Her eyes scan my body from head to toe as she adjusts her firm and perky breast in her dress.

"Black is your color; it matches your heart." She laughs, but we both know she is telling the truth.

"You look good yourself." I gently take her arm and pull her close to me. I catch myself. I almost kiss her. "Let's go get our money."

I never met the new connection, but as much as Stacy talks about these guys, I am able to place a name with a body upon entering the restaurant. Gorbachev is the big olive skinned guy sitting at the table. I am over six-feet tall, and he has me by a good two inches. He's a plain guy. I would think if his acquaintances and business partners are owners of international conglomerates, he would own tailored suits. The mass manufactured suit makes him appear common. He notices us as we pass the bar. He leans and whispers to the two gentlemen sitting next to him. The gentlemen stand, leave the bar, and walk to different tables on opposite sides of the restaurant.

Stacy enters the restaurant like a movie star. Gorbachev follows her with his eyes from the time she enters the restaurant until she arrives at his table. He stands, shakes my hand, never looking at me; his eyes are glued on Stacy. An inch of jealousy creeps in, and I remind myself she is not my woman. She is my chick. We discuss the logistics of the transaction and agree to meet in the safety of the Caribbean to make the financial and administrative exchanges.

"Where is your mind, J?" Stacy leans close as Gorbachev leaves the table to speak privately with his connections.

"I am right here with you" I lie. "Hey, you handle this business. Get your connection to give you a ride to your apartment; I will catch you in the morning." I pay the tab, grab my jacket and keys and leave. I stand outside of the restaurant for five minutes waiting for the valet to bring my car. I cannot concentrate on the meeting. My mind is on my children and their mother. I don't know where it comes from, but every once in a while I become anxious about them and have to be near them just for a moment. There are very few cars on the freeway tonight.

I speed down 85 South and take exit 37 to Fayetteville, Georgia. I drive ten miles down a dark road. The house is in the middle of nowhere. She loves this country life. She says it is good for the kids. It is late, so I turn the lights off before I approach her brick, ranch style home. A pink girl's bike with one training wheel lies in the middle of the driveway behind Lailah's minivan. I have offered to buy her a more upscale vehicle, but she loves the van for the children. All of the lights are off in the house, with the exception of the one in her bedroom. I sit in the car outside of the house. I wish I was worthy enough to be on the inside with them. I stay my distance because Lailah and the kids are the purest things I have in my life, and I will never fuck that up.

Chapter 7

I compare Jefferson's latest mug shot with the one taken six years ago. He has not aged. His confident smile is almost seductive. The contour of his shoulders and upper body is eye catching. Absent the orange jumpsuit, he would look as if he was at a photo shoot as opposed to a resident of Cell Block B. His jet black hair, flawless caramel skin and chiseled face could easily grace the cover of high fashion men's magazines. His well above average looks and brain has opened many doors for him. The sky could have been the limit for him. During the first prosecution, I thoroughly researched his life. Criminality is in his DNA. His mother, Mary Francis Thomas, has several misdemeanor charges and one felony charge for aggravated assault. All of his school records show his maternal grandparents as his guardian. There is no history of a father. He has no juvenile record. Though he has the physical build, he did not play sports. There was nothing remarkable about his life until high school, where he graduated valedictorian of his class.

He pretended to come from money. He had me and most everyone fooled. I thought he was from an affluent family possibly the son of a politician, an athlete, or an entertainer. He spoke with confidence. He was articulate and could converse with anyone on any subject. The problem is ninety percent of what came out of his mouth was a lie.

"Excuse me, madam." I turn the computer monitor away and switch to another screen as Beauty enters Mr. Badu-Bonsu's office. "I will need to copy a few files from the hard drive this afternoon to take to Accra."

"Sure, I will be finished in about an hour." I check my email and find a message from Trevor, begging to see me when I return to the states. I quickly delete the message.

"No hurries." She smiles and leaves the office. I switch the screen back to Jefferson's mugshot. I have to deliver this time. I am losing my edge. Three not guilty verdicts in a row are unacceptable statistics. Jefferson is the catalyst that will give me my edge back. I underestimated him last time, and he got away. This time, I will be prepared. His dark eyes emit an evil so intense, I have to look away from the computer monitor. A chill travels from the bottom to the top of my spine. A burning sensation travels from my chest to the back of my throat. I reach in my purse for an antacid tablet and pop it in my mouth. He has manipulated many people in our circle. Some know he is a criminal but are willing to turn a blind eye to keep his bribery money flowing. Jefferson is greedy and unwilling to play by the rules. It is hard to believe the choices he has made and the number of people who have suffered and continue to suffer because of his greed. I quickly switch the computer screen again as Ncheke enters the office with a duster attached to her apron.

"Excuse me, ma'am." She moves pictures, cleans underneath, and replaces them in the exact spot. I swear this house, with its maids and drivers dressed in crisp starched uniforms in the heat of the African sun, reminds me of an antebellum plantation house minus the antebellum style homes and white plantation owner. I erase the Internet history, shut down the computer, and remove my flash drive. I gather my files, go to our quarters, and pack for Accra.

Beauty's small plastic woven travel bags look out of place amongst the designer luggage that fills most of the foyer. Beauty accompanies the Badu-Bonsus when they travel. The rest of the staff is left behind to tend to the home in Kumasi. We are driven by chauffeured limousine to the Badu-Bonsus' compound in Accra. We pass a couple of wealthy, newly formed suburbs composed of beautiful mansions and perfectly landscaped yards. After a few miles, the landscape abruptly changes. We are stuck in bumper to bumper traffic as we drive through several large communities consisting of shanty homes made of tin, cardboard and anything salvageable. Children half-dressed run up to the car with their hands out, begging for money. I reach in my purse and remove a few bills. Osei takes them out of my hand. "We give to charity every year." I place my purse back on the seat and look out the window as we leave the shanty town and drive through bushy vegetation for another hour before arriving to the Badu-Bonsu compound in Accra.

Their rich lifestyle amongst vast poverty is overkill. The gated compound sits on two hundred hectares of land. The main house sits in the middle of the compound. An Olympic size pool separates the main house from a guest house that looks more like a starter home. A small maid's quarter sits behind the guest house. A colossal vegetable garden with a complete irrigation system sits on one side of the maid's quarters, and a massive professionally landscaped flower garden sits on the other side. The house is the most modern house I have ever seen. Solar panels cover the roof. The front of the beige stucco house is mostly glass, with custom blinds that deflect the intense heat from the hot African sun. The rooms are large and almost double the size of an average master bedroom in the states. Each bedroom has its own bathroom and sitting area.

From what I can tell, most of Osei's friends and acquaintances live this life, but the African experience for most Africans is quite different from the Badu-Bonsu experience. I have been in Ghana for over a week. I expected a full itinerary after the first week, but there were no plans to visit any of the tourist attractions. Not even a trip to the local market. In past visits when I ask for a tourist outing, I was always met with resistance. Osei used the children's age as an excuse, declaring they would be too young to remember. The Badu-Bonsus seem to have no interest outside of their small circle of friends. Mrs. Badu-Bonsu and her friends alternate visits between their luxury homes, upscale restaurants, and VIP parties. Local shopping is done by her personal assistant and Atta, the family's main driver.

"Osei, do you think we can visit the Door of No Return?" I have almost completed my task list and can make time to enjoy our trip. "You know I have always wanted to tour the site. You promised we could visit this trip. It is a must see tourist attraction for black Americans."

"Why do you want to go there?" His condescending tone and demeanor catch me off guard. The truth is, I want to get away from this house so I can think and meditate over my case. There is something about this case that is getting to me. D.A. Leslie is right; I have something to prove. Jefferson tried to ruin my good name, and the last three cases I prosecuted ended with not guilty verdicts. I can usually convince defendants to take a plea deal, but lately the criminals are coming up with the money to secure good legal counsel.

"Because that is where we were taken until they dragged us onto the ships." Although he has lived all over the globe, he has lived in Ghana the majority of his life. Surely, he is aware of the *"Door of No Return"* and the sanctimonious value to black Americans.

"How do you know that? How do you know your ancestors were from the west coast? There are fifty-seven countries in Africa."

"I didn't ask for a geography lesson. It does not matter; I want to visit." I feel strange having to explain my intentions especially when he is almost right. "I would like to take the children, so they can experience it."

"My children will not be going. If you insist on this foolishness, I will have Atta drive you. I do not understand why you black Americans spend so much time infatuated with such a horrid history."

"I am not infatuated with anything! What do you mean your children? What is it with your negative attitude? I have really had about all I can stand!"

"What time do you want to go?" He lowers his volume and totally dismisses me. "I will have a driver for you. The kids are having brunch with Mother, Mrs. Quarshie, and Mrs. Quarshie's grandchildren." I want to discuss his making decisions about the children without discussing them with me, but once again I let it go.

"Please have the driver ready for me in the morning before it gets too hot."

"Atta will gather you at 9:00 am. Shower and prepare for dinner." He continues with his authoritative tone. "And at the dinner table, please sit amongst the women. People are talking." He seems to be making subtle accusations, but I do not respond, and I honestly do not know the origin of this tone he now uses with me, but it makes me feel uneasy. I am in his country. I continue to ignore him.

The dinner table is filled with fresh fruit. Osei, the children, all of his siblings, and Mrs. Quarshie are dressed to the nines. Mrs. Badu-Bonsu cast evil eyes on me and whispered something in Twi as she shakes her head from side to side. I feel out of place in my jeans and halter, but I remain at the table. The maid served ground nut stew over gari with fried plantain on the side. A special pot without the spices was prepared for Che' and OJ. While the maid served our meal, Mrs. Badu-Bonsu served her husband and the children.

"Osei, your mother is enjoying the children. She will hate to see them leave." Mr. Badu-Bonsu's voice is deep, strong, and reminds me of the sound of an oboe.

"I know, Pop; we will visit more often. I promise."

"I was thinking; you and your family should move home. You do not have to worry about making partner at this substandard American firm." He tosses his hand in the air as if he is dismissing the Fortune 500 firm that employs Osei. "You are heir to your own business. You have your own fortune." My heartbeat quickly accelerates. My blood pressure elevates. Beads of perspiration congregate on my forehead and under my nose.

"Yes at some point that would be great. My dream is to return home." His smile is wide and authentic. He shakes his head back and forth, as if he is erasing the thought from his mind. "Thanks for the offer, Pops, but now is not the time. I need more experience, and right now Ayanna is doing well in her career; she just received a promotion."

"That will not be a problem." He smiles. Mr. Badu-Bonsu's teeth are so perfect, they almost appear false. "I will give Ayanna a position. She can have any position she wants and any expertise you need in continuing your development. I will be available to mentor you." He toasts his thin glass filled with palm wine towards me. I smile and look around the table to avoid eye contact with Mr. Badu-Bonsu; the childless sister and her husband, as well as Mrs. Badu-Bonsu and Mrs. Quarshie, are oblivious to our conversation and totally focused on the children. "What do you say, Ayanna?"

"I don't know, Mr. Badu-Bonsu." I am usually very honest and free to express my true feelings, but I do not feel safe giving an honest answer. My chest is tightening around my heart. It feels like my throat is closing. I am very cautious with my response.

"Papa, call me Papa. You are my daughter." Mr. Badu-Bonsu is very animated with his hands. In the states, his sexuality could possibly be questioned. "I am your Papa."

"Osei and I will have to discuss it. I would have to give my job notice, and we would have to sell the house. We would have so many things to think about before making such a move." I nervously touch Osei's knee and plant a small kiss on the side of his cheek. The muscles in my chest are so tight that I find it hard to breathe. A tingly, burning sensation travels from my chest to my throat. I reach in my pocket for an antacid tablet, only to find my pockets empty. Osei sits next to me, discussing the logistics with his father for almost an hour, as if he is actually considering the move. I am anxious, but a soft voice in my head whispers, "*Be cool.*"

We all leave the dinner table and sit by the pool and enjoy a bottle of wine Mr. Badu-Bonsu had shipped from France. I want to go inside and work on my case. However, I am filled with anxiety as I eavesdrop on Osei and his father discussing the positives of relocating to Ghana. My chest is burning. I have tablets inside my purse, but I do not want to miss any of their conversation. Osei converses in Twi, and they toast, and Mr. Badu-Bonsu wraps his arms around Osei's shoulder. Osei instructs Ti-Ti to run bath water for OJ and Che' and leaves the poolside for our quarters. I quickly follow him inside.

"Can you unhook my necklace?" I turn my back to Osei. "You are not seriously thinking about leaving the states, are you? That would be absurd." I turn around and face him and remove the necklace from his hand. I close the door and speak in a low volume to keep our conversation private.

"Why do you say that? What would be so bad about it?"

"I mean the kids."

"The kids?" His tone is harsh. I do not want to argue with him. "You rarely see the kids. Your little civil service job is all you seem to care about. Believe it or not, like many countries on the continent, Ghana is booming economically. As a matter of fact, many countries in Africa are growing economically at a faster rate than America."

"That was not part of our plan." I do not respond to his questioning of my relationship with the kids or his lesson in economics.

"So you say. You are engaged in a lot of things that are not part of our plan." His tone is accusatory. His stare is long and intense. He grabs a towel and goes to the bathroom leaving me with my thoughts.

I am anxious to leave this country. Mr. Badu-Bonsu changes our airlines tickets to depart Ghana from Accra rather than return to Kumasi. Mrs. Badu-Bonsu has taken total control of the children. The children start the night sleeping in the guest house with me and Osei. When I wake up in the morning, they are in bed with Mrs. Badu-Bonsu; this is how I learned Mr. and Mrs. Badu-Bonsu do not share a bed. Though I do not like her overbearing behavior with the children, I let it go. There is no use in starting a fight. In a couple of weeks, we will be back to our lives in the states.

"Good morning." I lightly tap on the door.

"Good morning to you, Ayanna. Did you ask Beauty to prepare your breakfast?" Her usual coldness dissipates. I am uncomfortable because she is almost friendly.

"No, I will have coffee. I rarely eat breakfast." I do not like the way she holds my children close to her heart. I make no eye contact with her. I focus on getting my children away from her.

"You know, Ayanna. I was thinking; you work so much. Osei says you rarely have time for the children." I am offended, but I keep calm and make a mental note to ask Osei not to discuss me behind my back with his family. "I am told his father has offered you both very good positions. Why don't you let the children stay here until you return?" She gathers her Indian Weave and secures it with a rubber band at the nape of her neck. A duplicitous smile is spread across her round, broad face. The tightness in my chest cuts off my circulation. I feel as if I am about to faint.

"Mrs. Badu-Bonsu, I don't think we have decided our next career moves. And besides," I manage to smile "the kids have friends and two other grandparents in the states. If we make this move, they will need to say their proper goodbyes." I walk closer to the bed with my eyes on Che' and OJ. I take both of their hands and guide them to our room.

"Come to Aunty, Che' and OJ!" Carol abruptly opens the door as I am in the midst of closing it. "Since you guys are leaving soon, do you mind if the children come with me? I will return them in time for brunch with Mother and Mrs. Quarshie. I am going to desperately miss them when they leave."

"I have not seen them very much since we have been here. I would like to spend time with them by the pool before it gets too hot."

"Don't be selfish! Didn't you make plans to visit your so-called history today?" His condescending voice is filled with chastisement. He is getting too comfortable using this tone with me. "We see the children every day. Go, Carol, you can take them with you." I manage a fake smile, but I want to damn them both to hell.

"Would you like for me to lay out a change of clothes for the children?" My tone is friendly, but my eyes are cold as ice.

"Don't worry, Mother had a children's buyer purchase the children a new wardrobe." She is unmoved by my menacing stare and proceeds to take the children.

"The driver is downstairs waiting for you. He is taking you to your dreadful door of no return." He says something in Twi to his sister. A slight giggle escapes her mouth. She quickly covers her mouth with her hand. His rudeness is transparent and on purpose. I am outnumbered. Rather than respond, I open the closet door and look through our luggage for something comfortable to wear.

The car is parked in the circular driveway in front of the house. Osei opens the front door, and the heat hits me like a ton of bricks. It is so hot it feels as if my body will go in shock. The Badu-Bonsus have massive backup generators. When the electricity goes out, the house remains cool. Atta looks like a giant standing in front of the open car door. Osei looks like a child standing next to Atta. Osei says something to him in Twi and places a stack of folded bills in Atta's hand.

"Mr. Atta will pay for whatever you want." I wonder why he did not give the money to me. I have my credit cards, so I don't complain. No need to initiate a losing battle.

"Where to madame?" Atta's jovial smile is contagious. I quickly forget about Osei and his antics and look forward to my trip.

"First stop, the door of no return!" It takes fifteen minutes to drive from the house to the main gate to leave the Badu-Bonsu compound. Atta waves at the armed security guard as we pass the guard station and drive through two electric metal gates. I don't know if I am happy because I can take my mind off work or if I am happy because I am getting a break from my husband.

I allow my mind to rest as we exit the compound to the rocky, government maintained two-lane highway. Although it is over ninety degrees outside, small chill bumps rise all over my skin. It feels as if a swarm of butterflies are taking flight in my stomach. I have been told to expect an array of indescribable emotions when visiting the slave dungeons. Trepidation, anxiety, excitement are the words that come to mind, but there are truly no words to describe what I am feeling as Atta drives past the sign that reads, "Five Kilometers to the Door of No Return." We drive approximately two miles before we see the packed entrance. Atta drives the car up a slight dirt embankment and into a VIP parking area.

"Are you joining me, Mr. Atta?" I am so excited I almost exit before he stops the car.

"No, I will wait here for you." Like Osei, Atta's attitude is indifferent. Perhaps if they were descendants of Africans who were dragged across the ocean in heavy chains, they could be more empathetic.

A crowd of people create a bottleneck at the gate's entrance. The humongous castle is white. Speckled sand washed up by the roaring sea covers much of the exterior of the castle. A slight breeze from the ocean carries a deathly stench that hovers in the air. A group of women in front of me are holding on to one another, balling and falling to their knees as they walk through the arch that encases two black, monstrous, wooden double doors. A macabre image of slaves handcuffed together, dragged to waiting boats flashes through my mind. On the other side of the door is a loud, powerful sea. Water usually symbolizes calmness and purity, but this water sounds angry and vicious.

Black men, appearing to be African American, hold tight to one another as they stand in front of the sea. A woman with an African American accent leads a group in a prayer for the ancestors. I am not an emotional person, but tears slowly fall down my cheeks as I walk back through two large wooden doors. It is disheartening thinking of my ancestors who were never able to return to dry land on this side of the door. It's hot and humid, but I am covered with chill bumps. I rub my hands along my arms for warmth. The hypocrisy of the slave owners and traders of human flesh is apparent. Ironically, a chapel sits next to the slave dungeons where the slave traders worshipped their God

Somehow, I find myself in the midst of African American women I have never seen; we are huddled together embracing one another as if we have known one another for a lifetime. It is as if a magnetic force unwittingly pulls us together. We leave the castle holding hands and embracing one another as if we are long lost relatives.

"We are going to Elmina Beach Resort for lunch. Would you like to join us?" I have no idea where Elmina Beach Resort is, but there is something about their spirits that makes me want to be amongst them.

"Elmina Beach Resort?"

"Yes, it is about thirty minutes from here."

"I will ask my driver to take me, and I will meet you there."

"Your driver? Are you ex-pat, too?" She embraces me. "I am Suzanna. I moved here about five years ago."

"No, I live in the states. I am here visiting my husband's family."

"Oh" Her beautiful smile is replaced by a disappointing frown. "I love when African Americans from the states leave the hustle and come home."

"You are actually the first Americans I have seen since I have been here." The chill bumps begin to disappear. I am so hot; I feel like I will have a heat stroke at any moment. "But my husband did tell me there are a lot of black Americans living here."

"Trust me, we are many. Our community is growing. People come home all of the time."

"Really" I didn't want to sound arrogant, but this is not my home. I cannot imagine changing the American lifestyle for this. "Let me tell the driver, and I will meet you at Elmina."

"Atta, do you know where the Elmina Resort and Restaurant is?" Atta stands outside of the car with the door open for me.

"Sure, I know exactly where it is." As always, a bright smile is plastered on Atta's face. I wonder if he is really happy all of the time, or if his smile is part of his uniform.

"I am going to meet a couple of ladies for lunch."

"Madam" He looks at his watch. "I was only instructed to drive to the castle."

"Okay, now I am instructing you to drive me to the resort."

"I will need to call Mr. Badu-Bonsu for permission." Atta reaches in his pocket, removes his cell phone, and begins to dial.

"Permission?" I hold my breath and count to ten. "Atta, I am an adult." My tone is firm. "I do not need permission from anyone to do anything. If you do not drive me, call someone to pick you up. I will drive myself."

"Of course, madam" He quickly puts the phone away. "Of course, please accept my apology." I do not like speaking harshly to Atta. I feel guilty as he bends forward with his hands together, profusely apologizing.

He opens the rear passenger side door. I get into the car. He gently closes the door, still apologizing. It takes thirty minutes of driving over bumpy roads in bumper to bumper traffic to get to Elmina Resort. The resort is one of the prettiest places I have ever seen. Tables reserved for VIPs sit on top of cement slabs encased in glass on the ocean shore. The smell of fresh fish and spices hover in the air. I feel at home as I walk through the maze of tables listening to familiar African American dialect.

"Madam, I will eat at the bar." I do not respond to Atta. I simply throw my hand up and wave him away.

"Suzanna." I wave to her.

"Ayanna" She motions for me to come to the table where she sits with three of the women I met at the castle. Of all of the women, I gravitate to Suzanna. I do not understand the attraction; I usually find dreadlock wearing women too radical.

"What made you decide to move here?" We sit amongst her friends, and I immediately begin to ask questions.

"I simply got tired of the hustle and bustle, the racism. I just wanted to breathe. There are issues here, too, but they have nothing to do with the color of my skin. The culture is very different and can be very classist and sexist, but it is what it is. My son drives a European car and does not get pulled over by the police because he is black." She sips from her glass of wine. "It is so unnatural how black Americans live in the states. I came with my husband on vacation, and within a year we were living here. I love it here!" There is a lot of enthusiasm in her voice. The Ghanaian government should hire her to work in the Department of Tourism.

"Is your husband Ghanaian?"

"No, he is American."

"What do you do to support yourself?"

"My husband has a fish farm; I conduct tours for people considering repatriating here, and we have rental properties in the states. Life is simple here. It does not take much."

"I am in the process of moving here with my husband." Carla is a very thin woman with shoulder length curly hair. "My husband is Ghanaian. We have three kids, and we decided to raise them in Ghana. The education system here is exemplary. It is a lot simpler here than in the States. The children can go outside and play. The community is very strong, and family is very supportive." Pride emanates from her beautiful smile. "Augustine has a very established CPA firm. He travels back to the states during tax season for three months out of the year." I listen to their stories of success and still wonder about the attraction. Ghana is nice to visit. I do not know how they live but even with the lavish life the Badu-Bonsu's have, there are so many things about the American life I refuse to give up. I sit amongst the ladies and listen to their stories for a couple of hours. I share my opinion on some of the latest political events happening in the states.

"Madam" Atta walks fast to our table. He greets the ladies and taps his watch. "I do believe we should be getting back. It's getting late."

"Yes, Atta, I agree." I look at my watch. "Atta, please pay for all of our lunches, and I will meet you at the car." He collects all our checks while I trade phone numbers and email addresses I have no intention of using.

Almost immediately upon getting in the car, I am overcome by exhaustion. I don't know if it is the wine, which contains more alcohol per volume than American wine or exhaustion from work, but I can barely keep my eyes open. I try to nap, but the road is too bumpy. Every time I find sleep, I am jolted awake.

We must have been gone a long time, as there is a shift change at the guard gate. Two armed guards allow entry to the compound. I am still groggy, but I notice Osei walking out of the house towards the car as we enter the circular drive. His arms swing back and forth. His pace is long and rapid. Atta parks the car but leaves the engine running. Osei snatches open the driver's side door just as Atta places his feet on the ground. Atta loses his balance and rolls out of the car, landing hard on the polished, stone, brown driveway.

"Osei!" He acts as if I am invisible as he yells in Twi at Atta. I do not understand what he is saying, but the English words idiot and fool stand out during his violent diatribe. Atta, who is at least a foot taller and thirty pounds heavier, moves away from Osei with his head bowed, unresponsive to the insults. After totally dismantling Atta's manhood, Osei redirects his wrath to me.

"You are not in America!" He grabs my arm, snatches me out of the car, and slams the car door so hard, I am amazed the window does not shatter.

"You had best let go of my arm or..." It feels as if a swarm of bees have stung me a thousand times when his open hand makes contact with my face. Atta quickly grabbed Osei's heavy hand just as it was about to make contact with my face again.

"Or what? What are you going to do?"

"Sir, please, it was my fault." Osei snatches his arm from Atta. His stance is stiff and intimidating. I walk away from him and towards the back of the house to the guest house. He is close behind. He grabs my shoulder and snatches me around; we are face to face. "This is not America! If you should get stranded, there will be no tow truck! There is no auto club to get you home! If you go missing, there will be no search party looking for you! Never do that again! Atta knows better!" There is a mean, angry look on his face I have never seen before. "Where were you?" I do not know this man standing in front of me. Our eyes meet, but it is as if he is looking straight through me.

I ignore him. I walk to the guest house, removing my clothes as I march to the shower. He is close behind. I slam the door as hard as I can and quickly lock it.

Chapter 8

We were given a nice and over the top bon voyage. Osei and I stand next to one another on the side of the first limousine with fake smiles plastered on our faces. It is as if we are on the stage performing Act II of the *Happy Couple*. On the inside, my emotions are topsy-turvy. I have never seen this side of Osei. Yes, his attitude has been stanker than stank, but to actually strike me? This type of thing does not happen to women like me. Even Atta is part of the cast. Surely, in his heart he has not forgiven Osei's blatant emasculation. Atta, dressed in his crisp and clean chauffer uniform, holds the door open with a wide smile on his face as I slide into the car. There is no sign of resentment towards me or Osei from the incident a few days earlier. I feel guilty because it was totally my fault. I should not have put Atta in that predicament. Atta obviously knows his place with the Badu-Bonsu clan. I have to remember Osei is from a different culture, and I am not acclimated to the rules of engagement amongst the Ghanaian classes. However, Osei's attack on me was unprovoked and out of character. I have not decided how to handle this. He shows no remorse. He did not apologize and behaves as if nothing happened. I am angry and want to act out, but I am smart enough to know I am in another country, and the rules are different.

"Atta"

"Yes, madam." I place my business card in his hand.

"Write your contact information on my card. I want to send something to your children when I return to the states." He dutifully writes his information and passes the card back to me, then walks to the other side of the car and opens the door for Mr. Badu-Bonsu.

We are driven to the airport in a two limousine caravan. Mr. Badu-Bonsu, Osei, the children, and I ride in the first limousine with our luggage. Mrs. Badu-Bonsu, the fashionista, and her parents have appeared out of nowhere; they ride in the limo behind us. I have no idea why the fashionista and her parents are invited to our send off. Perhaps it's a cultural etiquette Osei neglected to explain. We say our last goodbyes at the airport. I notice Mrs. Badu-Bonsu speaks with the fashionista in a closeness and kindness I have never experienced with her. I also notice the coldness the fashionista initially directed to Osei has disappeared. I may be overreacting, but the embrace they share before we board the plane lasts two seconds too long for comfort. I ignore it; in about nineteen hours, we will be back to our lives.

Osei remains antisocial the entire flight. We start the flight in our designated seats, with Osei in the aisle seat sitting next to me; OJ and Che sit close to the window. Once the "S*afe to remove seat belt*" signal appears, I release my seatbelt and go to the lavatory. When I returned, Osei sits next to the window; the children sit in the middle, leaving the aisle seat for me. Again, I ignore him. He and the children entertain themselves by flipping through pictures on his IPad. I remove a file from my bag and work on my case, the state of GA vs Jefferson Thomas.

"You are so obsessed with that little job! Would it be too much to ask you to put it away? We are still on vacation!"

"Osei, you are not talking to me, and when you do decide to talk to me again, we have things to discuss that have nothing to do with my job!" He continues to ignore me and only interacts with the children.

We are so exhausted when we arrive home from the airport that we leave our luggage in the garage. We arrive in the States on Sunday, and Osei and the children sleep the entire day. I have no time for sleep; I am busy preparing my case. I have papers spread out all over the floor as I examine Jefferson's financial imprint. He has gone through extraordinary lengths to appear legit. His records are in order, and he keeps his bank account balance low enough to make it appear that he struggles to maintain his lifestyle. I know better. He lives big. He thinks big, and he is too smart to leave a paper trail. I work nonstop until three o'clock in the morning before going to bed. Osei is sound asleep. When I pull the covers back on my side of the bed; he does not move. The rise and fall of his chest is the only indicator he is alive. The morning comes quick. I am so exhausted, I hit the snooze button a dozen times before I am able to fully wake up.

When I go downstairs to the kitchen, Osei is fully dressed standing in front of the stove making breakfast. "Osei, can we trade today? Can you pick up the children from summer camp? It is going to be a long day today."

"Of course, they are my kids, why couldn't I?" His attitude is flip, and it has gotten old. I have no time to address his issues. I have four days before I present my evidence to the grand jury. I will not be distracted by his foolishness.

I plant a light kiss on his cheek, grab my coffee, and rush out of the door twenty minutes early in a useless attempt to beat the morning traffic. Half of the city must have had the same idea. Where it normally takes twenty-five to thirty minutes, it takes forty-five minutes to reach the detention center.

The Juvenile Detention Center looks no different than an adult prison. There are no windows, just small squares of thick glass systematically cut into gray concrete. The slants must be for decoration, as they are too high for the average person to peek at the outside world. The noise is excruciating, and the guards are so flat and stern that the delinquents should be scared straight at the completion of their detention. Surprisingly, the recidivism rate is higher in juvenile detention than adult prison. I sign in at the front desk. There is a line of detainees, some as young as twelve years old, standing against the wall waiting to see their attorneys. They are chatting and laughing with one another as if they are in a school lunch line and appear unfazed about their legal predicaments.

Ashleigh is waiting for me in the interview room when I arrive. Her skin is radiant and unblemished. The stress lines that covered her face when I first met her have disappeared. She easily shares her smile and is totally opposite of the drama queen I met a month ago.

"Ashleigh, how are things going?"

"I am good. I will be happy when I leave this place." She looks down at the floor swinging her legs back and forth like an eight-year-old child as opposed to the thirteen-year-old she now professes to be.

"The social worker says you are ready to talk. Is that true?"

"Yeah, anything to get me out of this place." She looks up from the floor, and I stare into the prettiest, clear, light brown, almond shaped eyes. In spite of what I imagine she has endured, there is still a little girl-like innocence in her eyes.

"I am going to be perfectly honest with you. We are going to have to talk to your parents. The social worker informs me you do not want us to contact them, but we have to make a positive identification."

"I told you; my name is Ashleigh Michelle Scott."

"Yeah, but you also told us you were 17, and we know this is not true. The way this works is, you are a minor, and we have to make contact with your parents. It is the law." Her eyes are now glued to the floor. If it were not for the tear that slowly travels down her cheek, I would have thought her eyes were closed.

"Did your parents hurt you? Is that the reason you do not want us to contact them?"

"No," she quickly answers. "My parents are perfect! I do not want them to see me like this! They do not deserve a slut for a daughter!"

"Ashleigh, you are not a slut; you are a victim." She covers her eyes with her hands. Her cry is soft. I pull her close and wrap my arm around her. I am out of character. I never allow myself to get personal on the job. For me, it is all about the win. There is something about this child that reminds me of my own child. "Okay, we will get back to your parents." She seems relieved we are leaving the subject of her parents. "How do you know Mr. Thomas?" Her blank stare confuses me.

"I don't know who you talking about." Her denial appears authentic.

"You were arrested with him."

"I don't know him. He gave me a ride. The day the police put us in jail was the first time I saw him. I have heard his name mentioned. My roommate talked about him. I think he is Stacy's boss or boyfriend. I am not sure."

"Who is Stacy?"

"I think Stacy bought me from my friend's brother."

"Bought you?" My imagination takes me to a grocery store checkout line with a child on a conveyor belt.. "You mean actually paid someone money for you?"

"I saw her give my friend's brother a large envelope. Her brother took the money out and counted it. It made Stacy mad. She pulled her gun from her purse and placed it against his head said "all twenty Gs are there." She laughs. "My friend's brother got really scared. He knocked over a chair trying to get away from Stacy."

"Do you remember where this place is?"

"I lived with a couple of women in an apartment someplace. I don't know the address, but it is in a tall building where there were a lot of tall buildings." Her eyes are open wide. Her mouth stretches in a wide smile. "We have tall buildings in Charlotte, but not as many." The excited look on her face disappears and is replaced with sadness. "At first she was nice to me. Stacy would take me shopping, out to eat, and get my nails done. She took me to etiquette classes. I already knew which fork and spoon to use. Last year, I was a Jr. Debutante." She smiles. I make a mental note of this and become intrigued that she is obviously at the very least from a middle class family. "I didn't enjoy the etiquette classes, but I loved the modeling classes. My mom always discouraged it, but I always wanted to model."

"Ashleigh" I need her to focus. "Do you know the names of the girl you roomed with?"

"I can't remember. She had a weird name. I only saw her a few times. She was from Somalia and did not speak English. She worked a lot. I eventually had to start working to pay rent. I only worked for the China man. I heard Stacy tell my friend's brother I was exactly what the China man was looking for." A slight smile creeps across her face. "Mr. Ye was my only date. In the beginning he only came once per month, then he started to come twice a month and now he comes every week."

"Mr. Ye?" My mind goes back to the night Detective Davis picked her up and a Chinese diplomat was also detained, but quickly released due to diplomatic immunity.

"He is very rich, and I hang out with him for a week or so. The first time it was bad, but I got used to it. I would close my eyes and pretend to be at the mall or the amusement park. He pays Stacy a monthly fee to make sure he is my only date. Mr. Ye always asks the dumbest questions about black girls." I stand and leave the table. I am having a hard time processing Ashleigh's disclosure. She shows no emotion as she speaks. I return to the table, gently place my pen on my writing pad, and mentally count to ten to gather my composure. Anger cannot convey my emotions. A sick, vile feeling creeps in my stomach at the thought of a grown man violating a child. Vomit travels from my stomach through my esophagus to the back of my throat. The burning feeling makes me gag, but I manage to swallow it back down. Ashleigh speaks as if Stacy is the ringleader. I know this is not true. Jefferson works under no one. Stacy is the puppet, and Jefferson pulls the strings. I do not expect much from Jefferson, but it never entered my mind he would go this low.

"It is my fault."

"No, Ashleigh, this is not your fault."

"Yes, it is. I knew better. My cell phone was a birthday present. My mother told me not to take pictures and post them on the Internet. I learned about sexting in health class at school, but I did not listen. Everyone at school does it. Me and my friend were playing around and taking pictures with our phones and emailing the pictures to each other. She dared me to show my boobs. I should have never done that. Somehow, her brother found my pictures. Her brother was going to show my parents, but he said if I went to a party with him, he would not show the pictures. I snuck out of the house, met him on the corner down the street and went to the party." She is detached. It is as if she is narrating someone else's experience.

"Did your friend send pictures as well?" I found it strange she only talks about sending pictures but never mentions the friend sending pictures.

"Yes, but she only showed her boobs. Her face was not on the picture, but my face was."

"Where was the party?"

"It was at a house I have never seen before." She shakes her head and closes her eyes, as if she is trying to picture the house in her mind. "It was not on my side of Charlotte. I think we were probably on the south side, because the houses were kind of run down and old." I mentally note she is from Charlotte but not from the run down part of Charlotte. "I got myself into a bad mess. They must have given me something to make me pass out, because I don't remember anything that happened. When I woke up, I was lying on a hospital bed, but not at a hospital, and Nita was examining me to make sure I still had a cherry." The interview becomes more difficult with each disclosure. Her detachment from the experience bothers me; I have to constantly check my emotions.

"So after you left North Carolina, where did you go?" There is more than one city in America named Charlotte. If I could narrow down which Charlotte she is from, finding her parents is easy.

"One time we went to New Orleans to a party. Mr. Ye met us there, and we stayed in a really nice house on the water. I mostly stayed in the house with another girl who was always traveling for Stacy. I think her name is Courtney. She would always take me to Mr. Ye. But for some reason, the man you call Mr. Thomas took me the day I was arrested. I didn't want to do any of this, but when I saw what Stacy told Nita to do to one of the girls who was stashing money and jewelry one of the customers gave her because she was planning to leave I did what I was told."

"What did they do to her?"

"They wrapped the girl in a blanket, carried her out, and we never saw her again. Nita can make any of us disappear."

"Nita?" This is the second time she has mentioned Nita. I inconspicuously jot her name down on my clipboard. "Who is Nita?"

"Nita gets everybody ready for the parties and dates. She is our stylist. Supposedly she used to work for a lot of celebrities, but none of the girls believe her. She styles our hair and makeup. She does our wardrobe.

"When was this?" I am disturbed and shocked by Ashleigh's disclosure. I find myself wanting to leave the interview, check Che' out of school, and keep her with me forever.

"When was what?"

"When did they wrap the girl in the blanket?" I went back to the girl wrapped in the blanket. As she speaks, I am trying to remember a case about nine months ago where a Jane Doe was found wrapped in a blanket in the woods off Interstate 20.

"Like a week after I got to there."

"Do you remember what the girl looked like?"

"She looked like a girl." She is easily annoyed. I want to warn her that her eyes may get stuck if she continues to roll them to the back of her head. "Some girls say they killed her, and some of them say she went to work for another company."

"You mentioned other girls. How many other girls did you see?"

"I don't know. We didn't all live in the same place. Unless there was a special party, we did not see each other. Some of the older girls traveled a lot. Some were in college, and I believe one was married. We kind of worked in shifts because there were two of us to each apartment, but we were rarely there at the same time."

"How many apartments?"

"Stacy has several apartments all over the world in very pretty neighborhoods. One of them looks like the building my dad works in downtown." I note her dad works downtown in Charlotte.

"Ashleigh, we are going to have to get them, but you are going to have to trust me. We have to work together. We cannot allow them to get away with this. We call what they are doing human trafficking, and it is illegal." My tone changes from conciliatory to serious and firm. "We need to find your parents. I need for you to tell me who they are, because they need to know you are okay. They have probably been looking for you every day. Trust me, they are worried about you. They need to know you are safe."

"I am tired of talking now." She wipes long tear away from her eyes. "I am ready to go back to my pod."

"Ms. Williams, I think she is tired! We will let her get some rest now!" Mary abruptly opens the door and interrupts the interrogation.

"Thank you, Ashleigh, for talking to me." I ignore Mary. I am well-acquainted with the rules.

"Ms. Williams, you are not supposed to interview her alone!" She looks at Ashleigh, but it is not a look of concern. I can't place my finger on the look, but it makes me uneasy. "We are working on a group home placement." Mary softly squeezes Ashleigh's shoulder. "Honey, it will not be long." The detention officer opens the door; it seems as if Mary forcefully pushes her through the thick glass doors. "It will not be long, sweetie. I am going to get you out of here."

"I do not believe this crap!" I grab my bag. Mary and I leave the building and walk to the parking deck together.

"Did she give any new details?"

"We talked a lot before you came, but I didn't get much out of her. I am going to get this thug if it kills me." I look at my watch. I am late but too overwhelmed to rush home. "Mary, do you want to go for a drink?"

"Absolutely." She checks her watch. "I can seriously use a drink right now."

To my surprise, Mary is more than a Bohemian mother hen.

She put down three cocktails in less than thirty minutes and does not appear inebriated. I usually do not drink this early in the day, but my nerves are frazzled, and I need to pull it together.

"How long have you been in child protective services?"

"Too long, long hours, low pay I don't know why I've stayed this long." She swallows the remaining liquid in her third cocktail, motions the waiter over, and requests another one.

"Have you always worked in Georgia?"

"No, I used to work in Las Vegas, but as I got older I could not take the hot, dry weather. Bad asthma."

"I totally understand." I smooth my hair with my fingers and squeeze my French roll tighter. "I am not into dessert heat either. It does not agree with my hair." I take a long, hard and much needed sip from my Cosmopolitan.

"Married?" I look at the large, bright and clear diamond on her finger that makes my five carats look like a speckle.

"Nope."

"You?"

"Yes," I remove a family picture of Osei, Che' and OJ from my wallet. I'm not in the picture. I was working when the photo was taken.

"Nice family."

"My husband can be a pistol, but I am blessed." I hope I am blessed. I do not know the true status of my marriage. I do not know what will become of it. Everything is rocky. Osei has not apologized. He has yet to address the incident that took place in Ghana. I guess we both are pretending it did not happen.

Chapter 9

I park next to the first gas pump in front of the convenience store. The black Lincoln Navigator continues north on the two-lane highway. I walk into the store, pay for gas, grab two cups of coffee and return to my car. I peer over the gas pump and see the headlights of the Navigator extend past the side of the bank building on the adjacent corner. The Navigator has been tailing me all morning. She can do better than this. Surely, she knows she will have to enlist her top guns for this battle. Traveling three cars behind your target in the Surveillance Manual is elementary and out of date. Surely, they have GPS devices they can attach to my car and follow me from a computer, or she can track my phone as it pings on the cell towers. She is a cocky bitch. She wants me to know I am being followed. I first noticed the car when I picked up Stacy from the hair salon. This overzealous bitch has not learned. Her quest to make a name for herself led to many mistakes and ethical complaints in her attempt to bring me down. She will slip. I have no worries. She will attempt to find inconsistencies in my finances. I employ the best forensic accountant to ensure all of my financial dealings appear legit.

She is an opportunist. Ayanna does not care about me, my business dealings, or the citizens of this county. Her eyes are on her next political move, and she needs a big fish to fry. Ayanna is the typical politician. She wants to make a name for herself and will run over anyone who gets in her way, but there are rules to the game. She does not play by the rules. In our first trial, she attempted to hide evidence from the defense. She bought trumped up charges against people who I do not know and never had dealings with and threatened these truly innocent people with jail time if they did not testify against me. She even had the balls to offer a plea deal to me, and when the attorney I paid over a hundred thousand dollars had the nerve to present the offer to me, I had to take matters into my own hands. One would think she would have learned her lesson. She is not as bright as she thinks she is. Like most prosecutors, her winning streak is a result of poor people pleading to lesser charges out of fear of lengthy prison sentences. I am not poor, nor am I afraid.

She is back to her old tricks, but I put a damper on her winning record. I anonymously provided the finance for lawyers for the last three cases she prosecuted, and the jury returned not guilty verdicts on all of them. The brass at the capital is vetting her as the replacement for District Attorney when the current District Attorney retires. If she continues to lose cases, she can kiss her dream to political office goodbye.

She used me to gain public notoriety in the first trial, and it backfired. We were members of the same club. I pay a lot of money for my position in the inner circle of the political class. Most of the brass is in my pocket in some form or fashion. She envies my position amongst the elite.

She is resurrecting old feelings and old behaviors. The voices in my head that were once loud and screamed, "You are not good enough" had all but disappeared. I had almost arrived and was making a solid place for myself in a world that was determined to keep Mary Francis Thomas' boy out. I was young and fighting to get away from a fucked up past. I transitioned myself from the world of fast money, glitz, and glamour to a major player in the political class. She wants to make a name for herself at my expense.

I have worked too hard to allow Ayanna to pull me down. I expect neither accolades nor pats on my back. I have overcome many obstacles. I only want to be free to live the life I have created for myself in spite of my circumstances. I am Mary Francis Thomas' only child. I should have never been born. Quite frankly, I would love to find the pervert who impregnated my mother and cursed me at conception. I never knew my father, and no one seems to know who he is. I know he was not about shit and had to be a man with a fucked up moral compass. He is nothing shy of a rapist. My mother is mentally ill and has been all of her life. The words schizophrenic and voices were always whispered in my grandparents' home. He could have been an orderly but was most likely a doctor at one of the many hospitals she was admitted to during one of her many episodes, which would explain my high level of intelligence. My grandparents did the best they could to shield me, but I was an inquisitive kid. I would eavesdrop to find out bits and pieces to the story of my life. From their conversations, I gathered she was admitted to a mental hospital and came back pregnant. Grandparents are wonderful people, and mine were no different. They did the best they knew how to mold me, but grandparents do not raise children. They are not parents.

When my grandparents died, I went to live with an aunt up north. That did not work out because her husband had an affinity for touching little boys. I was ten and always big for my age, but my size did not stop my Aunt's husband from trying me, but I stopped him in his tracks. The Social Security check my aunt received for caring for me did not put a dent in the bucket for what was needed to run her household after I disfigured her husband's face and broke several of his bones. He tried to place the blame on me. He lied to my aunt and said he caught me stealing, and when confronted I attacked him. Of course, like most weak women with no identity outside of their husbands, she believed him, so I came back to Georgia and lived in my grandparents' house with Aunt Nell, their youngest daughter.

Unfortunately, Mary Francis Thomas never drifted far from my grandparents' home. I was often forced to see her. When she was not in the mental institution or in jail for stealing or excessive panhandling, she came around daily. There were a few special times when she would take her medicine and would appear normal and almost functional. She could actually look nice when she was medicated. She never came to terms with her illness, so it was rare that she took her medicine.

My grandparents tried to regulate her behavior. Crazy people can become violent, and Mary Francis Thomas was no different. I guess I loved her in my own way, but the embarrassment of your peers seeing your mother walk down the street in nothing but a sheet with her hair matted to her head, begging for spare change, or seeing her in a garbage can scavenging for food can damage a little boy's self-worth. They could have said, "That is Tyree" as I was known back then, "the smartest boy in the class and the winner of state spelling bees," but I was always in the shadow of my mother, Mary Francis Thomas. I was never allowed to bathe in my accomplishments. Her crazy antics outshined all of the great things I accomplished, but I changed that. Tyree was always Mary

Francis Thomas' boy. Jefferson Thomas is his own man.

I fought hard for an identity of my own, so I buried myself in my school lessons and made no less than one hundred percent on everything from kindergarten through high school. I was number one academically in every school I attended, but I could never escape Mary Francis Thomas. By the time I was in my teens, I totally cut ties with her. I would walk past her on the street and pretend not to know her. When she called my name, I would keep moving; no matter the distance I put between me and her, the voice always managed to find its way back in my ear.

I found solace in the beauty of my own brain. I knew my grades would get me away from my crappy life. I graduated top in my class. I received a standing ovation when I accepted the award money from the superintendent of the district. I was elated and proud. My smile was wide and bright as I scanned the sea of people standing and applauding after I completed my speech. Within minutes, it was as if a dark shadow commenced over the crowd when that voice whispered, *"You still Mary Francis Thomas' boy."* I almost tripped over myself in the hurry to leave the stage. I was born with a fucked up debt. The shame almost killed my spirit, but I fought back. I have paid my dues, and this bitch had best get out of my way. Ayanna is trying to erase all of the work I have done. She is trying to make me Mary Francis Thomas' boy again, but I am Jefferson Thomas, my own man.

I ignore the black Lincoln Town Car with the black tinted windows and continue to travel to my destination. I turn right off Martin Luther King Boulevard and into the Chicken Shack parking lot. The Lincoln slows and then stops. I roll down the window, stick my arm half of the way out of it, and wave. The passenger side of the tinted window rolls down half of the way and then stops. The driver blows the horn, slowly accelerates, and continues through the next light. This is Ayanna Williams 101. She thinks I will get nervous and slip. I am a formidable opponent. I will not slip.

I take full blame for this current predicament. I gave her the ammunition to come for me again. I expect her to run with it. She is a cold, calculating bitch that mostly likely waited a long time for the opportunity to finish what she started.

"What was that about?" She looks from the rear view mirror to the side mirror with quick, robotic like movements. She squeezes my hand with one hand and holds tight to the coffee with the other.

"Don't worry about it. Everything is okay. Just a little problem I neglected to take care of." Stacy is not convinced; her nerves are frazzled, and they should be. Ayanna does not give up. She is truly the devil's daughter. If she continues to fuck with me, I will send her to hell to be with her daddy.

We park in the rear of the building and sit for a few minutes to gather our thoughts. We enter the restaurant through the kitchen. The lunch line is almost out of the door. The local politicians both black white and everything in-between, are lunch hour regulars. We are known to have the best soul food in the city.

I greet Ms. Mamie and Ms. Ethel, the best cooks in the south, and immediately go to the office in the back of the restaurant. I hate coming to this grease pit; it takes hours to get the smell of fried chicken out of my nose. This hole in the wall is part of the charade. This business, along with my real estate, beauty salons and barber shops justify my lifestyle on paper. I pay a few credit card bills late and purposely get behind on my mortgage a few times a year to keep the government off my trail. I ain't got shit in my mama or cousin Pookie's name, because that is how clowns get caught and take their families down with them. They cannot justify the Mercedes or BMW parked in their garage, and their mama who is pushing paper in some government office or cousin Pookie who has no job do not have the income to justify it either. My known businesses are legit and registered with the state.

They will not find anything on me, no matter how hard they look. I learned a lot from those white boys at Ivy League. They were not wasting their time flipping burgers and working at the library or the bookstore. Many had trust funds and a lot of cash to buy all of the dope I could sell them. Some were my competitors in the campus dope game. I figured out a long time ago that an hourly wage is a trap and was not going to get it for me. I relied on my street skills at Ivy League. Ivy League nor Wall Street have nothing on Street Smarts 101. I didn't have a senator daddy or lawyer mother, and the scholarship money was not enough to keep up, so I utilized my street knowledge. I started out selling little baggies, then big baggies, and the next thing you know I was supplying all of the fraternity and sorority houses and a few faculty and staff members as well.

Though I am born and bred in the 'hood I looked no different from my wealthy classmates. I drove a European car and wore the best designer clothes. I never left the country, but I researched every country on the map in order to blend in. I hung out with the wealthy. I mocked their conversation. I mimicked their mannerism and studied their lives. If a classmate discussed vacationing in St. Barts, I could do the same and compare the shops and cuisine to those of the Seychelles, Paris or any tourist spot frequented by the rich and famous. By the time I finished the conversation, I had almost convinced myself that I am a world traveler, though I had never left the United States.

At Ivy League, things were going well for me, and in my mind, nothing could stop me. I was strong like Samson. But like Samson, I found my Delilah. I should have known the bitch was no good when we met. It was not about love. It was about image for her, and the come up for me. Pam's father was a senator. She had the right background and the right look. She was serious about the relationship. She would never admit it, but she was sent to college to get a husband. Her bougie parents created a picture of what the bougie life should be. I completed the picture. I was popular and known to throw the best parties. I had a list of people waiting for invites. I was in a back room at my apartment handling business before a big party. She walked in and immediately stormed out when she saw the bags of product. I ran after her.

"What in the hell are you doing?" She was causing an unneeded scene. I placed my hand over her mouth to get her to quiet down. I dragged her in the bathroom, got her attention, and convinced her the drugs were not mine. She was cool and eventually liked what she called the thug in me, until she made an unannounced visit and found me in bed with a random chick I met at the library. Two weeks later, my apartment was raided. They didn't find anything. I had delivered all of my stash and had not replenished it. They put me in the back of the police car. The officer got in the car, opened his glove compartment and threw a small bag of marijuana in the back seat next to me. I was in total disbelief. It was as if life was moving in slow motion. I demanded to speak with his superior. He laughed. That my first encounter with the law. I complained and wrote letters to the arresting officer's supervisor and the mayor. I was made and knew I would be a target. The money was more than good, but I was smart enough to stop my hustle because I was on the law enforcement radar. I had to move out of my luxury apartment into a rancid shit hole while I finished matriculating. The college would not allow me back in campus housing because of the drug charges.

After graduation, I found an entry level gig at a brokerage firm, but I was not satisfied. My classmates, most that ranked much lower than me, were not offered entry level positions in the corporate world. They entered as Vice President of this or Chief Operating Officer of that. I was not the only classmate with an arrest record, but I did not have the connections that could make a hiring manager turn a blind eye to my small scrimmage with the law. Making money playing by the rules was too much pressure. I love making money, but I want to enjoy the process. Dealing with racism and cronyism at the brokerage firm was something I was unwilling to do. I deserved to be on top. I cashed in my 401K, changed my name, and moved to Atlanta.

"J, you sure you are okay? You keep zoning out."

"I am cool. Have you taken care of that situation?"

"I will send one of Nita's connections in with a misdemeanor shoplifting charge. My connection will make sure she is assigned to the same cell block." She looks at her watch. "The problem should be solved very soon." She looks at me, then back at the numbers she is adding on paper. "I honestly do not know how you got caught like that anyway."

"Remember, I had to take care of a business deal because your favorite cousin didn't show up." I want to blame it on someone. I am having a hard time coming to terms with the situation I have put myself in. This was definitely not one of my smartest moves. "She was too busy putting a needle in her fucking arm."

"Needle?" She frowns. "How do you know it was a needle? The coroner documented her death homicide by overdose."

"I just assumed it was a needle. Ain't that what most junkies do?"

"Not really, and you should know; you used to make your bank on heroin, powder, and rock. Why would you assume it was a needle? The report didn't say anything about a needle."

"I don't know. Why does it matter? She is dead." There is something about the way Stacy looks at me that makes me uncomfortable.

"You don't have to be so cold. We all know she is dead." She stares into my eyes as if she wants to challenge me. I stare back harder. "The event planner contacted me about an upcoming convention next month. A lot of global business people will be here for the World Philanthropy Summit. I need fifty legs, no hormones." She feels the heat redirected towards her. She quickly changes the subject.

"Where are we going to get twenty-five untouched girls?" I take risks, but I am realistic. "I hope you did not confirm anything."

"We have no choice; we cannot pass on this opportunity. That is 10,000 per night, per girl for two nights. If we make this happen, we will get more international contracts. If you want to play with the big boys, you have to keep it international." She removes a smart phone from her purse and begins to press numbers. I immediately jump up, reach across my desk, snatch the cell phone out of her hand, and stomp it in the floor. I grab her by her freshly done hair, drag her out of her seat, and pull her across the desk; my initial reaction is to slap her across her face, but I stopped with my raised hand hanging in midair.

"What the fuck, J?" She raises her arms to block the anticipated blows. Her chest extends unnaturally outward with each breath. Fear resonates from her eyes. I feel remorse, which makes me mad as fuck, because remorse is an emotion I cannot afford.

"I told you no personal cell phones anymore when we are together!"

"I was not using it. I pulled it out to use the calculator." She smooths her hair down, straightens her clothes, reaches in her back pocket, and pulls out the prepaid phone I gave her a week ago.

"I don't give a shit; when you are with me, no fucking personal cell phones! Give me that fucking prepaid phone; it is time we destroy it and get another one." She passes the phone to me. I pass a new one to her. I feel guilty for going off on her like that, but she has to stay on her "Ps" and "Qs." I am not built to do time, and everyone knows they have all types of tracking devices in cell phones.

"We need to meet with Gorbachev and the Mexicans to fill the order." Stacy continues to conduct business as if she has forgotten I was two seconds from knocking her block off. "We expand our global reputation if we can pull this off. We can purchase the product for ten grand each, or we can rent them for five grand. We have to use them again at least four additional times in a twelve-month period." She senses the doubt in my expression. "Gorbachev says he can fill the order and guarantee the entire product is certified pure, untouched and disease-free." Stacy could have really done well in a legitimate corporation if she would have had the opportunity. "Of course, we will have them examined by our own people."

"What is the profit margin?" She uses the calculator on the prepaid phone.

"If we purchase twenty-five girls it will cost about 250,000 plus overhead like clothing, housing, food and transportation. It would take about two events to see a profit." She seductively throws her freshly done hair over her shoulders. I feel my nature rise. I ignore it; business before pleasure. "But if we rent them for the night and split the profit with Gorbachev it is straight up profit, with very little initial out of pocket expense."

"You think he will go for that?"

"I am sure he will."

"Yeah, I bet you are sure. That Hulk looking motherfucker has the hots for you."

"You can't be serious. This is a win-win; we are supplying the venue. He is supplying the companions. He gets the rental fee, plus a percentage of the profit. I am sure his motives are strictly business." She smiles. If I did not know better, I would think she is blushing. "You can't be serious; he has no interest in me."

"Oh, I am serious, but around here pussy is a commodity; make sure he pays." She does not respond, but she knows I am serious. "I will be out of town for a few days. I will need you to hold everything down."

"Sure" She looks at her calendar. "It is September. You disappear around this time every year. Where do you go?"

"None of your business."

Chapter 10

I have been texting her for days. School starts in two weeks, and we have yet to go on our annual vacation. Angst boils in me like a volcano. I have no right to be angry, but I am accustomed to her returning my texts within an hour. I thought of making a surprise visit and simply knock on her door. I often drive past her house, but I never stop. I am not sure what my reaction would be if I actually saw another man around my children.

"Hey, you!" I glance at the phone, see her picture pop up on the display, and press answer before the phone actually rings. I am happy to hear her voice. After texting her all day, she finally responds. My son decided to see if the phone could float in the toilet again. She had to purchase a new one.

"I have been trying to contact you for over a week. School starts soon. We have not gone on vacation."

"Are we still doing that?"

"Of course." I am disappointed. I thought she looked forward to this time as much as I did. "I will purchase airline tickets and get the hotel today."

"I don't know. The kids and I will be back tomorrow from visiting my parents. They may be too tired."

"They are kids; they don't have to go to work." She is reluctant but accepts my invitation.

"You are going to have to stop driving by the house." She pauses as if she is waiting for me to respond. "I need to move on." Four years ago, we went on vacation and came back pregnant. I tried to convince her to have an abortion, but she would not consider it. I made it plain and clear once again she was on her own and was to have no expectations from me other than finance. She did not react. Most women would have cursed me to hell and back, but Lailah was chill. There was something about her calmness that convicted me.

"Maybe we should go another time. I am going to be tired. I need all of the rest I can get before the school year starts."

"You can rest. I will take care of the children. I will purchase the tickets. I will text you the time to meet me at the airport." I am happy she finally agreed. I look forward to seeing the children and spending time with Lailah. If I were a different kind of man, she would be the perfect woman. Lailah's calming spirit is what I need right now. She is different than any woman I have ever known. Unlike Stacy, she is unimpressed with glitz and glamour.

I call my travel agent and purchase four first class plane tickets. I quickly call instead of texting and advise her to be ready tomorrow.

"So soon?" I detect hesitation.

"I will take care of the children; you can relax." I find myself pleading with her. It seems as if she has changed her mind about our vacation, but she reluctantly agrees.

I am extremely excited about spending time with Lailah and the children. I can barely sleep. My phone rings as I anxiously wait for Lailah and my children. I press the decline button. I have to get my emotions clear when dealing with Lailah. I don't want vibes from Stacy. She has been calling me all night. There is something about Lailah that makes me want to cleanse myself from Stacy before seeing her.

I notice her runway walk immediately. There are no signs that she gave birth three years ago. I wave my hand back and forth to get her attention as she crosses the parking lot. She is sexy as hell in a natural kind of way. She recently switched to an all vegan diet. She looks thinner, yet fit. She follows my instruction and simply brings a carry on. We will shop while traveling. She drags the small carry on with one hand and secures my son on her hip with the other. She walks so fast that my daughter has to run to keep up.

Her life is a mystery. She has become evasive. I have never seen her with another man. I periodically drive by the house she purchased for herself and our children. There is never a sign that a man is present. I have grown accustomed to her availability. Honestly, I do not know how I will feel if I come face to face with Lailah and a man. It was established early in the relationship that she is not to ask questions about my life. Other than financial support, she has no expectations. Our relationship is accidental. I did not plan for babies, but when the babies came, I reluctantly accepted them. I was always afraid to have children. Schizophrenia is hereditary, and I would not wish Mary Francis Thomas' genetic code on anyone. I am thankful my children appear normal and absent of the Mary Francis Thomas Gene.

I met Lailah at the library museum. I was meeting a connection when I was in the game and saw her sitting alone. Her hair was a mass of locks pulled to the top of her head. Large gold hoops dangled from her ears. Her profile is perfect. Her thin face reminds me of ancient Egyptian women painted on the walls of pyramids. She sat alone at the table and kept staring at her watch.

"He is obviously late. The question is, am I on time?" She was captivating. The gap in her teeth accentuates her smile. There were hundreds of people around, but I only saw Lailah.

"What makes you think I am waiting on someone?" She stood and placed her hands on her curvy, but thin hips, did that flirtatious sister girl neck pop, and smiled. Her gap tooth smile was wide, but it was her eyes that drew me in. I have never seen anyone with eyes so bright and clear.

"You keep looking at your watch and looking around the atrium. The evidence suggests you are waiting on someone."

"You got me. I have been stood up. I was waiting on my study partner."

"Student?"

"Yes, part-time. I teach second grade, and I am working on my master's."

"You mind if I sit?" She didn't answer. She simply pointed to the chair. Her conversation was refreshing. Her lifestyle was different from mine, but she put me at ease. We exchanged phone numbers. We spoke for hours every night on the phone before she eventually gave me her address. We saw one another every day for four months, but I immediately pulled away when she insisted I meet her parents. She was getting too close, so I abruptly stopped seeing her. No phone call, nor Dear Jane letter, no "*It is not you; it's me*" type bullshit. I abruptly cut all communication and blocked her number. Six months later, I was in Lenox Mall shopping when I saw her wobbling out of a baby furniture store. Her face was full. Her body was thin, but her stomach was full with life. Initially, I did not allow my presence to be known. I followed her to several stores, out of the mall, and to the mall parking garage. I grabbed the driver's side door before she could close it. She is startled. She looked deep into my eyes. Initially, we were both speechless.

"How far along are you?"

"Seven months."

"Do you need anything?"

"No, I am good." She reached for the car door and attempted to close it. Again, I stop her.

"Are you still in the same place?"

"Yes."

"It is mine?"

"Of course."

"I will send money."

"You do not have to."

There was no doubt in my mind the baby inside of her was mine. I can pinpoint the day we conceived. I knew she was pregnant at the moment of conception. We started out using a condom, but it broke. She tried to push me away, but I resisted. It felt good inside of her with nothing between us. I had never had sex without a condom before. Afterwards, we were both very tired. She was so drained; she slept the entire day. I had no intention of developing a relationship with the either of the kids. I only planned on sending money, but when I lay eyes on them for the first time, all of that changed. I felt something I have never felt for another human.

Kaycee runs to me with her toothless smile, as always. Jonathan kicks his legs back and forth and wiggles out of his mother's arms. His mother puts him down, and he follows his sister and runs to me as well. I carry both children in my arms, and we walk to their mother. We greet one another with a simple peck on the lips and go inside of the airport.

We stand in the long line at the security checkpoint with other travelers appearing to be the all American family. We place our carryon luggage on the conveyor belt for screening. The officer scans each of us including the children with his metal detector. We gather our bags from the conveyor belt, board the plane, and take our seats in first class. She is unusually quiet, but her smile softens as she watches me enjoy our children.

"Where are we going?"

"It is a surprise. Did you bring the children's passports?"

"Yes" She removes the passports from her purse and passes

them to me. She puts her earplugs in her ear and leans back deep in her seat. I am in total control of the children. They jump around like rabbits the entire flight. I sense irritation from other passengers, but I have a look that at first glance, most people understand I am not to be fucked with. I should make them quiet down, but I allow them to do as they please. Raising them has to be a hard job, and I have more respect for Lailah each minute I spend with them. We travel from Atlanta to St. Maarten. The airstrip in St. Barth is very narrow and cannot accommodate large commercial airliners, so we charter a private flight to St. Barth's. Lailah is exhausted by the time we check in the Villa.

"Jefferson, I am going to shower." I do my best to remain unfazed by her nonchalance.

"I have the kids." I chose St. Barth because it is laid back and relaxing. Your everyday Joe Blow cannot afford to bring his family to St. Barth's. It is one of the most exquisite of the islands. I run bath water and bathe my son while Lailah showers. She does a remarkable job with my children. I am almost envious of the affection and attention she shows them. I wish Mary Francis Thomas could have been normal. I wish she could have been my mother as opposed to my curse.

"Where are his pajamas?" I leave the bathroom with Jonathan tightly wrapped in a hooded Superman towel. Her skin is still damp from her shower. She sits on the settee and sips wine.

"I did not bring any." She opens the carry on, pulls out a white T-shirt, and throws it to me. "You told me not to bring anything. Remember?"

"We will shop tomorrow."

"Cool." Her continued nonchalance makes me uneasy. She stands, grabs her wine, and leaves the sitting area. "I am going to bed now. I will see you in the morning." I play with the children until they fall asleep. I honestly do not know how she does this. My body is in pain from them jumping on my stomach. My face hurts as they engage in a contest to see who could open my mouth the widest and who could push my nose up the farthest. When they finally fall asleep, I place them in their bed. Initially, I pass her room, go to my suite, but turn back. She is startled when I enter. Her locks hang free and drape perfectly around her face. She resembles a lion. She removes a rubber band from her wrist, bends forward, and wraps the rubber band around her hair.

"Aren't you ready for bed?" She removes her top. Though she has had two children, her breast are still beautiful. They slightly hang but are still full in a motherly kind of way. I sit and stare as she pulls her arms through her T-shirt and over her head in one movement. She doesn't notice me staring. She has had three glasses of wine and doesn't notice I didn't answer. I sit on the arm of the settee. She moves closer. I stand. She stands on her toes and places her lips on mine. I taste the bitter taste of merlot on her tongue. She softly places her hands on my face. "We have to stop this." I do not respond. She uses her tongue to part my lips. I am hungry. I softly suck her moist tongue. I lift her T-shirt and caress one of her small, soft, breast. I follow the patterns of the raised stretch marks that extend from her nipples. I slide my hand between her thighs and notice she does not have on panties. Soft moans escape her lips. I rub her clitoris with my middle finger. She grabs my hand, spreads her legs farther apart, and pushes my middle finger deep inside.

We walk in unison to the bed. I push her down on the bed until she is flat on her back. I caress the small stretch mark covered pooch at the bottom of her abdomen. She reaches down between my legs and massages until it stands at attention. She tries to pull me close to her; I resist. I slide down and place my head between her thin, yet muscular thighs. She began to quiver and move her hips as if she were an epileptic. Her juices are thick, slimy, and sweet. She is the only woman I will allow to cum in my mouth. I slide up and look in her face. Her eyes are watery. I kiss her. I have fucked a lot of women, but Lailah is the only woman I have ever made love to.

"Are you okay?" She pulls my face onto her and began to softly suck my lip. I feel her tears on my cheeks. I slowly slide inside. Her thighs close tight around my hips. I move slow and deep. I want it to last a long time, but I am so excited that I almost ejaculated as soon as I enter. It had been a long time since I made love. She grabs my ass and pulls me inside of her as deep as I can go and moves her hips with a slow rhythm. She moans; she screams and even cries before she releases.

"Thank you." She covers my face with kisses. "Thank you, Jefferson. Baby, that was so good." I wanted to stop and ponder her *thank you*, and how it sounds like closure, but I didn't want to disturb the mood. I take my time and stay in my groove for as long as I can stand it. It feels like the Earth is shattering as I release.

I was ready to go for the second round when she abruptly stands and goes into the bathroom. She returns in her bath robe. I pull her down on top of me.

"You need to go to your suite." Her face is turned away from mine.

"I want to stay with you and the children."

"That is not a good idea." She removes the rubber band from her hair; her locks fall to her shoulder. "Jefferson, it is time for me to move on. The kids do not need to see us play house a couple of weeks out of the year."

"Have you found someone?"

"What difference does it make? It does not matter."

"It matters."

"It does not matter. You set the course of our relationship. I went along with it, hoping..." She turns away and walks towards the fully stocked mini-bar in her suite. "The kids are getting bigger. They need more than a once per month dinner or an annual summer vacation."

"So you met someone?" It is more of a confirmation than a question. I do not make eye contact. I do not want her to see the rage in my eyes. I have never raised my voice to her. I have never struck her.

"It does not matter. It is time to move on."

"I will do better." I am surprised that I am pleading with her. I am out of character.

"You can't do better. This is who you are. You want no commitments. We are your disposable family. It is no longer good enough."

"I can't let you go." I am begging.

"What do you suggest?"

"I don't know. I can't make promises. I won't make promises to you that I cannot keep."

She takes a sip of her wine and comes back to the bed. I remove her bathrobe. She stands in front of me naked. I am excited again; I can actually feel the vibration of my heart beat against my chest. Her brown skin is moist with perspiration. I smell her scent and know she wants me. My rod is throbbing. She moves closer and stands between my legs. I touch her waist and move my hands down to her round, firm behind. I am anxious. She does not resist. I can tell she wants me to move faster, but I take my time.

"I never knew how to have a family." My voice trembles as I rotate my tongue around her nipples.

"You could have learned if you really wanted to." Her hand is soft to the back of my head. I am weakened by the tremble in her voice.

"Trust me; it is too late for me." I leave one nipple and bring my mouth to the other. I can feel her legs tremble. She massages the back of my head. I lean back on the bed. She lowers her body on top of mine. She slides down to my pelvis and places my rock hard shaft in her mouth. A disgusting scene flashes through my mind. She is not my whore; she is the mother of my children. My erection begins to dissipate. She has obviously been experimenting with another man. Fellatio was not her thing. I pull her back on top of me and roll over on top of her. I plant soft kisses on her face and lips. She guides my hand between her legs. I massaged her clit soft and slow. I slowly moved down to her stomach. I spread her trembling legs and kiss her thighs. Her spine begins to curve as I slowly licked her hardened clit. She moans this time it was not the soft whisper, but the roar of a lioness. She moved her hips hard against my tongue. She pushes my head away.

"Jefferson, I want you now! I want to feel you inside of me!" It was almost like a plea. I slide my body on top of hers; her legs are spread wide. I pushed myself inside of her skin to skin, no condom. Her soft moans reassure me I am getting the job done. I move slowly. She grabs my ass and pulls me in deeper. The lioness returns. She shouts and thanks me, the Creator, and Mother Earth as she adjusts her opening to take me all in. Her juices are all over me. I want to explore all of her insides. I look down at her; she is staring at me intensely. Tears flow down her cheeks.

"Cum, baby, let it go!" Her words were encouraging. "Let it go, baby." She moved her hips hard against me.

"Lailah," I gasped for air. "Baby...!" I began to speak in another language. I surprise myself. I am usually quiet and unemotional during sex.

"Yeah, baby, talk to me, baby. Her eyes were glued to mine as she moves her hips harder. "Talk to me."

"God, it is so good. You feel so good! Damn! Baby, what are you doing to me? I love you!"

"What?"

"I love you!" We are both in disbelief. I have never confessed love to anyone.

I collapsed on top of her shivering. The release feels good. I lay on top of her as she rubs my head. I was beginning to doze off when her phone rings.

"Hello" She sits up and quickly removes her phone from the night stand. "Why are you calling so late?" She grabs her robe and wraps it around her naked body as if I have never seen her naked before. "We are out of the country." She goes into the bathroom; I can still hear the conversation. "Yes, we are with him. I can't talk now. I will call you when I return to the states." She returns to the bedroom. Instead of coming to bed, she sits on the settee.

"Is that your guy?"

"Something like that."

"I don't know how I feel about that."

"You are confused."

"What is wrong with what we have?"

"Everything is wrong with what we have; the kids need a full-time father. We cannot be your standby family forever." She wraps the rubber band around her hair yet again. This must be a nervous habit she has recently acquired. "I should have moved on a long time ago. I stayed around hoping you would come to know that the children and I can complete you." She throws her arms up in the air. "I thought one day you would see we are enough for you."

"I am too damaged." I look deep in her eyes. I want to disclose my innermost securities. I want to tell her how fast I ran from Tyree. Tyree was hurting so bad until he found Jefferson. And the thought of losing her is making Jefferson scared. "I love you and the kids, but I am no good."

"You are good; we could not have created such beautiful and loving children if you were bad." She looks away. "I have to move on. I can no longer live like this."

I feel rage roaring inside of me. I have never hurt Lailah, but the rage is overwhelming. I need to leave. I put my clothes on. "I will see you in the morning." I lock the door and go to my suite.

We spend five days on St. Barth's. The tension between us is thick. We fight very hard to make sure the kids do not notice. Lailah and I do not make love again the entire trip, but we are very cordial to one another. She spends time in the spa while the kids and I take snorkeling lessons, play on the beach and enjoy a submarine to the bottom of the sea. I find myself growing despondent every time she moves away from me and the children to answer her phone.

"Please do not do that." My fists are balled so tight, my knuckles change colors. Blood vessels protrude from my temples. "Wait and talk to your friend when we get back to the states."

"Okay" She turns off her phone and places it in her luggage. I have no right. It is crazy for me to expect that she does not have a life outside of me, but love is sometimes crazy.

Chapter 11

"Take care." There is an unfamiliar, almost somber look on his face. If we were on good terms, I would suggest he seek the help of a therapist; his ill mood is lasting too long. I know it is hard for him to go to work and deal with a less productive co-worker's promotion, but everyone deals with shit on the job. He sits at the table reading the paper as he drinks coffee out of his favorite mug. I look at the mug that is chipped around the edges with the picture of Che' holding OJ and think of the number of times he has stopped me from throwing it away.

He holds the newspaper close to his face as if he is hiding. He is the only person I know who still reads the print version of the daily paper. Osei is very techno-savvy; I find it hard to understand why he does not read the paper online or on an e-reader. I glance at the clock behind the table. It is almost an hour past the time he normally leaves for work. He goes to the fridge, grabs a bottle of orange juice, and goes back to the table. He is dressed in tailored slacks and a crisp, starched, white shirt, but no necktie.

"Are you going into the office today?"

"No! Why do you ask? Do I need your permission to take a day off?" I am not an overly sensitive woman, but the continued hostility in his voice is beginning to cut deep.

"Of course you do not need my permission. I simply noticed you do not have on a tie." His mood swings are unpredictable; I seriously believe he has become bi-polar. Last night, we made the best love ever. There was not a place on my body his hands or lips did not touch. The passion was extraordinary and went on into the wee hours of the morning. We have not made love that intense in years. I am not the touchy feely type, but Osei held on to me all night. I would wiggle out of his arms, only to wake up to find them around me again. His spontaneous kisses disturbed my sleep throughout the night. His affection was beyond surprising and unexpected. This morning Bi-polar Osei is back. He has no patience with me. He acts as if it is my fault he was passed over for a promotion. His ill mood and impatience have intensified since we left Ghana. I know he is upset because he did not make partner. He deserves the promotion, but many of us do not get what we deserve. Besides, he is unwilling to play the game.

"We will see you later." Che' and OJ grab their bags and proceed toward the garage.

"No, I will take care of the kids!" He quickly stands; his chair turns over, as he weaves his way between me and the kids. He is so close in front of me I almost lose my balance. He grabs my arm to steady me. "You have a nice day at work. I will handle the kids."

"Are you sure? It is my turn." I hide my joy. Truthfully, I am very happy he is taking the children.

"I am sure. I have it." He kisses me on the forehead. I step away from him. He pulls me close. His grip is so tight I feel as if I am being embraced by a bear. He releases me. I grab the keys, kiss the kids, and leave.

Osei often takes the children in the morning, even when it is my turn; however, an unsettling feeling creeps inside as I drive out of the garage. The garage door closes; my instinct tells me to go back to the house and get my children. My spirit is suddenly restless. I turn into the neighbor's driveway, turn around, and drive back to my house. I park in front of the garage for two minutes. I see shadows of the children through the kitchen window. A light flickers off from our bedroom window. I am overreacting and chalk it up to work related stress. The muscles in my shoulders are tight. Pain shoots through my neck like a lightning bolt. I make a mental note to have Kate schedule an appointment with the massage therapist.

I coast to the security gate; I notice a black Cadillac parked outside of the subdivision. It catches my attention because it is out of place. Our neighborhood association bylaws prohibits tinted windows. I drive five miles north and turn into the neighborhood coffee shop. The car continues north, but I am uneasy. Instead of having my coffee to go, I drink it in the coffee shop. I stay in coffee shop for thirty minutes and leave. I drive my usual route and notice the Cadillac parked in front of the drugstore one mile from the coffee shop. A black Audi is backed in next to the Cadillac.

Both drivers have their window halfway down, engaging in conversation. I quickly check to make sure my doors are locked. I look in the rear view mirror and notice the two cars exit the parking lot and travel in different directions. The Cadillac continues to follow three car lengths behind me. I call Detective Davis and request him to meet me in front of my office building. I am uneasy. This is Jefferson Thomas 101. His goal is to intimidate. The driver makes no effort to be inconspicuous. I drive around my office building three times until I see Detective Davis' car. He flashes his lights and follows me into the garage.

I park my Mercedes GL in the middle of my two reserved spaces. Detective Davis stands outside of his car with his gun in his hand as I get out of mine.

"Are you okay?"

"Someone in a black Cadillac was following me." My nerves are frazzled. "Thanks for meeting me."

"That is what friends are for." He escorts me to the building entrance. "Did you get a look at the driver? Can you provide a good description?" He visually peruses the garage again, then places his gun back in the holster.

"I did not get a good look, but he appeared to be Caucasian."

"I am willing to bet he is one of Mr. Thomas' minions." He peruses the parking deck again. "All of this over a pimp charge? You know this is bigger than a pimping and prostitution charge. Right?"

"Of course, I wish the D.A. was as smart as you."

"I have a meeting this morning." He looks at his watch and scans the parking garage again. "If you need me, call me." I am safely in my building, but still nervous. I have placed a lot of criminals behind bars, but the only one bold enough to attempt to intimidate a prosecutor is Jefferson Thomas.

"Good morning, Mrs. Williams." Though my name is legally hyphenated, I am referred to as Ms. Williams at work to keep things simple. Osei dislikes my use of a hyphenated name and hates I use my maiden name in my professional affairs. Williams is simple. I do not have to constantly explain the origin, and Williams is more comfortable for an American to pronounce than Badu-Bonsu.

"Hello, Kate, please send my schedule as soon as you can." I walk past her desk and through the double mahogany doors to my office. I am going to leave this crazy shit with my husband at home where it belongs and concentrate on putting this bold, impudent, lowlife thug behind bars. Right now, my case against Jefferson is priority one. Osei is ungrateful. We live a good life. We both have six-figure salaries. We could grace the cover of Black Enterprise magazine as the poster family for success. Thanks to the one hundred thousand dollar wedding gift from his father, we were able to get a mortgage on a half million dollar mini mansion in an upscale gated community. We both drive new luxury vehicles. Our children attend one of the most prestigious private schools in Atlanta. So what? He didn't make partner. It is not the end of our world.

I am ten minutes late to my scheduled appointment with Ashleigh and Mary. I have wasted valuable time trying to make contact with Osei. I have called him over five times to invite him to lunch. We have not had a lunch date in months. I want to piggy back on our passionate exchange last night in hopes he will come to his senses and get acceptance about not making partner. The call goes straight to his voicemail each time I call. I give up, hang up the phone, and walk to the detention center to meet Ashleigh and Mary.

I hope our meeting goes well and she is willing to provide more insight on her relationship with Jefferson. Surprisingly, she has not lost all of her innocence. Jefferson Thomas is the devil. Jefferson is cunning. He believes his connections with the rich political class will shield him from scrutiny. Nothing could be farther from the truth. He is a pimp; not the average pimp, but a pimp nonetheless. All pimps operate from the same playbook; initially, they are caring. They draw their victims in with gifts, a lot of attention, and nice dates. They play the role of rescuer. Pimps have a charm that matches no other. Jefferson has an advantage on the average pimp, as he is clean cut with model-like features. He is a chameleon. He can mix with the lowest of the low and the highest of the high. We play the same game. The difference is I am on the right side the law.

He is too good to be true. After he was acquitted in the first trial, he interviewed with local and some national news reporters to smear the reputation of the District Attorney's office. He was almost successful in his endeavor. He campaigned to file a class action suit and tried to rally every defendant ever prosecuted in the county to join him. He never failed to mention my name. His allegation of prosecutorial misconduct received so much attention, it resulted in an ethics investigation that lasted six months. Thankfully, I was cleared of all wrong doing and the threat of a lawsuit disappeared.

I use my credentials to bypass the long line of people waiting to visit detainees. The noise in this place is painful to my ears.

"ID, please." I present my official county badge. The detention officer barely looks at it. "Place all of your belongings in the bag." She passes a plastic bag to me. I place my phone and keys in the bag and pass it to her. Again, she barely looks at it. It is as if she is on auto-pilot. I now understand how contraband gets into detention centers, jails, and prisons. "Give this to the officer, and she will return your items when you depart." I take a worn, laminated card from her hand. "Next!"

I enter the secured area that leads to the interview room. Ashleigh reluctantly agreed to talk with me on the condition that I do not ask questions about her parents. She also requests that Mary sits in on the interview. Mary is a good social worker, but she is overly involved with this case. If she ever asks my opinion, I will tell her she needs balance in her life. She is in the interview room when I arrive. Mary sits at the table embracing Ashleigh's hand. Red wavy lines mark the whites of her eyes. Puffy, dark bags sit so low at the bottom of her eyes they almost touch her cheeks. She looks as if she has not slept in weeks. Ashleigh's hair is pulled back in a bouncy ponytail. Her skin is flawless. She looks more like a child each time I see her.

"Hello, Ashleigh." She smiles. "How are you?"

"I am ready to leave this place. It's so noisy in here. These people talk nonstop. My mom used to say if a person talks more than three minutes at a time, they are probably telling lies." Her laughter is contagious. "You would think these people are on vacation." She laughs louder. I cannot help but laugh with her. I notice she has unnaturally perfect teeth. It is obvious she has had expensive orthodontic care.

I stare in her eyes, trying to gauge her mood before getting to business. "Ashleigh, we need to talk about testifying against Stacy and Mr. Thomas." She turns away from me. "We want him to pay for what he did to you. We want to make sure you are his last victim. Will you help us? Will you testify?"

"I don't know anything about the man you call Jefferson Thomas. He simply gave me a ride. I am dead if Stacy thinks I talked to anyone. She will make me disappear like Jessica."

"Jessica?" Other than Stacy and someone named Nita, she has never mentioned names in past interviews. "Who is Jessica?"

"Jessica is the girl they wrapped in the blanket." Mary pulls Ashleigh close to her. Ashleigh looks uncomfortable.

"The one you never saw again?" I recall her telling me about someone disappearing, but she never mentioned a name.

"Yes, that one." A look of sorrow replaces the glow on her face. It was awful." She wipes a tear away as she wiggles out of Mary's grip. "Ms. Mary said something about witness protection." She holds her head in her hands, looking more and more like an innocent child.

"We have to get you home to your parents."

"I want to go home, but I don't want my mom and dad to see me like this. They can't know anything about this!" There is a sense of panic in her elevated voice. I am still surprised she references two parents. Initially, I assumed she was a runaway from a broken home. "I would like to get in witness protection."

"Baby, you are only 13." I hope Mary did not pass bad information to Ashleigh. "We would like for you to go back to your parents. We can provide everyone with counseling, so your parents can understand what you have been through."

"Look, bitch!" She quickly stands. "I am not going back home! My parents deserve a lot better than me! They do not deserve a nasty, stank slut for a daughter!" The sudden change in her demeanor catches me off guard.

"You are not a slut. You are a victim." I gather my composure, reach across the table, and gently take both of her hands in mine. She snatches her hands from mine and turns away. I immediately change the subject. "We'll get back to that later. Do you know how long you have been gone from your parents?"

"It's just all messed up. I would not be here if it were not for those stupid pictures." She begins to cry again. "It is like I told you. The pictures I took got into the wrong hands. I didn't want my parents to find out about them."

"You are a child. You parents will understand that you have made a mistake. What were you doing in the pictures?"

"They will not understand! I was naked!" She turns away.

"Not totally naked, but I was showing my boobies."

"It's okay; calm down, we are going to work through this."

"My friend let her older brother see them. I should have run away instead of going to the party with him. I believed him when he said he just needed a date and then I could go on my way and never hear from him again."

"Did his sister come with you?"

"No, it was just me and her brother."

"Does the boy have a name?"

"Well damn, obviously he has a fucking name! Shit it should be obvious I don't want to tell you!" I do not press the issue.

"Okay, does the brother go to your school?"

"I don't know what school he goes to."

"What about the sister? Does she go to your school?"

"No, I think she is older. She said she was twelve, but she sounded older on the phone."

"Older?" Her story takes more turns than a roller coaster. "Ashleigh, how did you meet your friend?"

"I met her on the Internet; she was giving out free concert tickets in one of the chat rooms a lot of the kids in my school visit. It is really a cool chat room. A lot of kids hang out there; we trade athletic shoes and music. I emailed her my address so she could send the tickets. By the time she received my information, she had already given the tickets away." A wide smile stretches wide across her face. "She is good friends with my favorite rap group; she knows them personally. She even sent me an autograph picture of Three D, the leader of the group. All of the girls in my class fight over him."

"Ashleigh, what is your friend's name?" There are so many layers to this story, but with each interview the picture becomes clearer.

"I don't know her name. We use avatars in the chat rooms. My parents don't know I visit social network sites. Her parents probably did not know she was on the site either. I am only allowed to use the computer when we are all in the family room, but I sneak and use it when my parents go to sleep."

"Ashleigh, I need to know her name" I plead with her. Mary sits through the entire interview in silence, looking down at the table with one arm around Ashleigh and the other under the table.

"I don't know her name. Her User ID is Joy 24_7."

"What is the name of the group?"

"Grownups are not allowed. It is a place for kids to hang out."

"Ashleigh, I need to know the name of the chat room."

"No, I am not going to get my friends in trouble." She is adamant. I do not press the issue.

"How did you get to the party? Did the brother take you to the party in his car?"

"Yes, he took us." I want to expound on who "Us" is, but she is fragile and I do not want to push her. "There were a lot of old men at the party. I don't remember everything, but when I woke up, like I told you, I was naked on a hospital bed but, only I was not in a hospital."

"Did you try to leave?"

"What you think? He threatened to send the pictures to my parents!" She looks at Mary and points in my direction. "You sure she is a lawyer?"

"Okay, we will talk more later. What they did to you was wrong. I am going to do everything in my power to make them pay for what they did, but I need your help."

"I am just tired of being scared." Her demeanor changes again. "I want to be safe and happy again. I want to hug my little sister. I would give anything to hear Daddy lecture about the importance of taking my studies seriously. I used to think my family was lame and square. I would give anything to sit at the dinner table with them again."

"Mary" I stand. Ashleigh's emotions are getting the best of me. "I have scheduled a meeting on Wednesday. I will get everyone together. The D.A. will be there." I stretch my arms high above my head, to release the stress. "Ashleigh, everything will be okay." She stands and wraps her arms around me. I embrace her. It feels awkward. She holds onto me so tight, I have to peel her fingers apart to loosen her grip.

"I don't want to be afraid anymore."

"I know; I will see you again soon." She wraps her arms around me again and walks to the metal door. The loud buzzer stings my ears. Two metal doors open and then close with Ashleigh on the other side.

"Poor little thing." Mary's speech is slurred. "No child should ever endure what she has endured."

"Mary, has she had a psychological evaluation? She behaves as if she is manic."

"I am waiting until we get her in the group home. Of course, she is acting crazy." Mary looks over her shoulder to ensure Ashleigh's confidentiality is protected. "Quite honestly, I no longer believe anything the child says. She had drugs in her system."

"At 13?" Considering her pimp is Jefferson, I should not be surprised. There may be some people who can blame their environment, but not this Ivy League graduate. He has no excuse. He had the opportunity to leave the 'hood on a full scholarship but took the 'hood with him. Bottom feeding is what he does best. Jefferson has always had questionable morals. His moral compass needs recalibration.

I dial Osei's phone as I walk to my car. I must have called Osei fifty times today. Each time, the call goes straight to his voicemail. I order lunch and eat at my desk while I plan my prosecution.

"Osei, hi babe" He finally answers his cell phone. There is a lot of noise in the background; I can barely understand him.

"Let me call you back in a few."

"Just wanted to tell you I will be late. I will talk to you when I get home." He hangs up before I finish speaking. I place the handset back in its cradle. I flip through Jefferson's file, but I am unable to concentrate. There is something in Osei's voice that is distracting. His voice was shaky, as if he is nervous. Osei is never nervous; angry at times, but never nervous. My heart feels as if it is skipping beats. I grab the files, throw them in my bag and run out of the door. It normally takes me thirty minutes to get home in the evening, but I make it in twenty. As I wait for the garage to open, I notice the lights upstairs are on. I park on my side of the garage. Osei's car is not inside. The lawn mower he never used sits on his side of the garage.

I turn off the alarm as I enter the house. The house feels empty. Everything appears to be in its place, but the house feels empty. I turn on the entertainment system to drown the silence. I fill the bath with water as hot as my body can stand. It is 8:00 pm. and no Osei, Che' or OJ. I step out of the bath, dry off, and pour a glass of wine. I dial Osei's cell; the call goes straight to his voicemail.

"Osei, it's Yanna; call me when you get this message." I hang up the phone. I take the files out of my work bag and place them on the bed next to me. I cannot concentrate. I sit in front of the television and drink a second glass of wine. I remove all of the dirty clothes from the closets and take them downstairs to the laundry room. I come back upstairs, sit on the bed, and stare at the walls. I dial his number again as I flip the channel to the ten o'clock news. The call goes straight to his voicemail, but his voicemail is full. I hang up the phone and dial his friends, Mike and Diane.

"Hello," Dianne has been in the states over ten years. Her English is marginal, and her accent is still very pronounced. It is obvious she socializes very little with people outside of the small Ghanaian community.

"Diane, Yanna here."

"Hello, long time, no see. I missed you at Mike's birthday celebration."

"Yeah, I know, I have been so busy with work, Osei and the children."

"Ah, the overwhelming life of a career woman." I ignore the sarcasm; she is too insignificant for a response. If Dianne wants her legacy to be washing dirty dishes and changing dirty diapers, that is her business. There is nothing wrong with domesticity, but it is not for me. Besides, I am looking for my family. I have no time for subtle hostility from the unaccomplished.

"Have you seen Osei and the kids today? Are they with you guys?" Osei is not the cliquish type, but every once in a while he stops by Mike and Diane's with the children after work. He and Mike are very proud of their children. They meet up once a month, have a beer, take turns comparing the children's test scores, class rankings and bragging on their children's accomplishments.

"I have not seen them today. I spoke with Osei on the phone yesterday. Is everything okay?" Her sarcasm changes to legitimate concern.

"Yes. It's just that he is not picking up his cell, and it is kind of late."

"No, they have not been here."

"Can you ask Mike if he has heard from Osei?" I try hard to disguise it, but I am sure she hears the panic in my voice.

"No, Mike has not spoken to..." I abruptly and almost rudely disconnect the call and frantically dial Osei's number again. It goes straight to his voicemail. I am slightly relieved I am able to leave a message.

I sit on the sofa in the sitting area of our bedroom, pour another glass of wine, and wait for Osei to return my call. I have had way too much to drink. The room is spinning, and I am about to go crazy. I alternate dialing Osei's number, and the numbers to different local hospitals I have Googled on my cell phone.

"Ma'am, for the third time, no one fits the description. This is your third time calling in the last thirty minutes. Your family is not in this hospital. Have you called the other thirty hospitals in the city?" The receptionist's attitude is irritating. I hang up the phone, lie on the bed, and continue to wait.

I must have passed out. I wake up to an empty wine bottle in the middle of the bed. I hear the voices of the neighborhood children waiting outside for the school bus. Osei's side of the bed is cold and empty. I sprint across the hall to Che's room. Her room is empty, and her bed is perfectly made. I don't bother to look in OJ's room. I glance at the clock, and then sprint to my closet, peeling away my pajamas as I run. I slide into dingy, already worn jeans I grab from the hamper, stuff my ashy feet in the first shoes I see, and run out the door finger combing my hair, pulling it to the top of my head and securing it with a rubber band as I move.

Cars are lined up in the Kids' Academy drop-off lane. I park in the visitor parking space; I look for Osei's car, hoping to see him drop the children off at school. No Osei, and no children. I wave at familiar parents as they drop off their kids. I am anxious, as I do not know the whereabouts of mine. I sit in my car outside of the building for over two hours. When the drop-off lane is empty, I enter the building, walk past the receptionist desk, and straight to the classrooms. Gail immediately leaves her desk and tries to stop me.

"Mrs. Williams, you need to sign in!" I ignore her, walk past her to OJ's class, then to Che's class. Neither child is in their classroom. I rush down the hall and out of the building.

"Osei, what is going on?" I screamed into his voicemail so loud, I am sure I can be heard by everyone within a two-mile radius. I place the key in the ignition, turn the car on, shove the transmission in drive, and speed down Georgia 400, dodging in and out of traffic en route to Osei's job. I think about ignoring the blue lights that have been behind me for the last three miles. I am trying to find my children and have no intentions of going to jail. I exit the freeway at the next ramp and park on the shoulder of the road.

"Ma'am, are you okay?" The rotund, ruby cheeked officer inquires about my health with his hand secure on his weapon.

"I am fine. I am looking for my children. My husband didn't come home with them yesterday." My voice shakes as I fight back the tears. "He didn't bring them home."

"Can I see your license and registration?" I reach for my purse and find the passenger seat empty.

"Officer, I quickly ran out of the house. I must have forgotten my purse at home."

"Ma'am, please step out of the car." I open the door and step out of the car. The officer and I both look at my mismatched black sandals, one high heel and one low heeled. A river of tears flows from my eyes.

"Ma'am, have you been drinking? Are you under the influence of any substances controlled or otherwise?" He has removed his weapon from the holster. His hand is firmly on his gun. His stare is intense. His legs are shoulder width apart, and he appears ready for action.

"No, I am an officer of the court." I manage to pull myself together and put on my professional face. "I am Deputy Assistant District Attorney Ayanna Williams. I am second in command to District Attorney Leslie. Please contact the D.A.'s office, and they will confirm my identity." I take a deep and meaningful breath. "I will ask that you place your gun in the holster immediately." The officer does not like my tone. "You can verify my identity with the D.A., you can run my tags. As we both know, there are several ways to confirm my identity. I will ask again that you place your gun back in the holster. I am looking for my kids. I simply forgot my purse. I believe my husband has taken them out of the country."

"Have you filed a report?

"No. I was hoping I could find them."

"Are you still married?" He slowly places the gun back in the holster.

"Yes, we are married."

"Does he have reason to believe the kids are not safe with you?" He looks down at the two mismatched shoes on my feet.

"No, the kids are perfectly safe with me." After a brief interrogation and a call to the District Attorney's office to verify my identity, the officer looks through the glove compartment and finds my insurance and registration papers. He verifies I have a driver's license with my Social Security number and allows me to leave.

"You should keep your identification on you." I ignore his sarcasm. "Of all people, you should know the law."

"You are correct Officer." I get in the car, and rather than drive to Osei's job, I drive home. I know he is not at work. The signs were there. I was too engulfed in my own agenda to see this coming.

Chapter 12

"For the last time, I did not sign any papers to allow my husband to take my children out of the country!"

"Ma'am, your husband would have been stopped before boarding the plane if he did not have the proper documents. I can fax a copy of the rules and regulations."

"Yes, please do that."

"The only thing I can suggest is you come into the office and file a formal complaint; we will pass it on to the State Department."

"My husband has been allowed to take my children out of the fucking country using fraudulent fucking documents, and I have to file a fucking formal complaint?" I curse and scream for twenty minutes before I notice the dial tone. I reach for my third glass of wine. I normally do not drink before noon, but desperate ends call for desperate means. At the rate I am going, I may have to replace the carpet. I have walked from the fax machine to the desk a thousand times. I remove the fax, but I don't bother reading the regulations. In the back of my mind, I know it is a waste of time. The children have current passports, and it takes nothing but a few bucks to get a signature fraudulently notarized.

I use my hands to wipe a tidal wave of tears away from my eyes, as I rummage through the desk drawer in search of an old phone bill.

"Ay-Yee-Kooh" I immediately recognize Beauty's voice.

"Hello, Beauty. This is Ayanna, Osei's wife."

"Hello, ma'am, I will get the Mrs. for you." I wait patiently on the phone for five minutes before Mrs. Badu-Bonsu picks up the phone.

"Ay-Yee-Kooh."

"Mrs. Badu-Bonsu, how are you? She does not respond.

"Can I speak with Osei?"

"Osei is not available." She is direct; her voice is void of emotion. I detect no sign of empathy. She behaves as if a husband stealing his children is an everyday thing. Perhaps he inherited his coldness from his mother.

"I guess you know Osei has taken the children. I would just like to know they are okay." She remains silent. "We are both mothers." I plead. "I just want to know my children are okay."

"They are fine; the children are fine."

"Can I speak with them?"

"This is not possible!" She quickly hangs up the phone. I immediately dial the number again, but she does not answer. I call Osei's cell; the voicemail is full again. I fall back deep into the sofa. I must have cried for hours. I am lightheaded, and my sinuses are full with so much mucous I have to breathe through my mouth. My eyelids are so heavy, I can barely lift them. I pass the mirror en route to my bedroom. I barely recognized myself. I walk back to our bed and lay across my king size bed and rub my hands across the empty spot where Osei used to lay. The phone rings. I roll over and look at the Caller ID. The number is unfamiliar.

"Hello."

"Yanna,"

"Osei, Osei for God's sake, what is going on? What are you doing?"

"I had no choice." I detect a small amount of remorse in his voice. "I know you are having an affair. Divorce is imminent! I will not live without my children."

I am speechless. "What are you trying to do? What affair? I am not having an affair!"

"There is no need to lie. I have the pictures of you going to his apartment. I have spoken to his wife. How could you?" I am shocked that he spoke to Trevor's wife. I am not concerned about a confrontation with his wife; she knows her place. As long as he keeps the credit card open and she can attend lavish parties, she is good. Unlike Osei, she understands and expects men in Trevor's position will have special arrangements.

"Osei, it is not what you think." He does not understand the rules of the game. "Anything I have done is for our family. My sacrifice and efforts will open doors for Che' and OJ my parents could never have opened for me. They will never feel inferior to anyone."

"Don't bother yourself explaining." There is no emotion in his voice. "I hope it was worth it."

"You did not have to take the children!"

"I will not take a chance on losing either of my children." He laughs. "They are only backdrops to your stage. They are nothing more than props. The kids are with me, and they will be fine. You can come and see them in Kumasi if you like."

"It did not mean anything." I plead my case. "We can get through this."

"Shut up!?" He pauses. "You think I think you were in love, or even in lust?" I am unamused by his slight chuckle. "It was part of the job. Right?"

"Osei, please."

"How dare you? Who do you...?" The pitch of his voice has returned to normal. "I did not call to fight. I made the decision and it is a final decision. This is where we are going to be. You can visit if you choose, but my children will stay with me, where they belong. I am in my country now, and there is nothing you can do."

"Don't be so swift, Osei! It's illegal to interfere with custody! I am going to the State Department first thing in the morning! We have a treaty with Ghana!"

"Yanna listen to me!" He screams so loud, I have to remove the phone away from my ear. "I don't give a shit about a fucking treaty. Don't waste your time with that! Those foolish maternal laws in your country mean nothing to me. I am their father, and no one will take them away from me! No one will regulate when I see my children or how much they are worth! Be honest; you and I know you could care less about the children. Family means nothing to you. We were only in your life for image purposes. If I did not remind you, you would not even remember their birthdays."

"Osei" I count to ten and try with everything I have to gather my composure. I ignore his accusations. I have no energy to address them. "Will you file for divorce?"

"Yes!" His volume is low, and the anger begins to diminish in his voice. "I will not have a wife who believes spreading her legs to another man to advance her career is justified. You and I both know that was all it was. You should be happy you are in America. If you did this in Ghana..." He does not complete the thought. "I will not be regulated to second class citizenry. So I am back in my country. Here, all I know is first class."

"Osei, I work in a man's world. I do what I have to do to level the playing field! You know how hard I have worked. I have worked all of my life trying to be the best in my field. I am up next for District Attorney. I will be the youngest on the Federal bench if I stay on my path." I am screaming so loud, my vocal cords begin to hurt.

"You made your choice. You will continue to allow that little government job to dictate every part of your life, then you do that. My father would have given you any position you wanted."

"Can I speak to my children?"

"Absolutely not! They have to get adjusted to their new life."

"How can you be this cold?" I could care less about a position from his father. "How can you rip them away from me? I would never do that to you. When can I see my children? I cannot believe you have done this! You planned this! How could you look at me, sleep with me, make love to me while plotting against me?"

"You are not destroyed. Stop your antics! Save the theatrics for when you explain our absence to your colleagues. I will meet you in Kumasi if you want to see the children. Tell me when. I will wire the money for a ticket." His voice is calm. "I have taken the money from all of our accounts. Once I have the proper security in place I will wire money back to you." He hangs up the phone. I quickly grab my laptop and log into my bank accounts. A large, bright red minus sign followed by three red digits stand out against the white screen.

Chapter 13

I walk in the crowded boarding area in Sangster International Airport. I am not thrilled about meeting in Montego Bay, but Gorbachev insisted. The untidiness and overcrowded streets make me anxious. I take a seat and wait for Stacy to exit the plane. I traveled a day earlier from a private airport on a private jet to meet with my accountant to work out the financial logistics. I trust Stacy with most things, but I prefer to keep my financial contacts private. Expanding our services to an international clientele was a good business move and has proven to be very lucrative. However, this is a complicated business. It requires membership in an underground network of strangers you may have face to face contact with once per year, but trust them to hold and transport millions of your dollars.

The underground market is lucrative. If I were a betting man, I would bet it has more assets and conducts more transactions than Wall Street. The difference is, our cash is real. There are no bank drafts or electric finance; our markets never crash. We only deal in hard currency. You can't transport hundreds of thousands of cash dollars through Customs or on commercial airlines. The only way to survive and thrive is to have international connections with a network of wealthy partners with the ability to secretly transport currency to secure offshore accounts.

Under normal circumstances, I would have sent Stacy to handle this business on her own, but I don't trust the Russian, and Stacy has been acting strange. After almost an hour, she finally exits the plane. Her beauty stands out amongst the other passengers. I wave my arms back and forth to get her attention. She responds by a slight wave of the hand. We meet at the end of the first row of seats in the boarding area. She passes me her carryon luggage, and we walk to Baggage Claim. Normally she would greet me with a hug, or at the very least a smile. Dark shades cover her eyes. I am unable to read her expression.

"Did you have a nice flight?"

"It was okay." Her nonchalance irks me.

"How about you? How was your flight?"

"It was nice. The jet was small but very relaxing."

"You look tired." She looks at me over the rims of her sunglasses.

"I am tired; I partied all night with the accountant, his pilot, and some of his associates." We stand in front of the conveyor belt and wait for Stacy's luggage for what feels like another thirty minutes. I pass the carryon to Stacy, grab her luggage from the conveyor, and drag both pieces through the airport. I instructed her to bring one carryon. This is not a vacation. We are in Jamaica on business.

"Call your connection." I remove the pre-paid international phone from my pocket to give to her to call Gorbachev then change my mind. "I forgot the new pre-paid phone. This one is old. Just use yours." She immediately calls the Russian; the call goes directly to his voicemail. She pulls her sunglasses to the top of her head. She leaves a message and informs him she arrived safely. I detect a flirtatious sultriness in her voice. Her smile is annoyingly wide, and her eyes are unusually bright. My response to her flirting surprises me. She is my chick and not my woman. I don't like the relationship she has with the Russian. I don't own her pussy, but a woman will lose her mind to a man if she gives it up and he hits it right. Stacy knows too much about me and my operation. For her sake, I pray she does not become collateral damage.

"We could be on the way to the hotel right now if you would have listened to me! I told you to only bring a carryon!" She ignores me and places the cell phone inside of her purse. She's been different for the last couple of weeks. I can't put my finger on it, but she is distant. Last week, she was an hour late for our meeting at the Chicken Shack. I usually pick her up, and we ride together. When I went to her place, she was not there. Lately, she is spending more time in her own place. She used to want to spend the night with me every night. I used to have to demand spend the night at her own place sometimes to give me space. She is not my girl. She is my chick, but I do not share pussy.

"Who travels out of the country with one carry on? I thought that would look suspect." She looks straight ahead.

"When did I give you permission to think?"

"When did I need you to give me permission to think?" Her response catches me off guard. If there were no people around, she would be on the ground with two dotted eyes, searching for her teeth.

"Don't write a check your ass can't cash! You may find yourself in the middle of cross hairs!"

"Or overdosed with a needle in my arm?" We are making a scene. I lower my voice. We exit the airport and walk to our waiting car. She slides in the seat behind the driver.

"What's up with your attitude? You have been missing in action a lot lately. If you have a man, cool, but don't forget you are on the payroll."

"I don't have an attitude. You are imagining things again." The cell phone rings. Her eyes light up as she looks at the Caller ID.

"You have an attitude; I suggest you get it together." She answers the phone. There is too much happiness in her voice for my comfort. It is almost as if she is talking to a date.

"It's Gorbachev; he wants to meet in thirty minutes. He will take me to see the product. If everything is cool, we can give him the money for the passports and airline tickets.

"You go and handle business with him. I had a long week. I am going to take a nap. Besides, it is not good for us to be seen together."

"Cool" The excitement in her voice angers me. I am too tired to react, so I let it slide. We arrive at our hotel and have to wait in the long line of chauffeured cars trying to park into the circular driveway at the hotel entrance.

I stop at the reservation desk and get the key to the safe my connection rented prior to my arrival. I escort Stacy to her suite. She immediately hits the shower and changes clothes for her meeting with Gorbachev. I sit on the bed and watch her pull her hair in an upsweep and apply makeup to her flawless skin. I pass fifty thousand dollars cash to her for airfare and passports.

"Do you want to see the doctor's report first?"

"You can handle that. Make sure you check the passports to ensure they are authentic. Let him know I will wire the balance to his account in the Caymans when the product is safely on

American soil."

"I will let him know."

"Where are you meeting him again?"

"A restaurant on Cornwall Beach." She is vague. "Gorbachev reserved a private room." Surely, the restaurant has a name. I leave Stacy's suite and go to my own. I lay across the bed, but I am no longer sleepy. My mind is preoccupied with Stacy and Gorbachev. I don't trust the Russian.

I shower, change clothes, and walk to the beach. I remove my sandals to feel the warmth of the sand between my toes. Jamaican beaches are the prettiest in the world. The sand is almost snow white, and the water is deep blue. The beach is filled with people; most are vacationers from other parts of the world, as the locals do not earn enough money to enjoy their own paradise. I find a spot at a café next to the restaurant on Cornwall Beach. I sit and watch people run into waves in the clear, blue ocean water. The Caribbean is how I imagine heaven would look. It is almost a Garden of Eden. There is so much fruit and vegetation that it would almost be impossible to starve here. After almost an hour, I finally see Stacy and Gorbachev enter the restaurant. They are accompanied by two gentlemen.

I am on edge; I should not be here. I am always miles away from business transactions. If there is an event in Las Vegas, I may be in Mexico. If there is a request on the West Side, I am on the East Side. I look over my shoulder. I am paranoid. I should be somewhere, but not here. The one time I neglected to follow my own rule, I got caught with the product. I know better, but there is something about Stacy being with the Russian that does not sit well with me. Jealousy is a weakness I cannot afford. There is no room for weakness in this game. Weakness for money is why I am in this current predicament. I should have made the China man wait, and now I find myself once again in Ayanna's snare. I leave the beach, go to the bar, and find a seat in a dark corner. I watch stylish young ladies from various parts of the globe enter the private room Gorbachev reserved for the meeting. As requested, they are all well dressed and fit the description of the seasoned and well-connected traveler.

I enjoy the scene as I ponder my situation. Ayanna will work overtime to capitalize on this predicament, but I will not allow her to bring me down. She has stalked me for a long time, waiting for the opportunity to fuck up my life again. I am not one to be fucked with. Of all people, Ayanna should know this. I would give my right arm to be a fly on the wall when he confronts her. I sat in a rental car parked outside of her gated community and watched her husband open the envelope with sultry pictures of Ayanna and Trevor Bordeaux. The look on his face was priceless. He was so angry, the private detective was lucky to leave the premises with his life. I was too far to hear the conversation, but close enough to see the server run to his car, lock the door, and leave the property so fast, he left skid marks in their driveway. I felt little to no empathy when her husband grabbed his chest and hit his hand against the mailbox. He flipped through the pictures, then shoved them back in the envelope. He looked in the sky; a loud squeal escaped before he placed his hand over his mouth to muffle his rage. Hopefully, she will focus her energy on her new family crisis and less on fucking with me.

If things go as planned, my predicament will be over soon. She is betting the girl will testify. The girl can only say I gave her a ride. The day we were arrested was the one and only time she ever saw me. We have to make sure the girl does not make it to the witness stand to testify about our operation. I don't want the girl dead; she is too much of an investment. Ming Lee has contacted Stacy daily, trying to find out the status of the girl's release. Mr. Ye is beyond smitten; he wants to purchase her outright and ship her out of the country. One would think he would not want anything to do with the girl, but she is a commodity. Outside of Mr. Ye, the girl has never been touched. Mr. Ye pays ten grand a month to keep it this way. No, I do not want her dead; I just want to remind her to keep her mouth shut. Like all of our clients, Mr. Ye is rich, but perverted. People with sick, sexual perversions are like drug addicts. They always need a fix.

I sit and watch Stacy and Gorbachev exit the restaurant to a black chauffer driven Land Rover. The two men who accompanied Gorbachev leave the table and go in opposite directions. Stacy and Gorbachev look like a Hollywood power couple on a date. He walks out of the restaurant with his hand securely rested on the small of her back. He treats her in a romantic way, like one would treat their significant other; she will never experience that kind of softness with me. He stands outside of the door and assists her getting in the car.

I don't trust Gorbachev. We met at Peaches in Buckhead earlier this week to work out the details of our investment. He could not keep his eyes off Stacy. When Stacy went to the ladies room, his eyes remained on her from the time she left until she returned to the table. Like most black men, I am accustomed to racism and dismissive behavior from whites, but Gorbachev is pushing it. He addressed all business conversation to Stacy, as if she is running the show. What pisses me off is she is going along with it.

I don't blame Gorbachev for his attraction to Stacy; she is nothing shy of beautiful. Her look is exotic; she has perfect dark chocolate skin. Her thick, shiny, jet black hair hangs to the middle of her back. Her body is banging, and she is smart as hell. She blends in with the diplomats and global elite as if she is one of them. I hate to admit it, but I am jealous as hell when I see her slide close to Gorbachev in the chauffeured Land Rover. It almost looks as if they are having an intimate exchange. I don't know if I am pissed because of male ego or pissed from feelings I may have inadvertently developed for her. Stacy and I have a lot in common. We both have absent mothers. Stacy grew up in foster care in Las Vegas. Her mother was on the stroll and lived in the fast lane. She has never seen her father, and like me, she does not know who he is. Though she does not have a high school diploma, she has business smarts that will put Ivy League graduates to shame. She reads at least five periodicals a day and habitually watches three different international news feeds.

We both come from nothing. We grew up with nothing, but there was something, I don't know what it is or where it comes from, but there is something innate that told us that having nothing was good enough. Her official title in my discrete enterprise is Event Planner. She arranges hair shows for my barber and beauty shops, but our real money maker is arranging discreet, temporary companionship for some of the wealthiest people on the planet. We have high paying clients that have every sexual taste imaginable. Professional, powerful, and very wealthy women, some married to men, but occasionally want to discreetly enjoy the company of other women. There are married couples who pay top dollar to enjoy a discreet threesome. Many wealthy dignitaries from very conservative countries come to us to get their seven virgins on Earth. Surprisingly, the top money maker is married male clients who pay top dollar for discreet company with other males. I no longer offer serves to male clients who have an affinity for young boys. Stacy disagrees and believes we will make a killing, because that type of thing is in high demand. Our clients are wealthy and powerful international corporate executives of billion dollar companies that own other billion dollars companies most people have never heard of, or wealthy diplomats willing to pay big bucks for temporary and, in some cases, long-term companionship.

It's 9:30; I pay my tab, walk out of the back door of the restaurant, go to my suite and wait for Stacy to return. Until recently, I never worried about her double-crossing me, but I am concerned about this relationship with Gorbachev.

I am lying across the bed in boxers when I hear the door open. I hear the sound of her stilettos hit hardwood as she enters my suite.

"I know damn well you are not wearing fucking shoes inside!"

"Shit, Jefferson, I forgot. My bad." She bends down and removes her heels. "We are in a hotel. I did not think it would matter."

"It matters." I don't know why I have to keep reminding her to take off her shoes when she enters any place I lay my head, whether it is permanent or temporary. She passes me the bag filled with passports and airline e-tickets. She stands in front of the mini bar with the fridge door open and pours a shot of tequila. Her ruby red lips are so inviting, if I believed in kissing, I would put my tongue so far down her throat, she would choke.

I walk behind her and cup both breast in my hand and gently knead them. My shit is hard as a brick. She wiggles out of my grip and walks towards the door.

"I am tired. I am turning in early." She has never turned me down. I grab her and pull her back in front of me and untie the string from around her neck. The halter falls, exposing two perfectly round, perky breasts. I use my body weight and push her towards the bed. She snatches away from me and covers her breast with her hands, as if I have not seen them a thousand times. She walks toward the bathroom to get away from me. I grab her neck, drag her back to the bed, and throw her face down on the mattress. I am not too rough, but rough enough to put fear in her. I slide her dress over her hips and use my knees to part her thighs.

"What's up, Jefferson?" Her voice is shaky; she unsuccessfully tries to mask her fear. She attempts to get up. I grab her neck with one hand and press her face deep in the mattress. With the other hand I raise her pretty round ass in the air. "I am sweaty, Jefferson. It has been a long night. Let me shower first." The fear in her voice turns me on.

"Why?" I apply pressure to her neck. Not enough to choke her or leave marks, but enough to decrease her oxygen flow. "Did you just finish doing that pale ass Russian? I smell his cologne all over you."

"Hell no; you know it is not like that." She manages to wiggle free and crawl from under me. She rolls off the bed and makes a mad dash to the bathroom. I kick the door open before she is able to lock it. I grab a chunk of her hair and force her face down on the bed. "It's all about business. I swear on everything I love, ain't nothing going on with me and Gorbachev."

"I don't give a fuck, but if you do him, you had best be getting paid." I ram my shit so far inside of her, she screams. She tries to crawl from under me. I grab her hips and pull her back beneath me.

"You know it is not like that, you know it ain't like that! Why you tripping?" She continues to try to slide from beneath me. She finally gives up and stops resisting when I press my full body weight on top of her, making it impossible for her to move. I pull out of her, flip her over, and squirt in her face.

"Clean it off!" I put my dick in her face. "I said clean it off!" She sits up and reaches for the box of tissues next to the bed. I snatch the box away from her and throw it to the other side of the room. "Not like that. You know what's up." She reluctantly opens her mouth and licks my deflated rod clean from top to bottom. "Clean every drop!" I fall back on the bed. She lies next to me. Her body is stiff like a robot; her eyes are glued to the ceiling. She slowly gets up, walks to the bathroom. I hear the water running from the bathroom sink. She comes back to the bedroom, ties the string of the halter dress around her neck, pulls the dress down over her hips, and grabs her shoes.

"I am going to my suite. We can square up in the morning."

"Lock my fucking door behind you!"

Chapter 14

It's three o'clock in the morning. The moon is so bright that it illuminates my entire bedroom. The house is eerily quiet. I stare at the ceiling and pray for sleep. I have counted imaginary sheep, ducks, cats, and dogs, but sleep will not come. My thoughts bounce around in my head like a ping pong ball. One minute I am thinking of Osei and the children; the other I am strategizing a prosecution that will put Jefferson Thomas behind bars forever. I doze off a few minutes at a time, only to wake up reaching for the spot Osei occupied for over ten years. He and the kids were an integral part of my life plan. There are very few successful divorced female politicians. I never in my wildest dreams believed Osei and I would end up divorced.

This is Jefferson 101: find your opponent's weakness and exploit it. I don't call my relationship with Trevor an affair. It is a business arrangement. My eyes are set on sights much higher than the District Attorney's office, and Trevor Bordeaux with his three generation connections, is the key that will unlock many doors for me.

Jefferson is not on Trevor Bordeaux's level. There is no way Trevor disclosed our relationship to Jefferson. I don't know Jefferson's source, but I am aware he is acquainted with many of the movers and shakers in my circle. Trevor's wife has called nonstop for two days. My work voicemail is filled with her antics. She knows as well as I that infidelity is part of the equation when one settles as an accessory to a man like Trevor. My assistant called and informed me that Mrs. Bordeaux is waiting to speak with me. I have avoided coming to the office for two days to allow her time to come to her senses. Trevor is out of the country; I am confident he will take care of the matter when he returns. I am at the pinnacle of my career. Jefferson assumed wrong if he believed he could create a scandal to distract me. I will focus one hundred percent of my energy on prosecuting this case. I will not do battle with Osei over the children. He is the better parent, but I have to put up the appearance of a fight.

I call Fatima, a close acquaintance and college classmate. Fatima is also Ghanaian. She is the catalyst that bought Osei and I together; she invited me to the African Student Union party where I met Osei. Fatima received her law degree one year before I received mine. She was my mentor; I have always admired Fatima's drive. Unlike Osei, she was not born with a silver spoon in her mouth. She worked hard for everything she accomplished. The only thing she has in common with Osei is their home country. After graduation, she married an American student much below her status. I always believed it was for immigration papers, as they were such an odd couple. Their relationship was suspect, because after she was hired by the Ghanaian embassy, she immediately divorced the American. I call her office and speak with her assistant. I am given an immediate appointment to meet with her. I shower and drive through horrendous lunch hour traffic to the embassy.

I sit in the lobby for two minutes before her assistant greets me and escorts me to Fatima's office. She trots from behind the desk and greets me with a sincere embrace. After feigning distraught with a minute of uncontrollable crying, she tries to step away, but I hold on tight to her. "Oh, I am so sorry, sister." The compassion in her voice is sincere. She passes a box of tissues. "Don't cry; we will work something out." She leaves my embrace and returns to her desk. "I made contact with Osei after my assistant spoke with you, and he faxed a copy of all of the signed paperwork required to take the children out of the country."

"Yes, I know, but I did not sign any such papers. I did not give him permission to take my children! How would that look for a mother to do such a thing? Why would I do that?"

"Let us see what we can do." She removes her cell phone from her desk and calls the Ghanaian Ambassador on his direct line. She places the call on speaker, allowing me to listen. After a few brief niceties, she gets to the point.

"Yes, Fatima, I am well aware of the situation. The Badu-Bonsus' attorney called and gave me the heads up. As you know, the Badu-Bonsus are a wealthy, well-respected, law abiding family."

"Yes, sir, I am very familiar with the family."

"Mr. Badu-Bonsu declares his wife is a career woman who never truly bonded with the children. He alleges she works fifteen hour days. Can you imagine such a mother?" The judgment in his voice sickens me. "The husband believes she cares more for her career than the children." He clears his throat and lowers his volume slightly above a whisper. "Surely, if she works these many hours, the children are being neglected by their mother. In fact, to verify his allegations, the child care provider in America emailed our office a signed affidavit attesting to the father's outstanding parenting and alleging the mother rarely gathered the children, and when she did, she was frequently late." I make a mental note to have the Office of Regulatory services pay a visit to the school to teach Gail a lesson. He lowers his voice. "There are accusations of infidelity. You know American women can be somewhat promiscuous." It takes everything I have to keep quiet and not defend myself to the ambassador. I breathe deep. Fatima places her index finger on her lips. I follow her directive and remain quiet.

"Mr. Ambassador" Thank God Fatima appears to ignore the infidelity accusations and moves on to the issue. "The mother declares the children's travel documents are fraudulent."

"Yes, I see, but if the documents are fraudulent, he would not have been able to board a departing flight from JFK to leave the country. These are American children leaving an American airport on a flight out of the country. If this is her accusation, this is something she should discuss with the authorities in the United States. At this point, we feel there is nothing we can do. This is a family matter. Clearly this mother has misdirected priorities and loose morals. The father's concern appears to be for his children."

"Thank you, Mr. Ambassador."

"No problem, Fatima, as always, it is a pleasure speaking with you. I will be in the states next week; call my assistant, and let us schedule lunch."

"Yes, sir, Mr. Ambassador." She hangs up the phone. "His lawyers say you work fifteen hour days and did not have time for the children." She laughs. "When people ask why I am no longer married, I simply laugh. Men expect you to give up everything just because they place a ring on your finger. I am surprised at Osei; I would not have expected this behavior from my friend. He is way too modern and exposed for these types of Gestapo tactics."

"Yes, his behavior is shocking." I walk to the water cooler, remove the paper cone shaped cup, and fill it to the rim. "Fatima" I did not bother to respond to the infidelity and neglect allegations. "If I gave him the children, why am I looking for them?" She responds with an agreeing smile.

"Believe it or not, Ayanna, this happens all of the time. In this case, one thing we do know is Osei will allow no harm to come to the children." She opens her desk drawer and pulls out a business card. "This is the number to a private detective in Ghana. He is very good. I believe you will have better luck with him, as opposed to involving the United States State Department and the Ghanaian authorities. The Badu-Bonsus are very reputable, as I am sure you know. They are a very wealthy family and will bribe and pay the local authorities to get what they want."

"Thank you, Fatima." I take the card, grab my purse, and leave the office. I feel like I have lost about twenty pounds in the last three days. I am running out of food waiting for my credit card to arrive. It is hard to believe he took all of the money out of our account and canceled our joint credit cards. I totally underestimated him. Fortunately, I was smart enough to have credit of my own. I have one card he knows nothing about. I never used it, tore it up when it came in the mail, and opted to receive statements online.

I give my mother credit for teaching me to always have an ace in the hole. I think of what I will say to my parents. How will I tell them Osei has taken their grandchildren and unless they travel to Ghana, they most likely will never see them again? I don't want to hear an "I told you so" from my father. He did not like the idea of marrying across cultural lines. Like many Americans, his view of the continent is archaic. They will find out when they find out. Besides, I do not feel like going through the charade of the distraught mother with my family.

I stop by the grocery store and grab a bottle of wine before going home. I should be at work, but I am not willing to take a chance and run into Trevor's wife. He will be back in the country in a couple of days. He will remind her of her place, and things will be as usual.

I change into lounge wear and pour a glass of wine as soon as I walk in the door. I have to turn this predicament into an advantage. Very few divorced women make it in the political arena. It is a sign of failure. I remove the business card Fatima gave me and dial the number. I will create a paper trail that shows I made an effort to get the children back.

"*Me Chee Ya Wo*" I was about to hang up, as it took ten rings before the call was answered.

"Yes ma'am, my name is Ayanna. I would like to speak with Cedric Kwadwo."

"One moment, please."

"Yes, this is Mr. Kwadwo." He must have been sitting right next to the person that answered the phone because it takes all of two seconds for him to pick up the phone.

"My name is Ayanna." I did not provide my last name. "I am calling from the United States. I got your card from Fatima Oda."

"Yes, Fatima, I know her very well. I have known her since she was but a tot. She has made us very proud with her accomplishments." Mr. Kwadwo spends five minutes talking about Fatima's accomplishments before he paused long enough for me to interject and get to the nature of my call.

"I need to hire you." I get right to the point. I have no time for all of the Ghanaian niceties.

"Let me guess." He interrupts me mid-sentence. "You are married to one of my fellow countrymen; he has left the country with your children, you have no idea how to find them, and he has promised you will never see them again."

"Almost, but not exactly, I know where they are. They are most likely staying at the Badu-Bonsu compound in Accra. Are you familiar with the family?"

"Badu-Bonsu" I detect reservation in his voice. "You will never get them from the Badu-Bonsu compound!" His speech is rapid; his pitch is high. "That is impossible; it would take an army. Honestly, my dear, if they are with the Badu-Bonsus, they will be okay. You are very lucky. They are a much respected and very prosperous family."

"Yes, I understand they are highly regarded there, but the father has taken my children, and I would like to be reunited with them. Whatever fee you require, I am willing to pay."

"Perhaps you should speak with your husband and come to an agreement. I do not want to be pessimistic, but perhaps you should try to reason with your husband."

"I have tried to reason with him." I take a sip of the wine. It feels good easing down my throat. My muscles relax. My head feels light.

"I see. Give me your email, and I will send you a list of our services and fees." I spell my email address one letter at a time. "You should receive an email momentarily. I will wait for your response. Meanwhile, I will begin to research your situation."

Chapter 15

Each beat on the door feels like a sharp dagger penetrating my brain. I cover my head with the pillow and hope whoever is trying to beat the door down will simply go away. It is probably one of the neighborhood kids asking for Che' or OJ. I squeeze the pillow tighter around my head, but I am unable to drown out the sound. I throw the pillows on the floor, push five empty wine bottles out of the way, roll out of the bed, and stand up. It feels as if the room is spinning. I am dizzy and feel as if I am about to faint. I am having difficulty balancing my weight. I sit back on the bed and hope whoever is banging on my front door will go away, but the uninvited guest at the door is persistent. I take a deep breath and try to stand again. I hold tight to the walls as I navigate out of my room through the catwalk to the stairs. I flip the light switch, but the light does not come on.

"Who is it?"

"Detective Davis." I manage to make it downstairs to the foyer and open the door.

"Davis?" I open the door. My yard looks out of sync with the neighbors' illuminated yards. My lamp posts are the only posts not on. My house is totally dark with no inside light. The sun has set; the lamp posts in my yard should be on. "What are you doing here? How did you get in the gate?"

"I am a police officer. Remember?"

"Why are you beating the door down?" I massage my temple in an attempt to ease the pain.

"Your doorbell does not work." I wipe the sleep from my eyes but everything is still blurry. "What time is it?"

"It's 7:00 PM. Are you are okay? The D.A. is worried; you haven't been to work in three days."

"Really?" I grab my throbbing head and sit on the stairs in foyer. I flip the light switch again. "Why isn't this damn light coming on?"

"Did you pay the electric bill? Your entire house is dark."

"Of course, it comes out of our checking account automatically every month." I hit the wall. "Son of a bitch!" Detective Davis walks close to me and then takes two steps back. I sit on the steps.

"Ayanna, are you okay?" The concern on his face is genuine. It is one of friendship as opposed to professional colleague.

"My husband stole my kids, took all of the money out of our accounts, and left the country. Other than that, I guess I am fine."

"Is there anything I can do?" He steps to me and wraps his arms tight around me.

"Do you know someone in Kumasi or Accra, Ghana with more money and clout than the Badu-Bonsu clan?"

"I don't know anyone in Ghana, but I can get you a hotel until you get things straightened out. You don't need to stay in the dark."

"No" I slide out of his arms. "I will take care of the electric bill tomorrow."

"With everything you have going on, I hate to be the bearer of bad news; Ashleigh was attacked. She was severely beaten and has been hospitalized." I stand and then quickly sit back on the steps. The walls are spinning again. "Doesn't this remind you of the first time we tried to build a case against him?" He pauses. "If he is going to the trouble of having the child attacked, this sounds like something bigger than trying to beat a pimping charge."

"Let me get myself together." I stand and hold tight to the bannister rail. "Is she going to be okay?"

"She is in and out of consciousness. She has a severe concussion and some internal bleeding."

"I'll take a quick shower and meet you at the hospital."

"Hold on" He steps in front of me. "Unless you want me to arrest you for driving under the influence, I suggest you don't consider getting behind the wheel of a car. You smell like a brewery. I will drive you." It takes everything I have to climb the dark stairs. My legs feel like lead. I use the bannister as an anchor. I rummage through the dark closet for clothes and take a quick, cold shower then go downstairs where Detective Davis has remained sitting on the steps.

"You look better. It is amazing what a little water can do." He leans close and sniffs around my face. "You smell better, too."

"Yeah, I still feel like shit." I remove the house key from my bag and lock the door.

Detective Davis drives to the donut shop outside of the subdivision and comes back to the car with two cups of coffee.

"Drink this. You look like you need it."

"Do I look that bad?"

"Yes, you look bad."

"You do not have to be so mean."

"I am curious." He quickly changes the subject. "How long have you known Mary?"

"I really don't know her. She has assisted me with cases involving juvenile victims in the past. I know she has been with the county for years." His question puzzles me. "Why do you ask?"

"I just asked." I have worked with Detective Davis on a few cases, and I know there is a reason for his inquiry. He does not simply ask questions for the sake of asking questions. I don't push the issue. I don't feel very well, and my head feels as if it is detached from my body.

The hospital room is dark. The only noise comes from the many machines that record her vital signs. She looks like an alien in a science fiction movie. Both of her eyes are swollen shut. A thoracotomy tube sticks out of her chest. She was so badly beaten, one of her lungs collapsed. Mary is at her bedside when we arrive, performing her annoying surrogate, motherly duties.

"Mary," I greet her. "What are you doing here?" I stand by the hospital bed next to Mary. The child is barely conscious, so I wonder why she is here.

"I got a call from juvi." Mary's face looks strange. Her skin is puffy. She looks as if she has not slept in days. "They did a number on her."

"Do they know who attacked her?" I move closer to get a better look.

"Juvi is just as bad as or worse than adult prison. Probably some type of gang initiation. Who knows?" Mary's hands shake like a victim of Parkinson's Disease as she pats Ashleigh's hand. Her puffy eyes are blood shot red. "We live in a terrible world." Her mint gum exacerbates the scent of alcohol on her breath. I cannot judge; I have been in oblivion for days.

"Something tells me Jefferson has something to do with this.

This is definitely his modus operandi." Luckily, there are cameras in all of the common areas in the detention center. It will not be hard to find the culprit.

"I don't know." She stands and grabs her purse. "How could he infiltrate juvi? There are violent attacks in juvi all of the time. What makes you believe it is Mr. Thomas?" It sounds as if she is defending the creep, but she is right; fights happen all of the time in juvi.

"Don't underestimate him. He is a sick and very violent person." Our conversation ends when the doctor enters the room. He looks all of twenty-five and too young to be a doctor. Though Ashleigh looks horrible, her prognosis is positive.

"Has she spoken?" Mary talks to the doctor, never taking her eyes off Ashleigh.

"No, she hasn't spoken. She is heavily sedated, but we expect a full recovery." After the update from the doctor, Mary, Detective Davis, and I leave the hospital together.

"Mary, do you spend this much time with all of your clients?" Davis' question had an accusatory tone to it.

"No, not really, but this one has a special place in my heart." She looks straight in my eyes and it seems to avoid contact with Detective Davis. "Ayanna, are you okay?"

"I have seen better days."

Chapter 16

"Slow down." She is frantic. She has been calling my number nonstop for the last hour. When I finally check my phone, I have ten missed calls from Lailah. Between crying and the playful screams from the children in the background, I can barely understand her. "What is wrong?"

"People are following me! Two weeks ago, there was a car parked on the side of the house. I noticed it as I backed out of the garage. Initially, I thought nothing of it. For the last four or five days, I have been getting phone calls from private numbers! I don't answer calls from private numbers!" Her breathing is rapid. Her voice filled with fear. Lailah is usually calm and expresses herself with ease, but I am having a hard time following her.

"Calm down. I am on my way to you." I am concerned as well, as I have always kept Lailah and the kids away from my world.

"I don't want to go home. Meet me at the playground at Lucille Park."

"I am on my way." I remove my cell from my pocket and place it on the dresser. I remove one of my many prepaid phones from the drawer. Ayanna is upping the game. I am on her radar, but approaching Lailah and the kids was a bad idea. No one but Ayanna would be this bold. The people in my circle know nothing about Lailah or my children, and if they did, they would not have the balls to fuck with them. Ayanna will turn over every rock in Georgia looking for anything and anyone to help build a case against me. Her tricks are elementary. She will attempt to intimidate Lailah believing she can get information to use against me, but Lailah knows nothing about my business.

I speed down Interstate 20 and exit left on Joseph E. Lowery Boulevard. I pass several homeless veterans begging for money as I stop to make the right to West End. I would normally stop and pass a few bucks through the window, but I am on a mission. When I arrive at the park, the kids are running around chasing one another, oblivious to the homeless people who have made the park their home. Lailah is sitting at the picnic table with both hands wrapped tight around a cup of coffee from the neighborhood coffee shop. I think to myself she is too comfortable with the kids in this environment. When she sees me, she leaves the picnic table, runs to me, and falls into my arms. Her body is firm but soft in the right places. Her arms are tight around me. She is so nervous that she feels like a human vibrator.

"Why would anyone follow me? I am a simple school teacher and a single mother trying to raise my children." I release her, and we walk hand in hand back to the picnic table. The kids see me and run to me, screaming, "Daddy." I grab both of them in one scoop and plant kisses all over their faces. Lailah looks away. The fear in her eyes is real; she has reason to be concerned. I put the kids down and send them to play.

"Don't worry. I will take care of it." I think about the time I almost pulled the trigger and made her husband a widower. Taking her life is not an option right now. I hoped her new family dynamic would redirect her attention away from me.

"I never asked what you did for a living. I have seen you on television. I know you have a restaurant. I have seen your picture in local magazines. After the first kid, I figured it was too late to care."

"Let's not get into that; tell me exactly what happened."

"I am seeing someone. He is recently divorced. I first thought it could be the disgruntled ex-wife."

"Keep that shit to yourself!" I bang my hand against the metal picnic table. The vibration is so strong, it knocks her coffee on the ground. We both ignore the spill. I realized there was someone a while ago, but she should know she is not to mention that to me. "I hope you are not stupid enough to involve yourself with anyone who could bring harm to my children!"

"It was not her! He called her to put my mind at ease; it was not her voice." I try and stay focused, but if she continues to speak with me about a man, I am going to lose it. "The woman asked me questions about my life, you, and the kids. She asked if you were their father. I confirmed you were. The fury in her eyes scared me. I backed away from her, quickly got in the van, and sped out of the

146

parking lot to pick the kids up from school. When I came out of the school, she was in the parking lot. I grabbed the kids and threw them in the van. She came over and continued to question me about the kids. I tried to close the door. She grabbed the door and tried to keep me from closing it. I backed out of the parking lot with her still holding onto the door."

"What did you tell her?"

"I didn't tell her anything! Hell, I don't know anything to tell her." Her voice is elevated, which is out of character for Lailah.

"Calm down! What did she look like?'

"I don't know. I was nervous. It is not every day a stranger approaches me and asks about my children and their father. I quickly secured the children in the car, left as fast as I could, and called you. I was too nervous to pay attention to her."

"Do you want to move? I can relocate you and the kids."

"Move? You selfish fucking bastard! My life is here! Our children's lives are here! We are settled in our lives. I am moving on! Your life is too secretive. You are the father of my children and I know nothing about you. This is crazy." She cradles her face in her hands then looks me in the eye. "I don't want your money! Please do not send it anymore! I am moving on."

"Watch yourself, Lailah!" I raise my voice. I have never raised my voice to her before. "There is a lot you don't know about me." If my children were not present I would show her who I am. I sit still with my fist tightly clenched. She throws her hands in the air, grabs her purse, and calls for the kids. They run to her with smiling faces and are totally oblivious to the nasty exchange between me and their mother. "I don't know what kind of moving on you are talking about, but I will continue this relationship with my kids." I am surprised by my own reaction. They are my children, but in my life everyone is expendable.

"What relationship?" She smirks. "Once per month visits? And that is a maybe! Yearly vacations?" She places her hands on her hip. "Or is it the money you deposit every month? Is this what you call a relationship?" She takes the children's hands. "Tell Daddy bye." I don't like the way she says "*bye*."

I stand and step close to her. I embrace her shoulders a little tighter than normal and lean close to her as if I am going to kiss her, but whisper, "There are a lot of things you don't know about me. But know this; I can be a very dangerous man." I bend down, kiss the kids, and return to the table. I watch her put them in the minivan. She does not look back; instead, she gets in the van and quickly drives away.

Chapter 17

Images of Ashleigh's bruised and unconscious body in the hospital bed flash through my mind. Jefferson's actions are extreme. He mistakenly believed my family crisis would distract me from my mission. I am more determined than ever to take him down. He has actually made it easier.

Honestly, I am relieved. I would have gladly given Osei custody of the children. Having children was never my idea. I admit motherhood grew on me. He could have divorced me, and I would have been happy to accept weekend visits, but Osei crossed the line by giving me no choice. I love my children but would never have wanted full custody in the event of divorce. Now that they are gone, I will devote one hundred percent of my energy to the State vs. Jefferson Thomas.

I sent an email to the prosecutorial team, Detective Davis, and Mary, reminding them of the strategic meeting today. D.A. Leslie has missed all of our scheduled meetings but has promised to make this one. D.A. Leslie and I are usually on the same page; however, on this case we strongly differ in strategy. I want to go straight for an arrest warrant, but he demands I present the case to the grand jury. I know there are other pressing cases in the county, but his lackadaisical attitude about this one concerns me. It is as if he does not believe it is worth the energy and wants it to go away.

I remove my cell phone from my pocket, check the time, and see a missed call from Detective Davis. The team should arrive in thirty minutes; I do not bother to return his phone call. I advised everyone to bring their lunch and dinner if necessary. The grand jury has been seated for The State of Georgia vs. Jefferson Thomas. If he is indicted, I have three months to put together a seamless prosecution. Jefferson's financial statements portray a typical small businessman struggling to stay afloat. Although he has not been indicted, he has hired one of the top defense attorneys in the state. He is preparing for what he knows to be the inevitable.

There can be no slip ups. A successful prosecution is what I need to redeem my losing streak. No excuses, everyone must bring their A game. Shanna, my assistant, hates these strategizing meetings because they can sometimes go on past midnight. Kate, my secretary, hates them because she misses dinner with her husband and children. I often have to remind her that her familial issues are of no concern to the citizens of the State of Georgia. I make a mental note to call the temp services. If Kate whines about finding an alternative arrangement for picking up children and having to cook dinner for Bob, who looks as if he has never missed a meal a day in his life, she will be looking for another job tomorrow morning. It's not often I request work from her. She spends most of her day clipping coupons, organizing activities for her daughter's cheerleading squad, or online searching for recipes. I would have fired her when I received my promotion, but for reasons unknown to me, everyone loves Kate. I arrive a few minutes early to set up the projector and go over my PowerPoint presentation one last time before the team arrives.

"Mrs. Williams, how are you?" Detective Davis is early. He startles me as he enters the conference room. "I see you are prepared, as always. I left a message on your voicemail to let you know I was bringing a guest. Let me introduce you to Mike McAfee. He is with the local Feds. He wants to sit in if you don't mind? If this is as big as we think, there may be reasons for the Feds to get involved." Detective Davis looks like a giant standing next to the thin and balding McAfee.

"No problem." I shake Mr. McAfee's thin, pale, cold hand and direct him to the refreshments table in the rear of the conference room.

"You look better today than you did the last time I saw you." His volume is low as if we are in involved in some sort of classified, clandestine mission. I wanted to tell him how good he looks, but that would have been unprofessional; besides, I still need to play the role of a married woman. "So who are we waiting on?" His long and intense stare makes me uncomfortable. He turns away and looks at his watch. I am relieved.

"My staff, the District Attorney, a couple of detectives from the Sexual Victims Unit, and of course Mary will be here to provide an update on Ashleigh."

"Mary? Do you find her interest in this case strange? I have never known a more dedicated social worker than Mary."

"Yes" I did not know if his statement was pure sarcasm or for informational purposes. "She seems to be very dedicated. She must do this from her heart, because the pay is horrible."

"The pay can't be too bad. Have you seen the car she drives and the house she lives in?" I have never seen her home, but she drives a top of the line BMW. I assumed she was like many people that live check to check in order to invest in a luxury vehicle to project an illusion of status.

"Mrs. Williams, you are not going to believe this." I was going to ask Davis to further elaborate, but Trina almost knocked the door down. She briskly enters the conference room waving her hands back and forth in the air. "We found the girl's parents! They made a positive ID and are on their way here from Charlotte! I gave them my telephone number and will let you know when they arrive!" She pauses to catch her breath. "Also, I asked them to bring the computer she uses at home."

"Good job, Trina!" I wanted to jump up and down and kiss her, but as always, I maintain my professionalism. Trina has been the office paralegal for two years. I often encourage her to get a degree; she is much too smart to be a paper pusher all of her life. "How did you pull that off?"

"I kept going through the Charlotte, North Carolina's, Missing Children's databases, but there was no match for an Ashleigh Scott. I was on the phone with the missing persons division in Charlotte almost every day, but there was no missing child in their system by the name of Ashleigh Scott. After talking to them every day, they gave me a password so I can have twenty-four hour access to their database. I searched for children who have gone missing within the last two years but could not find an Ashleigh Scott." Trina is long winded. I keep waving my hand back and forth, prompting her to talk faster and get to the point. "You know I have been to Charlotte several times, I have aunts and uncles who live there. I read the transcript from the interview where she describes downtown buildings, so I knew we had the right Charlotte. You know there are several cities named Charlotte in this country. I wonder why there are so many." She shifts her weight to her left hip. I think to myself I am really going to encourage my staff to engage in healthy living. Trina is five, maybe six years younger than me, but her weight makes her look much older.

"Come on, Trina! Stay focused!" I glance at my watch. "We have a meeting in a few minutes."

"Okay, sorry, you know I am long winded. After not finding a match, I finally got on the phone with someone who transferred me to the runaway youth division, and we finally matched one of the runaways in their database to the girl we know as Ashleigh Scott. Her name is not Ashleigh Scott. Her name is Ansleigh Scott. The detective in Charlotte and I emailed photos back and forth. We were on the phone for over an hour. I may have a love connection." She smiles. Until now, I never noticed her deep dimples. "He is going to look me up next time he visits Atlanta, but anyway, we were shocked at the difference in the pre-missing pictures and the mugshot we have of her." She removes the picture from the folder and passes it to me. It is obviously the child we know as Ashleigh but she looks like a typical preteen child. Bangs cover her forehead, and a ponytail hangs from the top of her head to her shoulder. Her smile is beautiful, as I suspected, her teeth are adorned with pricey metal.

"I owe you a lunch for this! Good job!"

"Thanks, Mrs. Williams; I am free for lunch next Thursday."

"I will have Kate put it on my calendar."

"By the way, Ms. Williams, I like Jamaican food."

"You can have whatever you like and take a day off on me."

"Thanks, Ms. Williams." She claps her hands, jumps up and down like a preschooler, turns around and proceeds to leave.

"Trina" I stop her as she leaves the conference room. "When the parents call, tell them to give the computer directly to me."

The participants slowly arrive. The District Attorney arrives thirty minutes late and walks to the head of the table without greeting the participants. He is out of character. He is not fully engaged in the meeting. His attention is divided between his iPad and cell phone. I take a seat in the chair at the corner of the table next to him. The light from the projector is bright. Jefferson Thomas' mugshot, with a timeline of his alleged crimes, unfolds as the screen slowly descends from the ceiling. His eyes are dark, evil, and lifeless. It is as if he has no soul.

"I have an announcement more like a disclosure." I stand with perfect posture, straighten the lapel on my blazer, and walk in front of the projection screen. "I think it is appropriate to disclose this office has a former case against Mr. Thomas. This will be the third time Jefferson Thomas and I have crossed paths. We both attended the same Ivy League University, though I did not personally know him. As most of you know, I was unable to obtain a guilty verdict in the prior prosecution. After his case was dismissed, Mr. Thomas attempted to smear the integrity of this office. He filed many ethical and prosecutorial misconduct charges against me and this office, but we prevailed." I raise my thumbs upward and plaster the best politician smile I could muster across my face. His ethic charges were also dismissed. "Thanks to District Attorney Leslie, we get another shot."

"Are you serious? And you will be the lead prosecutor again?" She emphasizes "Again," as she looks at D.A. Leslie with a contempt that no other subordinate would dare. She is careless and making their relationship conspicuous.

"Yes, Nakia, I am serious. The District Attorney trusts my ability to successfully prosecute this case."

"That would be correct." District Attorney Leslie finally places his techno devices on the table, stands, and addresses the team. He makes no eye contact with me, and very little with the team.

"As I recall, there were some serious ethical violations you were accused of committing. Is that correct?"

"Yes, Nakia, you are correct. Again, those allegations were not substantiated. That was a very difficult case, but as fate would have it, we get a second shot. Let us stay focused on this case."

"Are there any questions?" I canvas the faces of the team. "Ok, let's get to our business."

I load the PowerPoint presentation on the laptop. Exhibit one takes five slides to show all of Jefferson's financial holdings on record. The famous Chicken Shack, five hair salons, three barber shops, a small apartment building, and three loft apartments generate over one half of a million dollars annually.

"Can he afford to live here?" Everyone is in awe of the mini-mansion in the exclusive gated community. "The homeowner association fees in this subdivision are thirty thousand dollars per year." I click on each thumbnail to enlarge the different amenities. Pictures of armed security guards standing next to a fingerprint recognition, high tech security entry gate makes the subdivision look like a fortress. The landscape is perfectly manicured; the grass looks like plush carpet. The Olympic size pool, tennis court and golf course are overkill for such a small subdivision.

"Were you able to get his loss and profit statements for the past five years?"

"Yes, of course." I distribute the handouts and place a magnified copy on the screen. The D.A. and the rest of the panel scan the financial documents. District Attorney Leslie taps his pencil on the table, an annoying habit that makes it difficult to concentrate. He does this when he is in deep thought. "It is a stretch, but it can happen." D.A. Leslie places the statements face down in front of him and turns his attention back to his techno devices.

"Ms. Williams" I turn my attention to Nakia, a subordinate who is still pissed I was given the promotion instead of her. According to the office rumor mill, she and the D.A. have had an ongoing affair for the last several years. Someone should have told her, spreading her legs to the D.A. would not elevate her career in the District Attorney's office. He does not have the political clout to make big moves for her. "It seems to me Jefferson Thomas is living the way a lot of people in this city live, paycheck to paycheck." I forward the presentation to the next slide that shows Mr. Thomas' bank statements. I pass a three-inch binder to the participants that contain the last seven years of his bank statements. His bank statements are unremarkable, reflecting a couple of insufficient fund fees, and a couple of late mortgage payment notices.

"Nakia, I propose this is all by design. What you see is what he wants to reveal in the event his operation ever comes to light." Hopefully, this meeting will teach her how to think forensically. "Notice May 2009, when his mortgage was behind; now look at his deposit and receipts from all of his businesses for the month. The receipts total thirty thousand dollars. He deposited thirty thousand to each of his business accounts in increments ranging from two thousand dollars to six thousand dollars." I place the pointer on each one of his business accounts and show that each have different Employee Identification Numbers; all of his accounts are at the same bank. "So he actually had 150,000 in deposits. Where did that money come from? Why is his mortgage late?"

"It could have come from anywhere. He could have gotten a loan." I think to myself, "Surely, the District Attorney is not this naïve."

"Sir, he does not think this way. Nothing on his credit report indicates he applied for or received a loan. As a matter of fact, there are no credit inquiries from any financial institutions for the last seven years after he purchased his home."

"Drug money?" Nakia smiles, as if she is saying something profound and brilliant.

"Allow me to interject, if you don't mind." I nod my head and allow Mr. McAfee to speak. He stands in front of his chair. "He makes transactions in small increments to circumvent Internal Revenue Service reporting requirements. He most likely has a connection at the bank because even small, frequent deposits are usually reported. He has different Employee Identification Numbers to throw off investigative agencies if he is ever audited. He will match those same receipts from his businesses to each of these Employer Identification Numbers. As Ms. Williams stated, the same amount is deposited in all of the bank accounts. If questioned about an account, he uses the same receipts."

"Mr. McAfee is right. Again, I ask the question, where did that money come from? He left the drug game a long time ago. The evidence suggests he is now trafficking women and children."

"Can you explain how you came up with this scenario?" The smirk on Nakia's face annoys me.

"He was arrested with this child." A picture of the child we now know as Ansleigh covers the projection screen. As I look at her face on the screen, I am creeped out at the thought of her having sexual contact with an adult male. "This Asian man in the picture was seen leaving the hotel with her."

"Where is the Asian?" Her tone is authoritative. "Was he also apprehended?"

"The Asian is a diplomat. He has diplomatic immunity. He could not be questioned." She taps her pen on the desk, a habit I am positive she picked up from D.A. Leslie. My stare is hard; Nakia nervously looks away. "I have interviewed the girl and have good reason to believe Mr. Thomas is involved with human trafficking on an international level." Nakia picks up the pen from the table and resumes hitting it on the desk. She is aware she is annoying me; I continue the presentation. "The next slide shows a detailed itinerary of his recent travels. His passport was stamped in Jamaica and Istanbul, Turkey, but there is no record of him leaving the country through an American airport during this time frame. We believe he travels by private plane and makes connections to other parts of the world through the Caribbean. How does someone with money issues travel around the world?" I return to my seat and pass the floor to Detective Davis. Detective Davis takes the pointer from my hand and passes his flash drive to me. An electrical charge travels from my fingertips and up my arms. I cannot deny, he exudes a lot of sexual energy. His shirt is tight around the arms and shoulders. His chest creates a perfect imprint in his shirt. I place the flash drive in the USB port and return to my chair. I have never been attractive to the blue collar type, and I am sure the slight attraction has to do with sleeping in an empty bed.

Chins drop, and long winded gasps escape mouths on shocked faces; the conference room becomes silent as Detective Davis reports statistics that place Atlanta as the number one hub for sexual trafficking of women and children. The only person who appears unimpressed with the statistics is D.A. Leslie.

"We believe Mr. Thomas has gone from selling drugs to selling young women and children. We believe the child we now know to be Ansleigh Scott is one of his victims. He is not the pimp on the street corner. His clients are wealthy diplomats, international business men and women, and a few high ranking politicians." Detective Davis advances to the next slide. A picture of a gorgeous and shapely female leaving one of Mr. Thomas' hair salons and getting into a white Land Rover with Mr. Thomas is displayed on the screen. He forwards to the next slide. A photo of a tall white male, Jefferson and the gorgeous, shapely female sitting at a bar is displayed.

"I will pass the podium to Mr. McAfee. He is our liaison with the Feds." McAfee walks to the podium.

"This gorgeous, burly white guy is Gorbachev Slizinsky. His claim to fame is identity theft; his passport has been stamped in some interesting places. Last month Slizinsky, Mr. Thomas and this lovely lady were in Jamaica. Mr. Thomas made a stop in the Cayman Islands."

"The Caymans?" Light bulbs are finally going off in Nakia's head. "He is hiding money in offshore bank accounts." I want to stand and shout "No shit!" But as always, I remain professional.

"He met with Everton Hylton. We know this because Mr. Hylton has been under surveillance for several months for laundering money for drug cartels. A week later, Gorbachev and twenty-five young women traveled from Jamaica to Atlanta. This Gorbachev is a world traveler and popular with the ladies. A week prior to the Jamaican excursion, Gorbachev traveled with the same group of women from Panama to Jamaica." McAfee returns to his seat and gives the pointer back to Detective Davis. Detective Davis advances to the next slide to a picture of a woman and two small children on a beach with Jefferson. "This woman is a school teacher. We believe she may be involved, but we are not sure at this point. We have subpoenaed her bank statements, phone records, and credit reports; we can build a profile on her pretty quickly." He pauses to ensure he has everyone's attention. "We can spend time dissecting his financial holdings; that can take forever, and we may come up with nothing. He has a cash business." He looks in my direction. "If his money is not adding up, the Feds will get to him. They have the best forensic accountants money can buy." I see a slight smirk on Nakia's face. "This woman here." He points to the beautiful woman on the screen. "She will give him up with the right amount of pressure. This will be the best way to get him. Once we get him on the human trafficking charges, the Feds can investigate and prosecute him for any related financial or tax crimes."

"I know that face." I point to the gorgeous shapely woman with dark, flawless skin.

"You should know her, Mrs. Williams. This is Stacy Lincoln. Her old man was part of Mr. Thomas' organization. You put her old man away when we successfully put several of Mr. Thomas' co-conspirators behind bars." He looks at his watch. "Unfortunately, we could not get Jefferson Thomas. He got away."

The meeting lasted several hours and past dinner. Luckily for Kate, she did not complain. Mary came at the end of the meeting to provide an update on the child we now know as Ansleigh.

"I am sorry I am late. Is there anything I need to know? Did I miss anything?"

"Well, you..." Davis squeezes my arm, leans over and advises we not discuss anything further right now. "You did not miss anything. Can you provide an update on the child?" Mary has nothing new to share. I wanted to tell her the child's parents were located, but I follow Davis' prompts keep everything hushed for now.

I grab my bag while Kate cleans the conference room and puts things back in order.

"Do you want to grab a bite to eat?"

"Yes, and you can treat."

"Cool, I will treat this time, but this is not a date." He laughs. "You know how you independent black women are. Where do you want to go?"

"Stoney's would be great. The mayor will be there." I leave my car in the parking deck and ride with Detective Davis. As I crawl into his cramped convertible Corvette, I think to myself, this is definitely not a family man vehicle. "Nice car."

"I like it." He gently rubs the dashboard.

"I gather you are not married." Although I have known Detective Davis for several years, our relationship is always professional. "Do you have children?" I look around at the different gadgets in the car. "This is definitely not a Daddy car."

"I was never married, but I have a daughter." He pulls the sun visor down. A picture of a toothy little girl around the same age as Che' with two ponytails on each side of her head stares back at me. I remove the picture and closely observe the child's happy, cheerful eyes. I smile, as I think of my precocious Che'.

"Where is her mother?"

"They both live here in Atlanta."

"Do you see her often?"

"Not as often as I would like. This job is not conducive to family life. Her mother is great. She doesn't keep me on a schedule. She is very flexible with visitation."

"If she is so great, why didn't you marry her?"

"Trust me. It had nothing to do with her. She is everything a man could ever want. I was the one who fucked up. Enough about me; I am boring. Have you heard from your husband?"

"No, I have a detective in Ghana working on it. I know where they are. His family is very wealthy. It will be hard trying to get them back. This is something we are going to have to work out."

"You are smart, and you will work it out."

"I am just praying my husband will come to his senses. He never showed signs that he would take the children. I am still shocked. I had no idea he would do something like this. I would have had no problem sharing custody if he wanted out of the marriage."

"Do we ever really know people? We can never predict what people will do." He takes his eyes off the road and stares at me. "Did you back him into a corner? You know we men can be difficult if we are backed into a corner." He pauses and looks away. "Sometimes the women we love force us to do some incredulous things."

"I don't know what happened. He became depressed when he did not make partner at his firm. He deserved it. He is brilliant. But this is America; many black people do not get what they deserve." As Davis drives, I think to myself I am not one of those black people. I will get what I deserve. The State bench is calling my name and when the time is right, I will answer. I have made the connections that will ensure my position. It is not my fault Osei was unwilling to play the game to get where he wanted to go.

"Yes, true, but your husband is not a black American."

"No, he is not." I don't want to talk about Osei. I don't want to think about my situation. I want to have a couple of drinks and relax.

We arrive at Stoney's and find a full parking lot. Stoney's is a small locally owned bar with an almost dismal food menu, but Stoney mixes the best drinks in the city. The atmosphere is so laid back it almost feels like home. It is crowded as usual, but Davis and I find a nice spot in the corner. Spending time with Detective Davis is different, yet pleasant. There is more to him than meets the eye. I would have never guessed him to be a world traveler. He takes a month off every summer to travel with his daughter. He does not strike me as the soft type. Yet the pictures he shares of he and his daughter show a very gentle side of him.

We sit at a table in the corner away from the crowd and watch the political players mingle. Stoney's is the gathering spot for politicians and business people, new money and old. The dusty walls are adorned with pictures in mismatched frames of Stoney posing with the last three mayors, the city's top brass, and several celebrities. Every once in a while, Stoney is generous, gives back by hosting a live band, but the majority of the time the music is pre-recordings of old Rhythm and Blues.

"It is hard to believe these drunken fools hold the keys to our city." His lips are turned up from the lime he sucked to make the shot of tequila go down smoother.

"I did not take you for the judgmental type. This room is filled with some of the brightest people in the city." I stare hard at the three empty shot glasses in front of him. He smiles, following my eyes to the empty glasses.

"I work hard, so I deserve to play hard every once in a while." He scans the room and throws back another shot of tequila. "These cats don't do shit but lie and steal from the public.

"Not all politicians are alike. Some are honest and care about the community they serve."

"I didn't take you for the naïve type, Ayanna. I have yet to meet an honest politician. They do not exist. Everyone in this place is making deals and buying someone off for personal benefit."

"It's getting late." I change the subject. I am not in the mood for debate. "We are both inebriated. How are we going to get home?" I stand but have to quickly grab the back of the chair to maintain my balance.

"My place is around the corner. I'll leave my car in Stoney's parking lot until the morning.

"What about me? I left my car at the office. Remember?"

"You can crash at my place. I have a spare room." He walks to the bar and pays our bill. Initially, I am reluctant to follow, but I realize I have no choice. Neither of us is in shape to drive safely.

"I need to use the ladies room." I stand and grab my purse. I notice Jefferson standing, conversing with one of the city planners and what I believe to be an aide from the governor's office. Though his back is turned to me, it is hard to miss his six-feet-four inch pit bullish physique. I didn't notice the petite, shapely woman with him until he sat on the bar stool. This Stacy Lincoln is definitely his type. She is flashy, long hair, beautiful flawless dark skin, and probably has a brain the size of a peanut. A Cage de' Cartier swings from her toned arm. Her hair is freshly done and precise, but none of this can hide the ghetto pedigree. There is something about a 'hood rat that even if you take them out of the 'hood and dressed them in the nicest Versace or classic Givenchy, you can still tell they are 'hood rats.

I am lightheaded. I am grateful I made it to the ladies' room. The light automatically switches on, as I enter the bathroom; the sudden change from dark to light makes me dizzy. I handle my business, flush the commode, walk to the sink, and stare at myself in the mirror. I have to stop drinking. My skin is dry. The makeup is not enough to conceal the dark, puffy bags under my eyes. I lean over the sink, splash water on my face, grab a paper towel, and pat my skin dry. His reflection in the mirror startles me. Initially, I am afraid. The space is small with only two bathroom stalls. The music and conversation are so loud, I doubt if anyone would hear if I scream. I step two steps backwards he steps two steps forward. His body towers over me. He is too close for comfort. My temperature rises. Beads of perspiration congregate on my forehead. I take two steps left. He takes two steps right in the same direction. His reflection in the mirror appears to magnify the evil in his eyes. He folds his large arms across his massive chest, props his weight on one leg and leans against the sink

"I see you have your bodyguard with you. You move on fast! You are one lucky lady. You have no idea the number of times I spared your love ones grief. You really should have left this alone. You are out of your league once again. You have people spying on some very important people in my life. I am going to need you to stay out of Fayetteville. You have enough family problems to deal with. Don't you think?"

"Mr. Thomas, my family affairs are of no concern to you. I have no idea what you are talking about. Fayetteville? What does Fayetteville have to do with me? Why don't you go and fuck yourself!" I take two steps forward towards the door. He walks two steps backwards and stands between me and the door. He turns to the side and locks the door.

He grabs his crotch. "I bet that African can't get down like me. Bend over the sink, and I will give you something you probably have not had before." He snickers. "But from what I saw on that video, you have a few good moves."

"Get out of my way!" He steps forward. "Should I be afraid?" I am sure my body has fear written all over it. The space is too small to lodge a defense if he attacks, and I cannot get around him.

"Matter of fact, you should be." He steps closer. I slowly step backwards. "You need to back down. You are playing with the wrong people. Don't fuck with me, and I won't fuck with you. How is Che'? Isn't that what you named her? Was that the African's idea? It is hard for me to believe you named your daughter such a revolutionary name." He laughs and continues with his mockery. "Her name should be Becky or Susie."

"I am going to give you two seconds to move away from the

door." I remove my cell phone from my pocket. He laughs, unlocks the door, and steps to the side; I cautiously step around him and exit the bathroom.

"Ayanna!" I pause in the foyer before entering the bar area.

"If you could have seen the look on your husband's face when he got those pictures; it was priceless." He laughs. "You have some really good moves. If you are ever low on cash, give me a call." I ignore him. He has one-upped me. He must have followed me or paid someone to follow me. His knowledge of my personal residence alarms me; however, I am more concerned that he is privy to my relationship with Trevor Bordeaux. "You need to back off, Ayanna. This can get really ugly for you. If the right people get wind of your clandestine affairs, you can kiss that appointment goodbye." I thought he was smarter. My destination exceeds the D.A. office. Once I win this case, nothing else will matter.

Detective Davis is standing at the front of the bar waiting for me. I rethink spending the night with him. I want to call a taxi instead, but this creep knows where I live.

We leave the bar. It is pitch black outside, but I feel safe holding onto Detective Davis's arm. I think of Osei and the children; a slight sadness comes over me, but the feeling quickly passes. Women have always had to make hard choices. Unlike me, some find mates that understand how the game is played. However, Osei is smarter and much savvier than I previously thought. Osei went so far as attempting to financially cripple me so I would have no resources to come after him. He planned this out well. I should have seen it coming.

I feel uneasy as Detective Davis inserts the key. I am one of the most sophisticated women I have ever known, one of the smartest women I know, and I am getting ready to fall asleep, more like pass out, in a colleague's home. The lights immediately come on as we enter the foyer. They are so bright that it takes time for me to focus. It is painfully obvious a woman does not live here. Everything is neutral. There are no pictures on the walls. No throw pillows on the sofa. Everything is the same color. This is definitely a man cave.

He escorts me to the sofa and goes to the rear of the apartment.

"Here, take these" He passes me a wash towel, and a towel. "You can shower in the guest bathroom. It is cleaner and rarely used." Just as I stand, the entire contents of my stomach fly out of my mouth and land all over us. I am embarrassed; I cannot control the flood of tears that began to flow from my eyes.

"Ayanna, you are a wreck." His face is serious. His concern is genuine. He goes back to the bathroom and returns with a damp towel. He wipes the vomit off me first, then himself. He helps me to the bathroom. My legs tremble as I walk. I am embarrassed; I cannot look him in the eye. He turns on the water in the shower and leaves. I stand in the tiny bathroom sick, feeling crazy, and off-balance.

"Hey" He knocks on the door. "Pass me your clothes. I'll put them in the washing machine." I am hesitant. "Don't worry; I have lived with a woman before. I've seen bloody pads, spotted panties, bras; you name it, I have seen it." He laughs.

"You're gross." My speech is slurred. The liquor has gone to my head. I shower and come out of the bathroom wrapped in an oversized towel. He passes me a T-shirt. "This is going to swallow me."

"I am a big man." He poses, tightening his muscles like a body builder. "Are you hungry?"

"I can use something hot on my stomach." He goes to the kitchen. The sounds of pots clinging and plates clapping permeate his small condo. It sounds as if there is a war going on in the kitchen. Twenty minutes later, he returns with a beautiful omelet and places it in front of me.

"Aren't you going to eat?"

"No, I'm not hungry." He sits next to me while I gobble down the food.

"Don't worry. I am not going to take it from you. You don't have to rush. Take your time." I laugh, placing food that falls out of my mouth back in. I finish my meal and pass my plate to him. He takes it back in the kitchen. I hear water running and then the hum of the dishwasher. He comes back to the living room wiping his hands on a paper towel.

"Are you okay?"

"I don't know."

"You will be okay. I will get your bed ready." He leaves, walks down the hall, then comes back to the living room with balled up sheets in his arms. "I changed the sheets. There is a television in the bedroom. The remote is on the bed." He goes to his bedroom.

He makes me think of Osei. He is much taller but has the same broad back, slim waist and tight rear. I leave the living room and walk down the hall to the guest room. I should feel guilt, but I don't. I am slightly unnerved. I think of my family, but I honestly do not miss the responsibility of the children or the demands of a husband. I should feel guilty that Osei found out about Trevor, but I don't. My arrangement was simply an arrangement that will guarantee I get to the next level. My parents were by no means poor, but I did not have the connections that would guarantee a high society lifestyle. You either are born into the network or you create it for yourself. Osei comes from a very wealthy family. I had to create the connections he was born with. I throw the covers off me and crawl out of the bed. I cannot sleep.

"Are you okay?" His body is covered with a spread from the waist down.

"No" I stand in the threshold of his bedroom door. My knees wobble. It feels as if my legs weigh a ton. I walk close to his bed. Although it is dark, the moonlight illuminates his sparsely decorated room and creates a shadowy outline of the muscles in his massive chest. His body looks powerful. Not in a sexual way, but in a protective way.

He opens his arms. I walk into them. He wraps them tightly around me. "I don't want to sleep alone."

"You will be okay. You have to believe that. It is not over. Your husband will come to his senses." I wish I could be honest and disclose the reason Osei left and took the children with him. I am sure if Davis knew it was because of an outside relationship with a well-known politician, the very people he abhors, he would think ill of me.

Chapter 18

I have been working with Detective Davis almost daily. It is not customary for the prosecutor to investigate a case along the side of law enforcement. Usually the detectives and police gather the evidence, and the prosecution puts the evidence together and builds a case. This case is special and deserves my undivided attention. Detective Davis and I are both equally invested in this case, but for different reasons. Davis is the good cop. He believes he makes a difference. On the other hand, I know for every thug he takes off the street, three more will take their place. Winning any case is good for a prosecutor's career, but this case will mean more. Jefferson is on the inside of the political class. Exposing his criminal enterprise will bring national attention, seal my position on the State bench, and increase my chances of reaching the Federal Bench. I have dreams that surpass City Hall, and Jefferson Thomas is my ticket to turn those dreams into reality. Jefferson is not an unfortunate casualty. He deserves all that is coming to him and more. Many believe him to be the pillar of the community. I know better.

Detective Davis and I worked hard to get him the last time. He is well-connected, and intimidation is his modus operandi. When he attacked my ethics, he also filed an excessive force complaint against Detective Davis. My ethics may have been questionable, but Davis is a good cop and did not deserve unwarranted scrutiny.

Stacy Lincoln is no less culpable. She and Jefferson Thomas operate from the same playbook. She, with the right amount of pressure, will help us bring him down. We have been staked out in front of her condo for hours. I should be at my desk working on my other cases. For now, the other cases will have to take a back seat.

Their businesses pay them well. She lives in an upscale Buckhead condominium with a concierge as well as a cleaning service. We are parked on the side of her building across the street from the garage. A couple of celebrities who have made Atlanta their home leave in expensive, fast cars as paparazzi stand inconspicuously outside of the gate snapping pictures. According to the county tax records, she purchased the property one hundred thousand dollars below the selling price of the previous owners four years ago. Her mortgage records show she paid a fifty thousand dollar down payment on the three hundred thousand dollar mortgage. She is smart. Her bank account shows consistent monthly deposits for the last five years, so the large down payment did not trigger an IRS audit. She earns just enough on paper to justify her lifestyle.

"Ayanna, did your team find out who the woman is in the pictures with Mr. Thomas?"

"My team is still working on that. We know her name and the children's names. We were able to get some information from the county school district. Her name does not show up on any of our radars. She has no criminal history and perfect credit. Outside of Mr. Thomas, she has no affiliation with unsavory characters."

"Who is the children's father?"

"The name of the father does not appear on either of the children's school records. The judge signed the warrant so we can have complete access to her bank records and credit file. We should have access to her complete life today. I can't imagine what he could be doing with a school teacher. School teachers are generally not the flashy type he usually associates himself with."

"Maybe he is using the teacher to get access to new recruits."

"Possibly, Detective, it's hard to believe a chicken shack and a few 'hood businesses can provide Mr. Thomas and Ms. Lincoln with the lifestyles they live."

"Mr. Thomas has a few rental properties in addition to his businesses."

"Who do you know making money from real estate now? That is a long-term investment, and almost everybody is upside down in their mortgages right now."

"True." She finally leaves her condo and exits the garage with her cell phone glued to her ear. We follow three cars behind. She stops at a corner coffee shop a block away and parks next to a grey Lincoln Navigator. A burly white male exits the Navigator as she exits her vehicle.

"That is Gorbachev." They embrace and kiss one another on the cheek, go inside of the coffee shop, and sit for over an hour.

"You think they are having a romantic relationship?"

"Who knows?" He shrugs his shoulders.

"I think they are. They are giving off a lot of sexual energy." After an hour or so, they finally leave the coffee shop. He walks with her to her car. This time, their embrace is longer. He kisses her forehead, and she gets in her vehicle. He stands in the parking lot and watches until she is out of view.

"Your job is interesting, but this waiting is boring." We continue to follow her three cars behind to a fitness center a mile away. Again, we park and wait.

"There is a lot of waiting in this job. It requires patience, but this is how we get the bad guys."

"She has been inside for over two hours."

"Criminals have to be health conscious, too." He laughs. "She is one of the prettiest criminals I have ever encountered."

"I did not know you were into 'hood rats."

"If a woman looks good, a man can't help but notice." He is right; Ms. Lincoln is very attractive. Jefferson has definitely upgraded her. I almost did not recognize her. She has more flair now than she did when she was on the arm of the drug dealer we put away a few years ago. I am restless and ready to request Davis pull her out of the gym when but she finally exits and returns to her vehicle. She opens the rear door of the SUV, throws her gym bag in the backseat, and proceeds to the driver's side door.

"We may as well get her now." Detective Davis presses the accelerator to the floor, parks behind her, and quickly exits the car. He approaches her as she opens the driver's side door of her Land Rover. She does not appear to be alarmed by the loud sound of Detective Davis' tires screeching against the asphalt. Detective Davis holds the door to prevent her from opening it further. He explains that she is not under arrest but would like for her to come to the station to answer questions. She puts up no resistance, grabs her bag, and closes the door of her vehicle. She walks next to Davis as if he is escorting her on a date, as opposed to the county jail for an interrogation.

"What is this about?" She sits in the backseat and crosses her legs as if she is in a chauffeured car. She exudes an abundance of confidence. It cannot be authentic. No one in her line of work has authentic confidence.

"We will talk when we get to the station."

"Is it necessary that I leave my vehicle? I can follow you."

"We figure you can call Mr. Thomas to come and pick you up from the precinct. He is the new thug in your life, isn't he?"

"Oh this is about Jefferson? Thug? I assure you Jefferson is not a thug." She chuckles as she looks at me. "I see you still have the hots for him. I figured by now you would have moved on." Her comments are unnerving, but I remain professional.

"No, it's about prostituting young girls. I hope he has the hots for you when this is over. At the very least, you will be charged with an accessory to human trafficking."

"You can't be serious." She uncrosses her legs and rolls her eyes. "You are very entertaining." She removes a tube of lipstick from her purse and slides it over her lips. "Jefferson is not to be played with. You should know this." She smacks her lips together to blend the lipstick.

"Jefferson does not impress me, Ms. Lincoln." I fold my arms across my chest.

"I guess we will have to have our lawyer contact the ethics board again." I ignore the subtle threat.

He drives into the garage behind the jail and parks next to the entrance to intake. We walk into the crowded intake section. A long line of women stand handcuffed against the wall, waiting to be processed. Some are hardened criminals, but many are mental health patients that need to be transferred to a mental health facility instead of the county jail.

"Why are you taking me here if I am not under arrest?"

"Ma'am, place your purse in this bag!" Her eyes hold contempt. She is reluctant to follow the detentions officer's commands. "Ma'am, I will not ask you again!" The six feet tall, female detention officer exhibits very little patience. In her world, everyone who steps across the security line is a criminal. "Place your purse in this plastic bag!" She reluctantly places the purse in the bag. The detention officer slips on gloves. "Any sharp objects or needles?"

"No, I am not under arrest! Why is this necessary?" The guard ignores her and goes through her purse with a fine toothed comb and places it on the conveyor belt to be X-rayed.

"Please step over here!" Another detention officer orders her to bend forward and place both hands on the table. Beads of perspiration congregate on her forehead as the guard spreads her legs and pats her down before letting her through the entrance.

"Was this really necessary?" Her brows furrow, and her lips turn up and slightly extend outward.

"We have to interview here." Davis' smirk is purposeful. "There were no vacant rooms at the precinct. We want you to get familiar with your future home. If I have my way, you will have a home here very soon." He escorts her to an interview room. I follow close behind.

Davis immediately takes a seat. I sit next to him. She stands in the corner. "This may take a minute; you may want to have a seat." She sits in the chair directly across from Davis and pushes her chest out, exposing so much cleavage that I am surprised her breasts do not fall out of her bra. Her demeanor changes. Her smile is flirtatious. She is definitely Jefferson's type. He has upgraded her, but the Gucci tennis shoes and purse cannot hide the raw, street nature. The well-groomed hair cannot mask her bottom-feeding instinct. Her body is toned and curvaceous and looks as if she could have once been familiar with a stripper pole. I have to give it to Jefferson. He invested a lot in her.

"We need you to testify against Mr. Thomas." I open a folder that shows a picture of Ansliegh in the hospital bed, black and blue with tubes in her body. "We know he is responsible for this."

"So now you think he beats up little girls." She takes the picture from my hand, scans over it, and slides it back to me.

"This is Jane Doe." Detective Davis removes a picture from the folder. "She was found in the woods wrapped in a blanket off Interstate 20. We have a witness who will testify you were one of the last people to see her." She glances at the picture of a decomposing young body and quickly looks away. "We know the 'hood businesses are fronts. We know he is pimping young girls."

"I am prepared to offer you complete immunity if you testify against him." I walk around the table and stand behind her.

"Testify against what? That he is a small businessman who employees people in low income communities?" She laughs. "I can testify about the many charities he sponsors and the amount of money he contributes to political campaigns for some of the most respected politicians in the county and state."

"No, testify about the real business and what happened to Ansleigh." I pause. "We can set you up with a wire. You don't have to go down with him."

"Set me up with a wire?" Her eyes become glassy. Her attempt to hide the nervousness in her voice is futile. "You have to be kidding me."

"Scared, you are scared." Davis' voice is strong, yet sympathetic. "You have that nervous twitch. You are unable to keep eye contact. I bet you have witnessed a lot of horror as Mr. Thomas' sidekick. You have more to worry about than Mr. Thomas; we have a child in the hospital."

"The child in the hospital was arrested with Mr. Thomas." I return to the chair next to Davis.

"Pimp? Is that what you think? I thought you were more sophisticated than that. Jefferson lead me to believe you were some smart Ivy League graduate. You actually believe Jefferson Thomas is a pimp?" She relaxes. "You think he is my pimp?" She reaches for her leather Gucci purse. "Are you going to charge me with anything?" She removes a tube of lipstick, rolls it across her lips, smacks them together, and puts the tube back inside of her purse. This has to be a nervous habit. Her lipstick does not need refreshing. "If you are going to charge me with something, please do so now so I can contact my lawyer." She looks at her Gucci watch. "I have an appointment this afternoon." She stands.

"Sit down! You got away last time. Your drug dealer boyfriend took the wrap for both of you, but this time you will not be so lucky." She reluctantly sits back in the chair. I sit on the table next to her. "I don't think he is your pimp. I think his business is so much bigger than that, and when we put the pieces together this is going to be big. Do you really want to go down with him?"

"Go down with him for what? If you have all of this information, why am I here?" Her confidence returns. The smirk on her face makes me angry when I think of the kid in the hospital that has been exploited to pay for the designer purse on her shoulder and the diamond bracelet on her wrist. "Why am I not in handcuffs? Why haven't you arrested him?"

"We are going to let you go for now, but think about your options. You have been here before. I don't need to explain them to you. Is he worth doing hard time?"

"Hard time for what?" She laughs. "If you have something, then charge me." His cockiness must be contagious, because she has the same demeanor as Mr. Thomas.

"We will, but I want to give you time to think about it first."

"Does he treat you as good as he treats her?" Davis removes another picture and slides it across the table in front of her. She glances at the picture, takes a deep, unnatural breath, and quickly looks away. Davis shows the picture of the woman we know to be a school teacher, two small children, and Jefferson. They are walking hand in hand on the beach with the children running in front of them. Stacy Lincoln and I are both surprised. I have not seen the picture. Davis is withholding information from me.

"Who is that?"

"You tell me."

"I have no idea. I have never seen these people before. Nice looking kids." She is lying. There is sadness in her eyes after she saw the picture. She stands and then sits back down. "Can I go now?"

"You can use that phone." He points to an antiquated phone on the wall that monitors and records conversation. "Have Jefferson come and take you to your car."

"I have a phone Detective" She turns away from me and bats fake eyelashes at Detective Davis. "Are you sure you don't want to give me a ride?"

"Sorry, Ms. Lincoln," His smile is almost flirtatious.

"Cool, but if you ever change your mind and feel like taking me for a ride, call me." She removes a business card from her purse and passes it to him. Detective Davis takes the card and places it in his pocket. He escorts her out of the interview room to the exit.

I am in such deep thought that I almost do not hear him re-enter the interrogation room. Davis and I stand side by side and look out of the window. Ms. Lincoln stands in front of the building. Her hands are swinging back and forth in the air as she talks on the phone.

"Did you see the look on her face when you showed her the picture of Jefferson and the teacher?"

"She is breaking; it's only a matter of time before she is ready to switch sides."

Chapter 19

Stacy is two hours late. Her behavior is a cause for great concern. I was certain it was Ayanna who approached Lailah and interrogated her about our children. I should have known better. Ayanna would have proudly bragged that she was the Senior Deputy Assistant District Attorney and given her a business card as she threatened her with made up charges she could file if she did not cooperate. I sent Lailah a picture of Ayanna and Stacy via text. She confirmed it was Stacy. Stacy must have followed me. She is not my woman; she is my chick. She is losing her bearings. She is no longer an ally. She has become a threat. Women do crazy shit over dick, even one that does not belong to them. When this deal is over, Stacy is history.

I went by her place. Her car was not in the garage. I drove to the gym and found her vehicle in the parking lot, but there was no sign of her. I enter the gym through the side door and canvas the entire facility, including the women's locker room. I flirt with the receptionist at the sign-in desk. I inconspicuously look through the pages while she writes her phone number on the back of a business card. She signed in at 12:00 and signed out two hours later. Her phone is turned off. Her calls are going straight to voicemail. It is as if she went off the grid; no one has seen her.

I am uptight. Stacy is out of pocket, and Lailah has my mind fucked up. I cannot afford to get distracted with confusion. If it were not for the kids, I would eliminate Lailah and dump her and Stacy in the same grave for fucking with my head.

Lailah does not want to see the other side of me. If she

believes she will take my children out of my life, I will show her something she has never seen. I call Lailah's cell, but she does not answer. I went by the house earlier. I knocked on the door; she did not answer. She was inside, as I heard the kids running around. If my kids were not inside of the house, I would have kicked the door in, but I used my better judgment.

I call Stacy again, but still no answer. Ms. Mamie calls and tells me I forgot to sign the payroll checks, so I drive back to the Chicken Shack. I sit in the office, sign the checks. I periodically dial Stacy's number; she does not answer. I go through my business files and remove documents that are ready for shredding. I quickly become restless. I leave the Chicken Shack and drive to Stoney's to have a few drink and chill. I call Stacy again, but she still does not answer. I am organized and a stickler to routine. Stacy, of all people, is aware of this.

I leave Stoney's and drive by the gym again. Her truck is gone, so I drive to her place. Her truck is in her assigned parking space. I touch the hood. It is still warm. I cover my finger with the sleeve of my shirt and use the keypad to enter the building. I take the stairs instead of the elevator to give myself time to cool off. I place my ear to the solid wood door. I detect no sound. I knock on the door. She does not answer. The peephole has darkened; she is in front of the door.

I wait five minutes. I beat on the door as hard as I can. I hear the hinges disengage as she moves the security latch on the door. I kick the door with full force as she opens it. The force is so great the door knob hits the wall, putting a hole in the sheet rock. The impact throws Stacy to the floor. She quickly regains her balance, gets up, runs to the living room, and grabs the phone. I knock it out of her hand. It flies across the room and shatters the mirror that sits over her fireplace.

"Who the fuck are you calling?" She makes a dash towards the bathroom. I kick over the chair in front of her. She trips over it. I grab her and smash her face into the floor. I pound her face so hard my knuckles begin to hurt. "Where were you?" She tries to speak but chokes on the blood pouring out of her mouth and nose. "I have been calling you!"

"I was with that woman D.A., the one you have been tangoing with for years. She and the cop we saw at Stoney's the other night picked me up from the gym. I tried to call you!"

"What did you say? They would not have gone to the trouble of picking you up and letting you go! That is not how she operates!" She folds her arms over her head to block my powerful blows. I am amazed her jaw does not crack. She slumps to the floor. I kick her in the stomach so hard, she slides across the hardwood floor.

"I didn't say anything!" My breathing is labored. I can barely catch my breath. She slowly stands and bends forward with her hand pressed tight to her side. She limps to the bathroom. I follow behind her. I am so close, she can probably feel my breath on her neck. Her crying intensifies when she sees dark circles forming around her swelling eyes.

"You have been acting strange and out of fucking pocket! If you ever cross me, I will kill you! You have made contact with some very important people in my life." I grab a handful of her hair, snatch her around, and pull her face as close to mine as possible without touching. "If you ever go near her or my kids again, I will kill you!"

"Kids? All of these years, Jefferson!" Her speech is muffled. "All of these years, and you have a secret life! You have kids! I wanted kids! I wanted a family with you!" I hit my hand against the wall. The impact creates a deep hole a hair away from her head.

"I don't owe you shit! I never promised you anything! If you cross me, I will make you regret the day your whore mother gave birth to you!" I grab her by the neck and smash her head against the bathroom mirror.

"When have I ever crossed you?" My hands are tight around her neck. I shake her back and forth like a rag doll.

"Call Ms. Mamie! I left a message for you that I was at the police precinct and I would get with you later! I didn't want to take a chance and call your cell or come by the shack." I grab a handful of her hair and drag her to the living room. She hobbles trying to keep up with my stride. Blood from her feet creates a trail from the bathroom to the living room. I pick up the cordless phone from the floor with one hand. The other hand holds a mass of her hair.

"Ms. Mamie, how are things going?" She goes into a diatribe on how busy the restaurant is and the need to hire another waitress and informs me that I did not sign a check for one of the waitresses. I do not address her concerns. "Ms. Mamie, did anyone call and leave a message for me today?"

"Matter of fact, they did. Stacy called and said she was someplace and can't make it to your meeting. She said she would call you later." She pauses. "But Mr. Thomas, we have to do something about this lunch crowd! The wait times are ridiculous. We are not able to handle it anymore, and Janice must have her check! She has to pay her sitter!"

"Pay Janice from the cash register, and make sure she signs for the amount of cash she is given."

"Any other messages?" I ease the grip on Stacy's neck. She hobbles to the couch, sits down, and picks glass from the broken mirror out of her feet.

"No, sir, that is all, but we really need to hire more help. These lunch lines are getting ridiculous." I ignore her and hang up the phone.

"Get Gorbachev on the phone and put him on speaker!" I can't say I feel bad. Stacy had it coming. She has been acting crazy since Gorbachev came into the picture. Her priorities are fucked up.

She reluctantly dials his number. He picks up on the first ring. She quickly informs him that he is on speaker and she is not alone. He greets the both of us.

"Can we meet in an hour to go over all of the logistics?"

"I am in Buckhead right now. I can meet you in thirty minutes." He pauses. "Will you be alone?"

"No, Mr. Thomas will join us." She ends the call and hobbles to the shower. She returns fully dressed. Her hair is pulled back. Her makeup is so thick, it looks like you can cut it with a knife, but it serves the purpose of covering her bruised face and blackened eyes, but no amount of makeup can hide her swollen and split lip. We do not speak to one another en route to meet Gorbachev. Part of me wants to apologize, but I want to leave something on her mind. We park next to Gorbachev's Lincoln Navigator. She slams the door so hard when she exits my vehicle it knocks the window off track. She continues to walk five steps in front of me to the restaurant entrance. Gorbachev stands and waves his hands back and forth to get our attention. He stares at Stacy from the time we enter the restaurant until she makes her way to his table. As always, he greets her with a kiss on each cheek. She does not remove the oversized Chanel sunglasses as she sits at the table.

"What happened?" He touches her lips like a concerned lover.

"Bike accident," He does not believe her bike accident story. He talks to Stacy but stares at me as if he wants to challenge me. I stare back. I back down to no man. He eventually turns away. I order a cocktail, and we get down to business.

"We have one week until the big event. I will send the limousine to pick up the girls at 3:00 pm to get their hair and nails done." I am speaking to him, but he looks at Stacy as if she is the one talking.

"I thought my people were doing the transportation?" He does not address me. His entire conversation is addressed to Stacy, and they both behave as if I am invisible.

"I guess there has been a change of plans." She shrugs her shoulders. I ignore her. She has a reason to be upset, but the side communication between them is irritating.

"Is there a problem?" I stand. "These are my clients."

"These are my girls!" He stands. "You have not made the final payment." I am not one to make a scene in public, so I chill. Any remorse I felt for kicking Stacy's ass has disappeared. There is no doubt in my mind; she is fucking the Russian. When this is over, Stacy's ass is done.

"Okay, buddy." My smile is deep but my eyes are deadly. I sit back in my chair. "I will have Stacy text you the names of the clients each girl is paired with and the pass codes to the hotel rooms. The awards ceremony will be over by 8:00 PM; have everyone in place by 7:00 PM. By then, everyone will be good and drunk and ready for action. The balance of your money will be wired to your account in the Caymans by midnight." We stand. I extend my hand. He reluctantly takes it.

"Hey, take care of my tab, big guy!" I grab my sunglasses off the table. "After tonight, you will be a very wealthy man."

"Черный ниггер, I am already wealthy!" I do not speak Russian, but I know the term for nigger in twenty languages. Stacy obviously knows he referenced me as nigger, as they have an "*I gotcha smile*" on their faces. Gorbachev escorts Stacy to the restaurant's exit and as usual watches until she is out of sight.

Stacy is silent the entire ride back to her place.

"Do you want to come over to my place tonight?" I have not had good sex in a minute, and she knows how to put it down.

"No, I'll go home."

"You have been acting strange. Don't forget who you are

dealing with."

"I have a lot on my mind."

"Are you sure?" I park next to the elevator that leads to her apartment. I reach across the console and pinch her nipple. She quickly pushes my hand away, exits the truck, and slams the door so hard, the window is now lopsided and has slipped half of the way down.

Chapter 20

I have been trying to make contact with the District Attorney since yesterday after my meeting with Stacy and Gorbachev. I have left several messages on his office phone; he has not returned my calls. He has been avoiding me like the plague, but he knows his game of hide and seek had best quickly come to an end. I scan the list on my phone for his personal cell phone number.

"What is this about?" He finally returns my call. I can barely understand him. His speech is rapid, and his voice sounds as if it is vibrating.

"Let's just say it is a mandatory meeting you cannot afford to miss."

"I am going to be tied up all day, Mr. Thomas. I really don't have time to fit a meeting into my schedule today. I have scheduled meetings on my calendar all day."

"Cancel them! I will see you at Stoney's in an hour." I open the bathroom vanity, remove the partition, open the safe and find my special envelope is still in its place. I call Stacy as I drive out of the garage. She does not answer. After tomorrow night, she will be history. She is making moves with Gorbachev that do not include me. There is no room for a third party in our arrangement. She and the Russian are attempting to outwit the wrong person. The Russian does not know me, but Stacy should know better.

I look for the District Attorney's car as I turn into the parking lot. He has not arrived. As usual, Stoney's is crowded with the local political brass and the people who own them. One would think with all of the money that comes in this place, Stoney would at least pay for basic remodeling and upgrades. I sit at the table in the middle of the bar, where he can easily see me when he enters. After thirty minutes, the District Attorney walks in with a fake smile plastered on his face. Everyone greets him as if he is Captain Crime

Fighter.

He shakes hands with patrons while cracking boring jokes as if this is an election year. We make eye contact, but he quickly turns away. He greets the mayor, chitchats with a couple of State Senators before making his way to my table. I am patient. I know he does not want to see me.

"Let's get down to business. I am going to have to call in that favor!" He tries to hold it together. He straightens a perfectly positioned necktie. He quickly downs the double shot of his favorite cognac I ordered for him in one swallow and motions for the waitress to bring another one. He has the physique of a child minus the slightly protruding abdomen. His county profile says he is five-feet and ten inches tall, but he is more like five-feet-five inches. He probably weighs 150 pounds soaking wet. "Your assistant D.A. is getting beyond herself and is once again trying to bring me down!" I swallow my tequila straight, no salt, no lime.

"I will not be bribed!" He has a good poker face. "I am the District Attorney of this great county. I will be respected!" He tries to maintain eye contact but quickly looks away.

"Of course, I have the utmost respect for you and your position! What you have done for this county is commendable. This is why I am going to provide evidence to put a heartless criminal away for a very long time." I ask the waitress to bring two more shots of tequila as she places his double shot of cognac on the table. "I need a deal, and I will give you that compromising video of you and your young friend. Mrs. Leslie, your children, and the citizens of this great county will never know our little secret." I throw a shot of tequila to the back of my throat. This time I ease it down by sucking a slice of lime.

"You set me up!" He grinds his top and bottom teeth together and hits the table with his balled fist. He scans the bar, hoping no one notices his outburst. He masks his anger with a fake smile and nods his head to onlookers. "I did not know his age!"

"This is Atlanta. We are very tolerant of all sexual orientations in this city amongst consenting adults. Unfortunately for you, Little Rico was two years shy of the age of consent, and the fact that you are married with children just may not come across too well with the citizens or the law." I throw back another shot. "I am sure you don't have to worry about the wifey. She probably already knows your sexual perversions. Just keep her in the finest clothes, that exclusive address on Peachtree, and just like the other political wives, she will continue to not give a fuck about what you do."

"You know damn well I did not know he was underage!"

"I know how you feel. We are in the same situation. I did not know that girl I was caught with was underage. Look at it like this, we are going to help each other get out of a fucked up situation. "

"What do you want?" He nervously rubs his hands over his balding head.

"Use your authority as District Attorney and force Ayanna Williams to back down. She is making this thing personal. She is coming after me when it is Stacy Lincoln who is the master mind behind a major trafficking operation that I knew nothing about."

"Stacy Lincoln! You are going to turn on her? I thought she was your woman?" His raised eyebrows make his eyes look twice their normal size.

"Nah, never my woman; just my chick. She is holding things over my head; she is bribing me. You know it is like the political game we play; many things are illusions. I have a buyer for that grease pit. I plan to leave town as soon as the deal is closed. You will never hear from me again, but I have to leave as a free man. I want to start over, move to the islands, and maybe have a family."

"What? You? Start a family?" His laugher insults me.

"I have plenty of evidence on Stacy Lincoln." I ignore his laughter and continue with my proposition. I remove a folder from my briefcase. "These are all of her financial transactions. This guy here..." I give him a picture of Gorbachev, "is a major trafficker in human flesh."

"You are unbelievable!" His eyes cast judgment on me; I don't give a fuck.

"Trust, Mr. Prosecutor, you are not the only person who has said that to me."

"And when she testifies about your involvement?" He leans to one side of the unbalanced chair and crosses his legs.

"What involvement? She has international contacts that have also threatened me." I remove a business card and write Stacy's personal cell number on it. "Check her phone records. You will find all of her contacts. She threatened my family; I believe her threats. She had her cousin killed."

"She killed her cousin?"

"Yes, about three or four months ago, she was found dead of

a drug overdose. An arrest was made, and as usual you assholes convinced an innocent man to plead guilty to something he did not do."

"You are something, Mr. Thomas."

"Let me know when I should expect Ms. Williams to close her case. I am sick of being followed and harassed." I order another shot of tequila. "Wait a week before arresting Ms. Lincoln; I have a few loose ends to tie."

Chapter 21

Her parents appear normal. They are professional, white collar workers. It is hard to reconcile in my mind that a set of normal parents could parent a child who could land in the seedy world of sexual trafficking. Her father is a doctor, and her mother is the principal at an elementary school. A young girl who appears to be five or six years old sits comfortably cradled in her father's arms as he lounges in a chair next to Ansleigh's bed. The mother lies in the hospital bed next to Ansleigh; mother and daughter appear comfortable spooned together.

Detective Davis and I enter the room at the same time. The father stands, gently places the little girl back in the chair, and shakes our hands. His grip is firm. Detective Davis escorts him out of the hospital room and into the lobby while I speak with Ansleigh and her mother.

"Hello, I am Assistant District Attorney Ayanna Williams." Ansleigh's mother eases out of the bed, slides her thin, perfect feet into a worn pair of Birkenstocks, and gently spreads the fallen covers back over Ansleigh.

"Laurel Stewart," She extends her hand. She is petite probably weighs 115 pounds, about five-feet-four inches tall. Her hair is pulled back into a thrown together ponytail. She appears loved and well-cared for. It is hard to know with black women, but she appears to be in her mid to late thirties. Her left ring finger is adorned with a simple wedding band, but her right ring finger sports a large diamond accented by two rubies. This was most likely custom made, a sign she and her husband have grown and prospered together over time.

"Has Ansleigh been able to tell you what happened?"

"I am not pressing her. I am just happy to have my baby back." She embraces Ansleigh's hand and softly rubs Ansleigh's hand across her face. A tear travels down her cheek. She makes no effort to wipe it away. "I can't believe they had her listed as a runaway." She is animated with her hands. "I kept pressing the police, telling them she would never run away." Our conversation is interrupted by a gut-wrenching squeal that echoes throughout the hall. Mr. Stewart stumbles back into the room biting his balled fist; a tsunami of tears flows from his eyes. Mrs. Stewart turns towards him, and they fall into each other's arms. The young sibling appears dazed and confused; she quickly leaves the chair and squeezes in-between her parents and begins to cry as well.

"I am going to kill that animal that did this to my baby! I am going to kill him!"

"Daddy, please stop crying! I am sorry!" He unwraps himself from his wife and steps away.

"Mr. Stewart killing him would be too easy and too quick." I remove the box of tissues from the side of Ansleigh's bed and pass it to him. Ansleigh does not speak. Tears fall on her pillow as she endures her father and mother's emotional breakdown. "Why don't we allow him to get tortured by people just as evil?" I have both of their attention and get straight to the point. "We need Ansleigh to testify, and we can put him away for a very long time." I pause to give them time to digest my request. "It will be a slam dunk. If she testifies before the grand jury, I will get him to plea."

"I will not put her through that. She has been through enough!"

"If we get her to testify before the grand jury, it will not go to trial. Trust me, he will take a plea."

"Daddy" Mr. Stewart takes two quick steps to Ansleigh's bed. His tall, lanky frame looks awkward bending over the hospital bed. He is as tall as Detective Davis, but much slimmer. The scattered strands of gray makes him appear much older than his wife. "I want to testify. I don't want this to happen to anyone else. It is my fault. I should have listened to you and Mommy. I should have never taken those pictures."

"Ansleigh, why didn't you come to me or your mom?"

"Daddy, I was ashamed. They said they would show you the pictures. I thought you guys would not love me anymore."

"Baby, there is nothing you can do to make me not love you." He kisses her forehead. "I will not allow you to be placed in harm's way. I cannot allow you to do this."

"Look at my teeth Daddy." Her two front teeth, that were perfect when I first interviewed her, are now chipped and crooked.

"We will fix your teeth as soon as we get back to Charlotte."

"Think it over." I pass Mr. Stewart my card. "Let us meet later and talk about how we can proceed." Detective Davis and I thank the parents for their cooperation and leave.

"Oh, before I forget, the young lady who contacted us asked that we bring this to you." She reaches into a bag next to Ansleigh's bed and passes a laptop to me. I am so nervous; I almost drop it.

"Does it still have the original hard drive?"

"Yes, this is our family laptop, but Ansleigh is the only one that used it. We don't allow Avril to use computers at all. She is only five." She frowns. "They are highly overrated in education." Mrs. Stewart follows us to the elevator. "It is hard for me to wrap my mind around the idea that someone could do this to a child." She extends her hand to us again. "We have never had a problem with Ansleigh. She was always a good girl."

"We really need Ansleigh's testimony at the grand jury" I plead. "Her identity will be hidden. Mr. Thomas is very popular and well-connected in this city, but I can guarantee no cameras will be allowed in the courtroom. Afterwards, your lives can go back to normal."

"Please don't placate me! Our lives will never be normal again." She wipes a tear away from her eye.

"I know. Normal is not the correct word." We shake hands again, and Detective Davis and I walk to the elevator.

"Is that what I think it is?" We both enter the elevator with wide smiles.

"Yes, this is the computer she used at home. The same one she chats with." I hold the laptop to my chest as if it is a precious baby.

"Are you tired? Do you feel like working?" The excitement in Davis' eyes invigorates me. I am tired and beyond sleepy but too excited to call it a night.

"No, I am not tired at all" I lie.

"Let's go to City Hall East. I have some people in Forensics that owe me a few favors."

"Cool, I don't have any kids or a husband at home. Let's get it."

"When has a husband or children stopped you from

working?" He smiles. "You are the hardest working prosecutor in the District Attorney's office."

When we arrive at his office, I am exhausted. I sit in a chair next to his desk and immediately fall asleep.

. . .

I feel my shoulder pushed back and forth. It takes a minute for me to focus. He passes me a cup of coffee.

"They found the chat room. Our sex crimes unit is busy analyzing 24/7's profile. We are throwing bait. Hopefully, she will bite."

"Oh my God, we are going to get him!" I almost want to cry. I stand and wrap my arms tight around Detective Davis. The embrace feels good.

"Don't you think you should go home now and get some sleep? I can have someone drive you."

"No, I want to stay and watch how this plays out."

The child sex crimes computer lab consists of six men and women housed in a utility closet that has been converted into an office. The unit peruses chat rooms and social media. They set bait for pedophiles in search of prey. Detective Davis and I grab chairs and sit behind the crew. The predators are slick. Some start with subliminal messages. They may start a chat on a new clothing line, and the conversation slowly gravitates to one of a sexual nature. Some are blatant and make their intentions known immediately and ask for a sexual encounter outright.

"We got a hit!" Charlotte is a thirty-year-old Forensics Specialist with the body of a teenager. Her cyber alias is Kari, and she has the prepubescent voice to match her body. "24/7 is in the house."

I almost run into Detective Davis rushing to take the seat behind Charlotte.

"Ansleigh says 24/7 hosts contests and gives away concert tickets and memorabilia of popular music groups. Start chatting about popular music." Charlotte begins posting typical teenage stuff. She comments about this week's top Instagram pictures and the latest music. Screen name 24/7 immediately chats back.

Kari: Bruh have you heard of that new jam by GigaMeister.

185

"She is not a guy; she is a girl." I whisper in her ear.

"Bruh is now a unisex term. Why are you whispering? She can't hear or see you." The crew's hearty laughter fills the room. I don't take it personal.

24/7: Yeah that jam is sweet. I was in the studio when they recorded that song.
Kari: GTFOH
24/7: Where u live?
Kari: Atlanta
24/7 GTFOH You know 8ball the lead rapper is gonna be in town 2nite. He is looking for people to ice with. How old are you?
Kari:14 sexy w/ lotta swag
24/7: Sorry Bae you 2 young.
Kari:I am 14 but everyone thinks I am older + I got a fake ID
24/7: I don't know if this is a good idea
Kari: I get in all the clubs. I don't look my age
24/7: You sure
Kari: Phvck yeah!
24/7: What you 00 like?
Kari: 5'4", 120 lbs all A$$, blue eyes, blond hair
24/7: Send a pic. I will send it to him and see if he wants to hang out. I can't promise anything
Kari: K put in a good word for me☐

We wait a few minutes while Kari goes through saved pictures of decoys to find one that matches the description. I am exhausted. I stand, stretch and remove the pins from my hair.

24/7 You banging. I hope this is not too personal, but a lot of girls want to hang with 8ball. Can you send a picture of something more personal?
Kari: ????
24/7: You sound mature you know those body parts that will make him go wild!!!LOL
Kari:negative what if someone finds out?
24/7: Only me and 8 ball will see.
Kari: you sure?
24/7: course
Kari: K give me a sec

We quickly scan through a folder on her computer that contains jpeg images of risqué photographs of decoys posing as underage girls. I am biting my nails, praying she will take the bait. Kari returns to the thread. She uploads a picture of a female from the neck down with her shirt pulled over bare breast and her shorts almost pulled down to the bottom of her pelvis. I remove my shoes and sit Indian style, praying 24/7 takes the bait.

Kari: think he will like me?

247: Hell yeah. You hot. If I liked girls, I would like you. LOL. Can u party 2night?

Kari: Can we hang 2morrow? I need to study for finals. I have exams 2morrow.

24/7: Sorry Bae, maybe next time I can hook ya'll up when he comes back in town. 8Ball catching a bird early in the AM. I will take pictures of the party and send them to you. You are really going to miss a good time.

Kari: Wait maybe I can study after I get back. Can he meet me somewhere? I don't have a driver's license.

24/7: Sure Bae where you want to meet? What will you be wearing? Make sure it is sexy. He O_O for girls for the next video.

Kari: OMG! Are you serious? K will meet you at 7 downtown at the Five Points train station. Tell him I will be wearing a white mini dress. It makes my A$$ look bigger. Think he gonna like me?

24/7: Course you hot

Kari: Will he be riding in a limo?

24/7: He doesn't travel like that he like to be incognito cuz of the paparazzi following him all the time.

Kari: K, I understand

24/7: He will be in a black Hummer

Kari: I will be there ttyl

We all stand and scream. I am so elated, I forget I am sleepy.

"We have two hours!" Detective Davis immediately takes control. "Kari, get the decoy ready!" She logs into the computer sex crimes database and finds the recruit in the photo she sent to 24/7. "Nate, activate the undercover unit in zone 3! I will call the captain and let him know what is going down."

"Are you ready to go home Ms. Williams?"

"Hell no! I would not miss this for a million dollars!" I grab my purse in one hand and shoes in the other and follow Davis.

"You have got to be kidding! I will lose my job if I let you ride with me and something happens to you!"

"Try and stop me!" I slide my feet in my shoes, stand with my feet shoulder's width apart ready for battle.

"Let's compromise; I will activate the camera on my computer; you can see everything from the comfort and safety of my desk." I walk behind him shouting commands. He ignores me.

"I am going!"

"You are not going!" He abruptly stops and turns around. I almost run into him. He stands in front of the door. "I am not losing my job, and I am not putting you in danger!" He is right. I am being selfish. I digress. "When I call you, turn on the videoconference monitor, and type in these numbers." He removes a torn piece of paper and scribbles numbers on it. "You will see everything from my office."

"This is it." I take the torn piece of paper from his hand. "We are really going to get him."

"Yes" He places a moist kiss on my forehead. "We are going to get him. You look nice with your hair down. You should wear your hair loose more often. Take a nap. I will call you when we get in position." I grudgingly accept that I can't accompany the team. I want to be present when it happens. While I wait for his call, I check my voicemail and notice a missed call from an international phone number. I listen to the voicemail on speaker. "Hi Mommy." It is Che'. It sounds as if she is whispering. "Pick up the phone Mommy!" There is urgency in her voice. I end the voicemail and stroll back to the call log, write down the number, and call back. No one answers. I call again and allow the voicemail to answer and listen to the entire greeting. I do not leave a message. I place my phone in my pocket, sit in Davis' office chair, and wait for his call. Thirty minutes later, the phone rings.

"Turn on VCT and type in the numbers I gave you." I turn on his computer, press the green button on the VCT and type in the numbers. "Can you see?"

"Yeah." The footage, initially blurry, slowly becomes clear. The area is crowded with people making last minute rounds before boarding the trains. Although a lot of effort has been made to extend the nightlife in downtown Atlanta, most shops and restaurants close by seven o'clock, when most people leave the city. The area is filled with a diverse socioeconomic dynamic from street vendors, drug dealers to executives of major corporations. Each dynamic usually keeps close to their defined socioeconomic group. I scan the area for several minutes until I spot the decoy. The decoy is slim with a rotund behind. She stands out. It is 7:00 PM. and she is in in a white, tight, cheap dress and platform stilettos. I am on pins and needles; the decoy does not look the part. She looks cheap like a common streetwalker.

The decoy sits on a bench at the bus stop with her legs crossed, smoking a cigarette. She needs to tone it down. She looks more like a prostitute than a groupie. A thin, young black male who appears to be in his early twenties approaches the decoy. He is moving his hands back and forth. The voices are muffled; initially, it is hard to follow their conversation. I adjust the bass and treble until they are audible.

"What's up?" He grabs the crotch of his sagging jeans.

"Ain't nothing." She stands, turns around as if she is looking for someone. Her dress rises with the slightest movement. She walks a few feet towards Alabama Street and sits on the bench in front of the Five Points station. The thin male follows her.

"Are you Kari?"

"What?" She pretends to be annoyed. "Yeah, how you know?"

"I saw your picture. I am here with 8ball."

"What?" Her demeanor instantly changes. She squeals like the excited teenager she is pretending to be. She jumps from the seat, grabs him tight around his neck, and raps her legs around his waist. "Where he at?" Her tight dress rises above her behind. She releases the thin male, pulls her dress down, and pokes her bottom out further than natural. "Oh my God, where he at?" She uses her hands to fan her face.

"Calm down, Bae. He is coming; he wants to make sure you are not one of those crazy groupies or the paparazzi." He stands and waves his hands motioning for someone to come to him.

"Hey, I am cool." She continues to use her hands to fan her face. "I can't believe I am actually going to meet 8ball!"

"Come on, let's go; our ride is pulling up right now." An older model BMW with flashing hazard lights stops in front of the train station.

"I thought 24/7 said he was pushing a Hummer." She stands back and away from the car.

"He is incognito." The thin black male opens the passenger side rear door. The decoy walks close to the car.

"You sure everything is cool?" She walks in front of him and stops in front of the opened rear passenger door.

"Where he at? Where is 8ball?" She bends over and leans in the car.

"He gonna meet us at the club." He walks behind her and lightly pushes her inside the car. He slides in the back seat next to her and quickly closes the door.

"You sure? This doesn't seem right! Stop! Let me out of the car! Tell me the name of the club. I can get there on my own."

The hazard lights flicker off. The broke down BMW quickly exits the curb and travels two miles south on Peachtree. An army of police cruisers and unmarked police vehicles surround the car as it reaches the corner of Peachtree and Trinity. The decoy quickly exits the car with her gun drawn and pointed at the head of the driver. Detective Davis exits his vehicle and immediately shoots all four tires of the suspect's vehicle. He then aims his gun at the occupants and demands they exit the vehicle. He grabs the passenger as he exits and throws him on the asphalt. An officer with his face covered in a thick, black ski mask quickly runs next to the fracas, lifts one of the suspects from the ground, throws him against the car, and removes the contents from the suspect's pockets. A city contracted tow truck quickly drives in front of the downtrodden BMW, passes paperwork to one of the officers and tows the car away. The driver and the passenger are quickly pulled off the asphalt and placed into different patrol cars.

"Ms. Williams, we got them!" I should be asleep, but I am too excited.

"Davis, make sure you keep the cell phones!"

I grab my bag instead of going to directly to intake. I leave Davis' office and walk across the bridge to my office, where I keep a change of clothes. The light is on in D.A. Leslie's office. It is not out of the ordinary for him to work odd hours. I do not disturb him. I lock my purse in my desk, go the bathroom, freshen up, and change clothes. I walk out of the side door and cross the bridge back to the Detention Center. I am at the intake desk when Davis arrives.

"Excited?" His smile becomes sexier every day. If I were into blue collar workers, Detective Davis would possibly have a chance.

"You know it."

The larger of the two struggle the most. He is escorted through intake by a uniformed police officer. The officer releases him to Davis and leaves. The suspect makes accusations of police brutality through swollen lips. He demands to speak to a supervisor. "Next time, try and keep your balance." Davis bypasses the long line of other detainees that are waiting to get processed in the jail. He places the suspects in separate rooms adjacent to one another and closes the door. He removes two chairs from the intake area and sits them in front of the one-way mirror. "Have a seat."

"Aren't we going to question them?" I proceed to walk around him to the door of the interrogation room. He stands in front of me and stops me from opening the door.

"Let them simmer; let's watch them to see which one is the weakest." The scrawny male sits nonchalantly in the hard plastic chair. He lays his head on the desk and appears to fall asleep.

"Do you have their names?" He removes their driver's licenses from a brown envelope.

"The sleepy one with his head on the desk is DaQuan Phillips. The one on the other side making the ruckus is David Harris. DaQuan has a rap sheet a mile long."

"What about Harris?" Harris paces back and forth like a caged animal. He screams at the one-way mirror.

"Harris has no record. He will be our target." Davis points to the hulk beating on the one-way mirror. He is moving his lips, but we cannot hear him. He looks like he should be on a football field, as opposed to a detainee in the county jail. "He is the weakest; he will be crying like a baby in a few minutes."

"When are you going to give him his call?"

"Never." He laughs.

"That's against the law and policy."

"When have you cared about the law and policy, Ms. Williams?" He laughs. "We need to see what he is going to say before he gets that call. We don't want him to talk to the wrong people. These are not the people we want. We don't want them to tip off the people we really want."

"You have a point." I stand outside of the interview room as

Davis enters. The detainee paces back and forth; he immediately begins to plead his case and confess his innocence of all charges, though no charges have been filed.

"I was just giving someone a ride. I don't know shit about nothing."

"You are in a lot of trouble." Davis sits at the table with his hands folded across his chest. He presses the intercom and record button on the table. "You can make it a good or bad day. Right now you have a kidnapping charge, child exploitation charges, all felonies. Big bubba is going to have a field day with you and your tight ass."

"Kidnap? I did not kidnap anyone!"

"We have it all on film. The undercover officer can be heard asking you to let her out of the car. You continued to drive. Sit down!" Harris sits in the chair across from Davis.

"Look, I was just giving my homie a ride."

"Save it. We don't want you! We want the person who sent you to pick up the girl."

"I can't give you that! Snitching is not my thing!" Harris throws his hands up. "Man, my life would not be worth two cents."

"Suit yourself." Davis stands, presses the button to turn the intercom and recorder off and pushes the chair back under the table. He methodically turns and slowly walks to the door.

"What kind of deal can you give me? I can't go to the pen." Davis returns to the table but does not immediately sit down.

"I will see if the D.A. will drop the kidnapping charge. The misdemeanor child cruelty charge will stand. You are looking at probation and a fine." Davis sits back in the chair across from Harris.

"Damn! I can't snitch! Old head, you serious?"

"When I get out of this chair and leave this room, I am going to speak to DaQuan. Trust he will rat you out! He will paint you as the mastermind. When I leave this room, I will not give you this opportunity again." Davis stands, pushes the chair under the table, walks to the door, turns the door knob, and slowly opens the door.

"Wait! Wait!" Harris quickly stands.

"I don't have time to play with you!" Davis steps across the threshold.

"I will tell you everything I know, but I am going to have to do my probation out of town! These people do not play!" Davis closes the door, walks to the table, sits down, and presses the intercom and record button.

"Who is 24/7?"

"I only saw her once. Was shocked as fuck to find she was an old ass lady. Bitch looked like she could be my grandma." He shakes his head. "We met her to get money she owed Quan for a previous delivery."

"How long have ya'll been doing this?"

"I provide transportation for Quan. That is all I do. I have only done it four, maybe five times for 24/7, and a few times for his other contacts." He shakes his head. "I needed the money. It is hard turning down 500 a pop. My girl is pregnant, and we needed the money."

"I don't give a fuck about your or your pregnant girlfriend! Stay focused, and answer my questions! Other contacts?"

"DaQuan signs into a secure website he calls the clearinghouse to get the transportation jobs."

"Let's stay focused on 24/7 for now. We will come back to that." Davis shakes his head. A look of disgust covers his face. "Where did you meet her?"

"Some raggedy ass bar downtown full of old ass niggers."

"When was this?"

"Bout two months ago."

"Describe her."

"Just a regular old lady. You know them type that dress in African clothes, shiny flat dollar store shoes everybody grandma be wearing and shit. Old hag drove a nice ass Mercedes though." Davis turns around and stares at the glass in my directions. I can see him, but he cannot see me.

"Call her on the phone." Davis removes the phone he confiscated from Harris and passes it to him. "Tell her the girl did not show!"

"She is not going to answer. She only communicates with DaQuan by texting. DaQuan texts her, and within a few minutes she will text back." Davis takes the phone, quickly leaves the interrogation room, walks past me, and retrieves DaQuan's phone. I glance at Daquan. He is asleep with his head face down, cradled in his folded arms.

"Which number is hers?" Davis returns to the interrogation room and stands next to Harris. "DaQuan calls her Grandma."

Davis leaves the interview room and goes to his office. I follow him.

"Ms. Williams, you need to go home and get some rest!"

"Not on your life." He ignores me. He is engulfed in his work.

"What are you doing?"

"Texting Grandma." He leaves his office, and stands on coffee-stained carpet in front of 15 cubicles in a space designed to comfortably accommodate ten. "Everybody listen up; we're having a meeting!" The members of his team all leave their desks and stand almost in unison on the side of their cubicles. I think to myself, Surely this is not how you hold a meeting. "We have some bad guys to get off the street and some people to protect!"

"Cuz that is what we do!" All 15 detectives shout in unison, as if they are in a cult.

"Tammy, I need for you and your partner to stakeout Ms. Lincoln's place and bring her in. I don't care if it takes days; make sure she is alone when you bring her in!"

"Sir, do I bring her here or to the intake?"

"Take her straight to intake, and make sure she gets the complete detention experience. Charge her with anything you can think of; we will find something that sticks!"

"Jason."

"Yes, sir!"

"Get a search warrant for the County Family and Children Services; we need the names of all of the children on Mary Beckham's caseload. Do background checks on each and every one of the children past and present. Find as many as you can and interview them!"

"Well, are you going to tell me the plan?"

"Stacy Lincoln is going to turn on him! Offer her the best deal you can." He continues his work as if I am not there. "Neal, please get the names of everyone on staff at the juvenile detention center the night when Ansleigh Stewart, AKA Ashleigh Stewart, was beaten."

"Davis, I am right here! Are you going to tell me what's up?" He continues to ignore me and walks to his office.

"You political types are all narcissistic."

"Hey," I stand in the entrance of his office and place my hands on my hips. "I thought we were on the same team?"

"Nope, Ms. Williams, I am on the team that gets the bad guys off the street. This is all politics for you."

"Fuck you!"

"Fuck you! You were right about one thing. This thing is big; some of your colleagues are involved in this bullshit!" He picks up the phone and places it back on the cradle. "I am out of line. I apologize. Prepare to give Ms. Lincoln the best deal you can. Go home and get some rest. I will talk to you tomorrow."

Chapter 22

Detective Davis and I usually work well together. Mistrust has somehow entered in our relationship. He distrusts all political figures; however, I thought I was the exception. I charge his attitude to exhaustion. We both endured several hours without sleep, but I am concerned and feel betrayed that once again he has come across information he is unwilling to share. He is smart and strategic. He has something up his sleeve.

I am beyond exhausted, and there is nothing left to do but sleep. I drive home and park my car in the empty garage attached to my empty house. I make a mental note to call a realtor as soon as possible. Now that Osei and the children are gone, I can place the house on the market. I never wanted a house. If it does not sell in thirty days, I will sell it below market to get rid of it. A penthouse condo in the heart of Buckhead is more suitable to my taste. I go upstairs to my empty room and flop on my empty bed. I turn on the television to hear noise in the house. I am exhausted, yet restless. I text Trevor Bordeaux and wait for his call.

"What's up?" He immediately returns my call.

"I was thinking about you."

"I am surprised; you never call this late."

"I have a lot of time on my hands. The husband and the children are gone."

"When are they coming back?"

"They are not." I pause to allow those words to sink in. "They are not coming back. He took the children to Ghana."

"Oh" The elation in his voice is annoying. "When did this happen?"

"A few weeks ago."

"And you are just now telling me?" Trevor sometimes fantasizes about me leaving Osei and he leaving his wife and making our relationship official, but that is not part of my plan. He can help me get to the State bench, but that is as far as he can take me. My goals exceed the State bench. If all goes as planned, I will one day be the youngest African American woman to get appointed to the Federal bench. Trevor is a good source of information and a good confidant, but I am not looking for ex-wife drama or kids having to visit every other weekend that would come along with him. I am sure his wife is a nice person, but basic women do basic things. Her complete identity is based on Trevor's accomplishments and his family name. She would most likely lose her mind if he left.

"I have been busy working on my case, but I could use some company. Can you get away?" He can do whatever he wants. She knows her position. Mrs. Bordeaux does not question Trevor. She has very little power in their relationship. I am sure it was what Trevor was trained to think he wanted. Trevor is very smart, and most smart people need stimulation. She has been a stay at home mom since their wedding. Talking about the kids, PTA meetings and the wives club meeting can only fill up so many minutes of conversation.

"What time will you be at the apartment?"

"Come to my house."

"What?" He sounds like a virgin boy getting prepared to get laid for the first time. "I am on my way."

I sit on the bed and remember the international phone number in my purse. I remove it and dial the number while I wait for Trevor.

"Ay-Yee-Kooh" His voice sounds different. His accent is thicker.

"Osei" He does not speak. "I miss the kids."

"You miss the kids? Is that even possible?" He pauses. "You never noticed when they were around. That fucking job is your life. You need mental help."

"I will not apologize for having goals and for being smart enough to pursue them." I pause. "Once you get out of your emotions, hopefully we can figure out a way to co-parent."

"You still don't get it! You are not the only smart person who pursues their goals in the world!" He sucks his teeth, an annoying thing Ghanaians do. It is like saying "Fuck you" without saying the words. "You have no true interest in the children, and we both know it."

"I did not call to argue!" We are both silent. I close my eyes and try to envision his expression. His brows are most likely raised in an arch. He is most likely shaking his head from side to side. "I would like to see the kids."

"They miss you. OJ cries for you all of the time." His tone is softer. "Most days, he is inconsolable. Believe it or not, Che' also cries for you. When do you want to visit the children?" He emphasizes children. "My security is in place."

"Well, I am almost done preparing my case for the grand jury and…" I continue conversing for several minutes before I realize he has ended the call.

My cell rings, initially I think it is Osei, but it is Trevor. He is at the security gate. I press the button to allow him to enter and run downstairs to open the garage so he can park inside.

He exits the car carrying my favorite bottle of wine. His smile is wide and lustful.

"I can't believe you are letting me come to your house."

"I live alone now. Why not?" He enters the kitchen and places the bottle of wine on the counter. My cell phone rings as I close the door to the garage.

"Ms. Williams?"

"This is she."

"This is Stacy Lincoln. I am ready to make that deal."

Chapter 23

Ansleigh was released from the hospital to her parents. Mr. and Mrs. Stewart denied my request and refused to allow Ansleigh to testify. My attempt to use judicial persuasion by threatening to follow through with pending solicitation charges against Ansleigh was met with strong laughter from Mrs. Stewart. She stood in front of me, placed a call directly to the governor's personal cell phone, and shoved the phone in my face. The governor's voice caught me off guard. I trade a few niceties and assure the governor the criminal case with Ansleigh in Georgia would be closed and Social Services in Charlotte would follow up with Ansleigh in her home with her parents. I was extremely disappointed the Stewarts could not see the value of Ansleigh's testimony. Ms. Lincoln's call was a gift from the heavens.

I am running on empty. My plan was to stay in bed and catch up on my sleep. My rendezvous with Trevor did not help. Trevor and I were up half of the night. After hours of freaky sex, something I rarely had with Osei, I am tired and want to sleep. Sleep will have to wait. After I present my evidence and get the indictment against Jefferson, I will have plenty of time to sleep.

Stacy Lincoln and I agree to meet at the Coffee House at 8:00 AM. I arrive at 7:30, thirty minutes early. I am seated in a booth in the back of the restaurant when she arrives. She is dressed in urban gear, and instead of her own car, she travels by taxi. Dark shades hang off her nose, exposing half of her eyes. Her long ponytail hangs out of the back of a baseball cap. She looks much younger and almost innocent without makeup. I almost pity her, but I remind myself she is responsible for or at least a co-conspirator in inflicting unimaginable pain on an innocent child.

"What do you have?" I get straight to the point.

"Everything" She takes a sip from the cup of coffee she

brought with her. "I have names of his co-conspirators, financial records of political officials on his payroll, and this." She slides a flash drive across the table.

"What is this?"

"My assurance that I am not prosecuted and you win your case against Jefferson Thomas." Her smile is coy and nervous. She raises her sunglasses and secures them on the top of her head. A dark ring around her eyes stands out against her flawless skin. She removes a laptop and another flash drive from her bag. She places the flash drive in one of the USB ports. The video is grainy, but there is no mistake the person on the video is D.A. Leslie. He slowly walks down the narrow hall to Stoney's private bathroom. He constantly turns his head, looking backwards, as if he is looking for someone. He opens the bathroom door. He does not close it shut but leaves a slight opening, then walks to the bathroom sink. He stands in front of the mirror and checks his profile. He removes his jacket and hangs it on the hook on the back of the bathroom door. He leans his back against the bathroom sink, folds his arms across his chest, crosses one ankle over the other and stands so still, he almost looks lifeless.

A few minutes later, a thin young male creeps down the hallway to Stoney's private bathroom, opens the door, and locks the door behind him. I inhale deeply to catch my breath. I am speechless when District Attorney Leslie unzips his pants, pushes them down to his ankles and exposes his erect penis. The thin male stands in front of D.A. Leslie, drops to his knees, and places D.A. Leslie's penis in his mouth. "Jefferson will try to make a deal with the D.A. and bribe him into forcing you to drop the case. He will throw me under the bus and name me as the mastermind behind his operation."

"The District Attorney having a sexual encounter with a man is not a big deal! This is Atlanta; no one cares about sexual orientation."

"Take a closer look. This 'man' is a 14-year-old boy."

"How do you know this?"

"He is in foster care. Jefferson arranged for him to meet the D.A. at Stoney's."

"Are you serious?"

"Yes, very serious. You, and maybe a few others, are probably the only people in the county Jefferson does not own." She removes a file from her oversized bag. "This is a list of names and key players on his payroll." I take the list from her trembling hands and scan it.

"Mary Beckham, the social worker?" I am surprised.

"Where do you think Jefferson got the boy? Honestly, it surprises me that no one notices the number of runaways on her caseload. She was my social worker when I lived in Las Vegas. How do you think I got in the game?" She quickly changes the subject. "He no longer trusts me. He is going to kill me. My days are numbered. I need a good deal."

"We can place you in a safe house. No one on this level will know your location. I will not even know." She opens her bag and removes a pile of papers. She bows her head and places her hands together as if she is in prayer. "You have to be honest and disclose everything. If it is found that you have lied about one thing, the deal is off."

"I know." She opens her purse and removes another jump drive. "Everything you need is on this. He makes monthly deposits in the bank accounts of some very important people." She place the jump drive in an empty USB port and opens an Excel spreadsheet. I glance at the worksheet and notice the name of the CEO of Morgan Airport with a monthly entry of five thousand dollars next to his name.

"Tavis Bailey of Morgan Airport?" I am shocked. Tavis Bailey is not only the CEO of the airport, but a very popular minister.

"Tavis allows Jefferson to travel back and forth to the Caribbean without checking his baggage. This is how he gets large sums of cash out of the country."

"Ms. Lincoln, you have got yourself a deal. Once we have him in custody, a team will escort you to your home so you can gather a few things." She sits still, as if she is in a daze. I remove the flash drive from her hand.

"I don't need a safe house. Trust, I would not be safe in one anyway. I have made plans to leave the country. I have another favor. My friend is from Russia. I know he is on the radar. We both want safe passage out of the country."

"You are asking for a lot; I will only agree to a deal for you."

"I have more." She takes a deep breath. "The Philanthropist Awards will be held at the Convention Center in a couple of days."

"Yes" I have heard about the awards ceremony for years.

"It has been getting a lot of press the last couple of days. Jefferson will supply entertainment."

"Entertainment?"

"There will be several celebrities, moguls, and diplomats attending. Many have requested his services."

"Services?"

"I am sure you know, the restaurants, barber and beauty shops are all front businesses. His real money comes from his companionship services. He owns an encrypted website with over three thousand members. The annual fee for membership is fifty grand per year."

"You have got to be kidding me!" I shake my head in disbelief.

"It is a very sophisticated interactive website that arranges dates for some of the wealthiest people on the planet with our in-house supply of companions." She types in the website address, enters a user ID, password and places her index finger over a small reader attached to a USB port to show me. "The clients choose their companions, wire the fee to his Caymans account, and a date is confirmed with the available companion of their choice."

"Impressive, but dating sites are not illegal."

"You are right. Dating sites are perfectly legal with consenting adults. Many of our companions are not adults, and most are illegals who cannot consent." Her braggadocios smile irritates me. "Some wealthy people have unusual appetites, and anonymity is guaranteed with our services." She passes me a spreadsheet that contains the list of clients and companions attending the awards ceremony. "Is this enough to get a deal for my friend?" I do not respond. I want more. She passes a folder that contains copies of passports. "These are the girls that will be at the event. We purchased these companions along with the passports a couple of months ago." I scan through the passports and see one for Ansleigh, only her name is still Ashleigh. She notices my interest.

"The Chinese man that was detained with her wants to purchase her and take her out of the country. Jefferson thought he would have her back and planned on selling her to Mr. Ye at the event."

"You have a deal for you and your friend!" We both stand.

"Thank you." She wipes the tears away from her eyes. "This will be my opportunity to make a fresh start. Thank you so much."

I almost want to console her, but I remember she is part of a team that traffics human flesh.

"I will contact you in a day or so." We shake hands and leave the coffee shop. I get in my car; she walks in the opposite direction.

I immediately call Detective Davis. He picks up on the first ring.

"You will not believe who I just left." I do not allow him time to respond. "Stacy Lincoln. You were right; she is ready to make a deal. Call your detectives off."

"Damn, that's good news, but do you ever sleep, Ms. Williams?" He laughs.

"Winners do what we have to do. Sleep comes when the job is done, but that is not all. I have something in my possession that you have to see."

"I am tired! Unlike you, I am not half-vampire." I hear the sultry voice of a female in the background.

"Let's meet later this evening."

We agree to meet at his office in a couple of hours. I am extremely exhausted and running on adrenaline. I cannot sit still. I run errands to kill time and then drive to Davis' office. He is there when I arrive. I enter his office and take the liberty of closing his door.

"What do you have that I will not believe?" He places his feet on his desk and leans back in his chair with his hands folded together behind his head. I turn on my laptop and place the jump drive inside of the USB port. "So Stoney films people in his private bathroom?"

"That is against the law, but check this out." I fast forward the video to start at the thin male entering the bathroom. Davis takes his feet off the desk and moves closer.

"You got to be fucking kidding me. Isn't he married? According to the rumor mill, he is having an affair with one of your female colleagues!"

"It is not a rumor. He is having an affair with Nakia Winbush."

"That looks like a kid!" Davis turns his head away.

"It is, and guess who his social worker is?"

"Mary Beckham?"

"None other, this is incredible." I remove the spreadsheet from the folder that contains names of public officials on

Jefferson's payroll, along with their monthly payments and bank account numbers. He goes through the spreadsheet in detail.

"You are something, Ms. Williams. I will get the arrest warrants."

"We have to work fast. Ms. Lincoln spoke of an international gathering being held at the Convention Center next week. Mr. Thomas' services were contracted for entertainment. We can get a lot of the international players, and with this evidence, diplomatic immunity will not apply." I throw my hair over my shoulders. "This could be big for both of our careers."

"I will leave the politics to you. My mission is getting the bad guys. That is what I do." He shakes his head as if he is judging me. "I will contact McAfee. This time no one will get away. I will have everything in place on my end tonight."

"One more thing" I remove Ansleigh's fake passport from the envelope and pass it to him. "He planned to sell her at the event to the Chinese man you briefly detained when she was arrested."

"You have got to be kidding me!" He stands. "Let's do this, Mrs. Williams! We have a lot to do in a very short period of time."

We leave his office together but go separate ways. I stop by my office to get my list of media contacts. I pass the District Attorney's office. His lights are off. I open the door and turn on the lights. I sit in his oversized, leather chair and prop my feet on the desk. If I smoked cigars, I would light one now and bask in my moment.

I use D.A. Leslie's office phone to call my hairdresser on her personal cell phone and make an impromptu appointment for tomorrow. I need a fresh look. In a few days, I will receive my just reward for hard work and sacrifice.

My daydream is interrupted when my cell phone rings. I move my feet off D.A. Leslie's desk and grab my phone. D.A. Leslie's number is displayed on the Caller ID.

"Ayanna Williams." Although this is my personal cell phone, I answer his call professionally.

"Yes, Ms. Williams." His speech is slurred and faster than normal. "I need to meet with you right away."

"Of course, sir. Can you tell me what this is about?"

"I will speak to you in person. Can you meet me in my office in thirty minutes?"

"I will be there." We never have private meetings. We meet

as a group to discuss cases. I turn off his light, close his door, quickly walk to my office, and wait for his arrival. He must have been in close proximity, because he arrives in less than ten minutes after the call. I give him a few minutes to get settled before our meeting. I grab my bag, turn off my lights, and lock my door. I stand outside of his office.. His door is slightly open. I knock on the door frame lightly. He stands in front of his desk and uses hand gestures to invite me in.

"Thanks for meeting with me on such short notice." He removes a tissue from the box beside his phone and wipes his desk in the spot where I positioned my feet earlier. He doesn't look like himself. His skin is puffy, and it appears as if he has not shaven in days. A somber look covers his face. "I have some bad news." He walks to the front of his desk, stands in front of me, and leans on his desk. "You have to drop the case against Mr. Thomas. We are getting a lot of pressure from people in high places. It turns out that he was simply giving the young girl a ride. They never met prior to the day they were detained."

"Are you serious?"

"Unfortunately, I am." He adjusts his necktie. "You have done a great job putting this case together; all is not lost. Ms. Stacy Lincoln, a woman this office has had contact with in a prior prosecution, is the mastermind of an elaborate human trafficking operation. Mr. Thomas recently learned of her exploits. When Mr. Thomas became aware of her illegal exploits, he fired her. He is willing to testify against her." He walks to the back of the desk, removes an envelope from his desk drawer, and passes it to me. "All of the information you need to prosecute the case against Stacy Lincoln is in this file." I take the file from his hand, briefly flip through it, and place it on his desk in front of him. "Are you going to open it?"

"No, I don't need to." I stare in his bloodshot eyes pupil to pupil.

"You are taking this better than I expected." He smiles.

"I am not dropping the case against Mr. Thomas, and Ms. Lincoln will get full immunity from prosecution." I remove my laptop from my briefcase. I dig deep in my pocket and remove the flash drive with the video of the underage male performing fellatio on D.A. Leslie, and place it in my laptop. He trembles; a small stream of perspiration drips from his face to his neck and rolls down to his chest. He uses the back of his hand to wipe the damp spots from his face then turns his head away from the laptop. "Don't worry, you can keep that. There is one more copy. It will remain in a safe place until after the trial. Jefferson cannot bribe you any longer."

"Are you sure?" He begins to cry like a baby. "I am so sorry. I was simply experimenting. I am not gay, and I had no idea the young man was underage."

"No need to be sorry." I stand and grab my bags. "After Mr. Thomas is arrested, there will be a press conference. You will announce your resignation."

"What?" His bloodshot eyes open so wide, it appears as if his eyeballs are protruding from the sockets. He quickly stands. "I will not step down until my term is over!" He uses the back of his hand to wipe mucous away from his nose. I almost feel sorry for him, but this is a big boy game, and we all play to win.

"You will step down. You will be taking a job in the mayor's office for the next eighteen months until you are at retirement age. Your pension will not be affected. Please wear black to the news conference, so we can match; we need to make this appear to be a mutual decision. This office cannot deal with any more scandals. I have taken the liberty of typing your resignation letter." I remove it from my bag and pass it to him. He is reluctant but takes it. "Sign it, and give it to the governor first thing in the morning. He is expecting it, so he can announce me as your replacement at the press conference." I leave the District Attorney's office and allow D.A. Leslie to enjoy his last days as the District Attorney.

Chapter 24

Stretch limousines line up bumper to bumper in the Convention Center's circular drive. Men and women dressed in top designer gigs exit luxury, chauffeured vehicles. Flashing lights from high speed cameras light up the sky like a fourth of July celebration. Journalists and camera crews from news affiliates all over the world fight through the maze of onlookers, vying to get snapshots of celebrities, politicians, and local and international dignitaries as they walk onto imported, plush red carpet.

The richest global capitalists in the world converge in Atlanta every year for this international event. This is the opportunity for the normally recluse high money moguls to shine and take their place in the limelight. Every year, they give billions of dollars to a variety of charities. The ceremony includes emotional speeches from recipients of their generosity who were saved from tragic life-altering events such as war and famine. One lucky charity is awarded five million dollars at the ceremony to support their mission. After the ceremony, the philanthropists host a party so extravagant, the money they spend can eradicate hunger on the entire planet.

"Hey brother, you got any change? I am trying to catch the bus. I am a little short." I take in all of the glitz and glamour, oblivious to the antics of the homeless man sitting next to me on the bus stop bench. He makes me uncomfortable; his sudden movements and conversations with himself remind me of Mary Francis Thomas. I continue to ignore him as he alternates scratching his arm and head incessantly. This is everything and more Stacy and Gorbachev said it would be. "I need sixty-five cents." He puts dirty hands inside of his trouser pockets and pulls out dirty coins mixed with small balls of lint. "That's all I need." The spittle caked in the corner of his mouth disgusts me.

I reach into my pocket, remove my money clip, slide a fifty-dollar bill from the stack, and pass it to the filthy man that smells like two weeks of funk. Initially he is hesitant to take it, but then grabs it out of my hand, removes his tattered jacket and runs across the street to the liquor store on the corner, leaving a grocery cart filled with useless junk. I walk away from the bench and stand in front of the telephone booth on the corner close to the Convention Center. I remove the handset and place quarters in the coin slot as if I am making a call. A voice in my head whispers, "*You should not be here.*" I am the brain child of this business, but I stay behind the scene. Stacy is the face of this business; I am here because I no longer trust her. I should leave, but there is something about Stacy being here with the Russian that does not sit well with me.

I know I should listen to my inner voice. I cannot afford another mishap. Ayanna has been lying in wait, praying for me to slip. I have fallen deep into her snare and find myself once again on her radar. I hate to admit it, but I admire her and wish we were on the same team. She is determined to make a name for herself. She has made the right connections. The top brass at City Hall has her next in line for District Attorney. I have tried on many occasions to persuade them to look at her rival, Nakia Winbush, as the better replacement, but she does not have Ayanna's panache or networking skills. Nakia thinks too small; she is too busy slobbing on D.A. Leslie's balls. Unlike Nakia, Ayanna thinks big. She will easily surpass city hall's expectations. Her connections are in high places. She knows how to play the political game, and she is winning.

I thought I could beat Ayanna at her own game. I planned my strategy after seeing her at Stoney's with a top State official. Stoney's is the gossip hole for the political brass. Most of the clientele are local and state politicians. Every once in a while Stoney's gets an important visitor or two from the State Office or Washington, D.C., for photo shoots as favors to the locals. However, his clientele is mostly local and State politicians. When the State Attorney General started becoming a regular, everyone was shocked except for Stoney. All of the local big wigs gathered around like vultures, salivating to get in his circle for the possibility of an endorsement for their next political move.

"You are moving up, Stoney. The State Attorney General is actually visiting this dump regularly. This is the third time I have seen him here."

"He comes around once or twice a month or so and always has drinks with that new Assistant DA. You know the one who had you by the balls a few years back." He laughs.

"You mean Ms. Goody Two Shoes is cheating on Kunta?" We both laugh.

"I did not say that." He laughs. "But hell, everyone in here is cheating on someone. They are all politicians, so who knows." My mind goes from zero to a hundred in two seconds. Ayanna is one of a handful of people in City Hall without a price. I have paid more politicians for favors than I care to count. I tried to buy her allegiance, but she would never take the bait.

Instead of forming a mutually beneficial alliance with me, as many in the political circle have done, she found it more lucrative for her career to become an opposing force. It is not personal with her. It is all business; I am well-connected and a big catch. Bringing me down will quickly further Ayanna's career. I thought I would make her feel some of the pain she has inflicted on me by giving her husband the pictures of her rendezvous with Trevor Bordeaux. I was wrong. She has not missed a beat.

I put myself in this situation. I can blame no one but myself and greed. I should have made Mr. Ye wait, but the lure of international business and the money to be made, in my mind, was too good to risk losing. I was wrong, and now I find myself once again in the grip of a formidable nemesis.

I thought I had her. She and the Attorney General get together at his private condo every third Wednesday of the month. For Ayanna, it is business. It is obvious the attorney general is getting caught in his feelings, as he makes no attempt at being inconspicuous. He did not seem to care who noticed them making out like two desperate lovers in the garage at his secret Buckhead Condominium.

One would never believe Mrs. Prissy had some freak in her. She has moves better than a porn star. In one of the videos, he lifts her, places her on the hood of her car, and drops to his knees. Her head is thrown back. Her hands hold his head in position as she thrusts hard against his tongue. After she makes a few fuck faces, he stands, picks her up, throws her legs over his shoulders and places his face between her thighs. She makes a few more fuck faces, he squats and he places her back on the ground. They walk hand in hand out of the parking deck, stopping periodically to engage in passionate kissing before finally getting on the elevator to enter the building.

"*Leave!*" The voice has returned; the volume is now loud and demanding. "*Leave!*" I stand ready to leave when I notice the line of luxury cars gets shorter, as most of the VIP guests have entered the convention center. I tighten my eyes to focus better and finally spot Stacy and Gorbachev exit a black Cadillac Escalade Stretch Limousine. They look like a Hollywood couple stepping onto the red carpet. She smiles and waves to the cameras like a seasoned celebrity.

It is obvious she has shared information with Gorbachev that should have remained confidential. One can tell when one is the subject of background conversation by the vibe when in the presence of people that are engaging in those background conversations. I am yards away from them, but I can feel his vibe, and I do not like it. We met at Peaches Restaurant in Buckhead earlier today to work out the last details of our investment. He could not keep his eyes off Stacy. When she went to the ladies room, he eyed her from the time she left until she returned to the table, a sign she has spread her legs, and a sign he likes the way she gets down. Gorbachev, like many Caucasian men, disrespects my position. During our meeting, he addressed all business conversation to Stacy, as if she is running the show.

I don't blame Gorbachev. Stacy is beautiful, and tonight she is exceptionally stunning. She spent three grand on the evening gown she is wearing. She is a triple "A" act. She blends in with the diplomats and global elite as if she is one of them, yet she has street smarts and a 'hood edge that is sexy as hell to those of us who are members of the underground economy. A fury I cannot describe explodes inside of me when I see her stand close to Gorbachev, smiling for the cameras and whispering in his ear. She is making side deals. I am insulted she believes she can tango with me. She is smart, but I am the king of smart. It almost looks as if Stacy and Gorbachev are having an intimate exchange. The Adonis sized Russian is standing next to her with his hands resting at the bottom of her spine, almost touching her ass. It is my ego. I remind myself Stacy is not my woman; she is my chick. I liked having her on my team, but she has become a threat. She crossed boundaries by following me to Lailah's, and she has added an uninvited player to our enterprise. A woman can't serve two dicks; eventually, she will cross one.

Stacy is a survivalist and will take the arm of the highest bidder. She is always on the prowl for an upgrade. If I would have put the bait out when she was with Earl, she would have bitten. I totally understand why Earl was in love with her and took the fall for her, but she was not worth it. As soon as he went to prison, she moved on with no remorse. She may have put a couple of bucks on his books, but she was in my bed in a matter of weeks. Likewise, I know whatever bait Gorbachev has thrown, she has bitten.

Stacy and I are a lot alike. We come from nothing. We grew up with nothing, but there was something I don't know what it is or where it comes from, but there is something innate that told us that nothing was not good enough. We were going to get something by any means necessary.

Her official title in my enterprise is Event Planner. She arranges hair shows for my barber and beauty shops. Our real money maker is sex, and it is a lucrative business. High paying clients have every taste imaginable. Professional, powerful, and very wealthy women, some married to men, but occasionally want to discreetly enjoy the company of a woman. Some very normal couples want to enjoy a discreet threesome but hold high society positions, and discretion is a must. Many dignitaries, from very conservative countries, use our services for discreet, wild sexual fulfillment that is forbidden or looked down upon in their home countries.

Some of our clients are on the Rent A Bitch plan. Business men, some gay and some straight, who may not have wives or significant others, sometimes need arm candy to accompany them on extended business trips, vacations and sometimes month long excursions. All of the members are wealthy millionaires and billionaires of conglomerates that own international businesses or are Chief Executive Officers of international corporations. Others are diplomats willing to pay big bucks for a discrete good time. If all goes as planned, when the night is over, I will be one quarter of a million dollars richer and my feet deeply planted in the international trade.

I reach in my pocket for my cell phone and see Ms. Mamie's name and number on the Caller ID. I do not feel like dealing with anything from the Chicken Shack. I should have informed her and the staff that I was selling it. The new Korean owners agree to keep the current staff, so all is well. The phone rings again. I reluctantly pressed the "answer" button then immediately end the call when flashing lights on top of unmarked black cars abruptly grab my attention. There is an uncanny silence; it feels as if the world has stopped and stood still. My heartbeat accelerates. A sharp pain grasps my shoulder and travels down my arm. My chest is so tight, it feels as if it will implode. My instincts say run, but I manage to keep my composure. I walk back to the bench at the bus stop. Just as I was beginning to sit, S.W.A.T., city police, and the Federal Police cars surround the Convention Center at lightning speed. I am over one hundred yards away, but I can hear police commands from bullhorns, frightening screams, and the hustle and bustle of bystanders trying to get out of the way. Black shadows run on top of the roof. Red dots from their sniper guns look like a laser show as they move and take their positions.

Several rounds of gunshots echo in the air, followed by total silence. I grab the dingy, worn hooded jacket the drunk left behind, throw it on, grab his cart, and walk closer to the Convention Center. A police van converges on the sidewalk. Screams of "*diplomatic immunity*" ring loud as the officers escort tuxedo clad men and women adorning the finest evening wear outside where they form a line next to a parked police van. I push the cart behind a crowd of spectators. Minutes later, a line of scantily dressed young women exit the building and stand next to what appears to be a tour bus. I spot one of Gorbachev's sidekicks exit shackled to a dark skinned Middle Eastern male with a red and white head wrap. Their pleas for "*diplomatic immunity*" are unheard as they are thrown into the back of a city police van. I wait for several minutes to see if Stacy and Gorbachev are detained. Another drove of police cars converges outside of the Convention Center, followed by more news media. I leave the crowd and push the cart down a dark street behind the train station. I quickly remove the jacket, ditch the cart, and walk to the train station to get my vehicle. I drive back to my house and wait for a call from Stacy. The call never comes.

I grab the remote from the night stand and press the green button. All regularly scheduled programs have been interrupted. The raid occupies all local and cable news channels as footage of my Jamaican, Turkish and Cayman colleagues in handcuffs flash across the television screen. I rush to the closet, grab a duffle bag, and throw some clothes in it. I sprint to the bathroom and open my safe. I grab cash and the envelope with my flash drive. The envelope feels light. I open it. It is empty. "Stacy!" I am so dizzy, I can barely stand. I quickly gather my composure and leave the bathroom. I pass the television in my bedroom and see news crews following behind armored police trucks crashing through the security gate of my subdivision. I drop the duffle bag, turn off the lights, and run to the back door.

Chapter 25

He sits in a beat up, black, faux leather swivel chair. Everyone involved in the case is gathered around conversing, sipping champagne, and enjoying Chinese takeout and pizza. There are over fifteen monitors displaying news coverage of domestic and international law enforcement executing warrants and making arrests. Several news affiliates are positioned at the Convention Center. Bright lights and flashing cameras are reminiscent of a Christmas celebration. A caravan of luxury limousines occupies three blocks and a parking lot along the side of the Convention Center.

The center's entrances and exits are blocked and guarded by heavily armed law enforcement; no one can enter or exit without presenting identification. A long line wraps around the building as law enforcement officers use official photos to identify and separate Jefferson's clients from legitimate attendees. Those detained pass news reporters using their jackets to cover their faces as they form a line and stand outside of police vans. Another line is formed for young women in revealing high end designer clothing. They stand outside of a rented tour bus as Federal Police match their faces with the passports Ms. Lincoln provided.

I stand in front of the monitor that displays my local media contact outside of Mary's house as police kick in her door. Moments later, Mary emerges in her nightgown with her hands cuffed behind her back. She is led to an awaiting police car parked in front of her house. My contact places the microphone in Mary's face and asks for a statement.

"Bitch! Get that shit out of my face!" Mary's eyes are bloodshot red. Her hair is in disarray, and she looks ten years older without makeup. Another crew of cameras is stationed outside of the CEO of the airport waiting for the police to arrest him. There will be arrests all over the United States, Jamaica and Turkey, but I am eager to see Jefferson Thomas with his hands tightly cuffed behind his back.

It has been over two hours since the raid began. Finally, the largest screen in the room displays a caravan of three armored police tanks positioned in front of the gate to his subdivision. A news helicopter hovers over his home. An officer exits the first vehicle and approaches the gates. He attaches a device at the opening, presses a few buttons, and sprints back to his vehicle; the gate does not open. After several attempts, he gets back into the tank, moves forward and forces the gates open with the armored tank. The tanks followed by several marked and unmarked police cars, enter the subdivision and stop in front of Jefferson's house. A line of detectives in bulletproof vests kick in the door and enter. Five minutes later, Jefferson emerges in handcuffs. Laughter and applause fill the room.

"Good job, Ms. Williams!"

"Good job, Detective Davis!"

"We should celebrate!" He passes me a flute filled with champagne.

"I am finally tired, Detective." I take a sip of the champagne and set it aside. "I am truly not a vampire. It is time for me to get some sleep." I grab my bag and leave Detective Davis to celebrate with his colleagues.

Epilogue

The prison attire is two sizes too small for his above average height and muscular build. His thick, ashy ankles are shackled together. His large hands are bound with tight metal cuffs. He takes baby steps to the lopsided metal chair stationed in front of the thick, unbreakable glass partition. I sit with my legs crossed on the other side of the partition as the guard removes the cuffs from his wrists. We pick up the phone at the same time.

"This is not over!" I am not surprised; he has not accepted his defeat.

"I think it is. I think you will be going to prison for a very long time." The smile on my face is authentic and confident.

"This was all about you. You could care less about crime and putting criminals away! Bringing me down guarantees your position as the next District Attorney!"

"That is correct, Mr. Thomas." I smile. "It is all about me."

"When I am done with you, you will hate the day you ever tried to tango with me. I am looking forward to the trial, bitch!" He slams the handset so hard in the cradle, the phone detaches from the wall. I stand with my hands folded across my chest as he turns and stumbles out of the visitation room. He steps in front of the steel door. His stare makes me uneasy. I quickly turn away. I leave the jail and join the former District Attorney in front of City Hall for our press conference.

The flash from the cameras is bright and almost blinding. The water fountain in front of the county justice building is clean and free of debris. New county and state flags wave back in forth with the cool breeze from the wind. This is my time. This is my moment. I am at my best standing on the podium next to the Governor, former District Attorney, the mayor, and the federal police as we answer questions from the news reporters. The former

District Attorney is a true thespian. His acting skills are impeccable. The smile on his face as we stand before the reporters, thanking me and Detective Davis for our work on this case, appears genuine.

Our photo shoot with the press is perfect. We stand side by side with wide smiles plastered all over our faces, shaking hands. The applause is almost overwhelming when the Governor announces me as the new District Attorney, replacing the great and retiring D.A. Leslie.

Also By

Regina Neequaye

"360 Degrees"

Zero Degrees

I heard a loud, hollow pop followed by an eerie, echoing silence. I slowly walked into my parents' room. Momma was a folded heap in daddy's arms. Blood oozed out of her head and slowly dripped down daddy's bare shoulders. Daddy sat still; his mouth was wide open, but there was no sound. Tears rolled down his face one at a time. The house was so silent the quietness was more frightening than the morbid vision of my momma and daddy. I was numb and in shock. I did not feel anything. I was twelve years old; I knew I was supposed to be scared, crying or something, but I was numb. I left my parents' room and walked down the hall. Khalid stood still in the threshold of his bedroom door. His eyes spoke what his mouth could not. His eyes were blank, looking at me but not actually seeing me. He knew something happened that would end our lives the way we knew it. I ordered him back inside of his room. He walked backwards into his room, climbed onto the bed, and curled his body tight in a fetal position. I tip toed to his room and closed his door. I walked back into my parents' room and picked up the phone.

"911 operator."

"My daddy hurt my momma!"

"How did he hurt her?"

"I think he shot her with a gun."

"Honey stay on the line! Help is on the way!" The operator sounded frantic. I thought she was supposed to remain calm and reassure me. Instead, I felt the need to reassure her.

"Does your daddy still have the gun?"

"I don't know."

"Is your mom...?" I placed the phone down and squeezed my head between daddy and momma. The room was so quiet I could actually hear our hearts beat.

Blue lights flashed through the curtains. A faint knock echoed through the house. I could not move. I wanted to answer the door, but I sat still. I could not move. A loud bang reverberated through the house. I heard an army of footsteps coming down the hall towards momma and daddy's bedroom. There was what seemed like a thousand policemen in full riot gear standing in my parents' room.

"Turn the girl loose!"

"Let the girl go!"

Daddy did not move. He appeared oblivious to the small army occupying the bedroom. He continued to hold momma and sat quietly with tears rolling down his face. The police had guns drawn and pointed at daddy's head. I heard the click of a gun and squeezed out of daddy's arms. An officer abruptly grabbed me and rushed out of the room; the police officer did not wear the standard blue uniform. He was dressed in faded jeans and a sweaty, dingy, gray t-shirt. I felt cold, hard metal on my leg, as he held me over his shoulder and ran with me out of the house.

Everything went fast. The ambulance's spinning red lights made me dizzy. I thought they were coming to take my mother to the hospital and make her better. I did not realize she was actually gone until I saw her neatly wrapped in a thick, black, plastic bag. I remember thinking; I wish they would open the bag, so she can breathe. I wanted to scream. I wanted to shout to momma here I am please come and get me; I'm over here. I wanted to cling to her and feel her soft chest close to my face one more time. I wanted to feel her warm arms tightly wrapped around me. I wanted to see her beautiful smile; her smile was always reassuring. I knew this was not going to happen ever again.

I don't know how long I stood outside before the police officer brought Khalid to me. The sullen look on his face made me cry. It was a sadness I have never seen on anyone's face before. A deep, penetrating melancholy pierced my heart. I have never felt sadness like this before. Khalid and I were both crying. He ran to me. He jumped into my arms, tightly wrapped his arms and legs around me, and buried his face in my neck. He was almost as tall as me; I cannot believe my skinny legs were strong enough to hold the both of us. We stood outside for what seemed like an eternity while the policemen were talking to one another, going back and forth, inside, outside, and around the house before they took us to the police station.

Grandma was at the police station when we arrived. She sat in a dingy room; the musty smell of mold permeated the air. The walls were made of cinder blocks covered with chipping, gray paint that appeared centuries old. The room was sparsely decorated with a light that hung down from the ceiling over an old, wooden table. Grandma seemed small sitting at the table. Her eyes were puffy. It seemed as if her whole body was shaking. Khalid immediately ran to her. I stood motionless, unable to move. Grandma came over and gently touched my shoulders. She attempted to pull my rigid body close to her. I put up as much resistance as my thin body would allow.

"Don't worry baby; Grandma will take care of you. I am going to take good care of you." I could not respond. It was as if I were dreaming; the kind where at the end of the dream you figure out it's not real, but you still can't wake up and leave the dream. This was not a dream. I would not wake up and run to my momma and daddy's room and snuggle close between them where even if they didn't wake up, feeling their warm bodies made everything okay.

Grandma's house was no longer the same to me. My relationship to this house had changed; it was a place I used to come and visit but then return to my own house. Now I would have to live here. I was no longer going home to my own house to my own things to my momma and daddy.

I was lying in the bed tired but trying not to fall asleep. For the first time in my life, I was afraid. I was afraid, but I did not know what I was afraid of; it was not an object but a feeling I could not touch. I could not describe this feeling. I could not call it a name. There were no words to describe a feeling so sad. This was the first time in my life when I woke up, I would not know what the day would bring.

Momma was ritual. I knew every morning she would come into my room and gently touch me. Though I would already be awake, I would not get out of the bed until she came into my room. She would either make oatmeal or French toast on weekdays, or she would make a three course breakfast on the weekend, but I no longer knew what would happen. I was fearful, and I was hurting. It was an abysmal hurt that cut deep, a continual pain without relief.

The sunlight peeping through the blinds woke me. I scanned the bedroom looking for something familiar when I saw the blood stains on my shorts. The rose colored splatter brought me back to the present. I pushed my head back and deep into the pillow and cried. I cried because my momma would never hold me again. She would never part my hair straight when I cannot see the back of my head. She would never come in the bathroom and wash the part of my back I cannot reach. She would not see me grow into a woman and see herself in me. I cried because I wanted to be in my own home. I wanted to be in my own room in my own bed. Grandma came into the room. She attempted to touch me. I did not want her to touch me. She tried to hold me. I wiggled out of her arms and ran out of the room.

"Thandisha! Thandisha!" She looked helpless, but I was too absorbed in my own pain to feel her pain. I ran down the hall crying and screaming, "I want my momma." Grandma looked broken. She looked tired and worn. She came closer to me with her arms spread and her hands open in a come to Jesus stand like Reverend Deal does on Sunday at the end of church service when he invites the congregation to come to Jesus.

"No! Don't touch me Grandma! Don't touch me! I want my momma!" I did not want to feel anyone's hands but momma's. I did not want to feel old, hard, wrinkled hands. I wanted momma's soft, perfect, and loving hands to touch me.

"Thandie, baby, your momma is with God. God has called her home." She slowly walked towards me. I walked backwards and away from her moving my head from side to side in disbelief at Grandma's words.

"I hate God! Why didn't he call you home? You are old and tired! I want my momma! Where's my daddy? I'm calling him to come and get me out this house!" She walked towards me, a stream of tears flowed from her eyes and down her bronze cheeks. Her hands were together as if she was praying. I walked towards the phone screaming so loud I could hardly talk. My throat and neck were hurting. I picked up the phone and began to dial. I hoped daddy would answer the phone, come to grandma's house and take me back to my own house with my own things. I wanted to be in my own bed.

"Thandie, remember last night Thandie!" She screamed while snatching the phone away from me. "Your daddy killed your mother! He killed my daughter!" Her words were piercing; they cut deep. They took away my final hope last night was a dream and That Day really didn't happen.

"You're a goddamned liar Grandma! Don't say that to me! Don't you dare say that to me! Don't you lie to me Grandma! You're a liar! Where is my daddy?" She slapped me so hard my neck popped. Her face was tight. It seemed as if every blood vessel in her face was at the surface of her skin.

"Don't you ever mention that man in this house again!" I ran to the kitchen, opened the backdoor, and ran out of the house. I ran hard and fast; Grandma could not keep up. She shouted to Mr. Nance, her neighbor, for help. Grandma and Mr. Nance ran after me. I ran faster. They were behind me. David, Mr. Nance's son, joined them. He caught me and tackled me to the ground. I kicked and screamed. They held me down, and I passed out. When I woke up, I was in bed with Khalid still in Grandma's house.